DARK NATION

Escaping Anarchy

Enduring Anarchy

Surviving Anarchy

RELAY PUBLISHING EDITION, MARCH 2022

Grace Hamilton is a pen name created by Relay Publishing for co-authored Post-Apocalyptic projects. Relay Publishing works with incredible teams of writers and editors to collaboratively create the very best stories for our readers.

www.relaypub.com

ENDURING ANARCHY

DARK NATION BOOK TWO

BLURB

They survived annihilation. But the real danger has only just begun…

When Molly, Colton, and their group of high school students narrowly escape a field trip gone wrong, they return home to find their town in shambles. An EMP has devastated the world. And life has been reduced to a daily battle for survival….

After a derailed train throws what's left of the town into chaos, Diego, the father of one of Molly's students, quickly takes charge. At first, he seems determined to help the survivors and clean up the train's wreckage. But it soon becomes clear that he has a sinister motive of his own for taking over. And Molly is certain he can't be trusted…

Things become much worse after a failed attempt by the local police has Diego seizing control and drawing a line in the sand. It isn't safe for anyone and Molly is ready to head to the woods, but not without all her students. Colton might be the Marine, but she isn't leaving anyone behind.

Molly will do anything to protect her students. But can she lead them to safety when the entire world has fallen into chaos?

CONTENTS

1

MOLLY

Despite the distant sunrise, the trees lining the road remained eerily dark. With every step, as her foot met the road, Molly's heart pounded. Shadows looked like people. The innocent snap of a twig in the undergrowth sounded like the loading of a gun. The wind on her back felt like movement; the movement of a body walking too close behind her, following her, preparing to attack. Someone who was armed. Dangerous. Looking for revenge for what Molly did in the prison or looking to steal whatever the group might be carrying that could be useful in this dark new world they'd found themselves in.

Molly shuddered. The image of an imaginary attacker wavered and bled into her memories of Dougie. Although her eyes were open, she could see him in front of her; the way his body had slumped onto the ground after she shot him. The glassy look in his eyes as his last breath left his body.

She'd had no choice but to do it. It was the only way to get the kids out of Fairfield. It was the only way to get them safely back home.

But that didn't mean she was okay with it. She had taken a life and there was no way—even if circumstances had allowed it—that she could go back to her old life. She was different now and, although the kids didn't seem to have noticed it, she sensed that Colton understood.

Beside her, the retired Marine stopped walking and grimaced as she looked at him. He was resting on his cane and looked extremely pale. Despite his injury, he'd made it out of the prison and had—until now—gritted his teeth through his obvious pain. The last thing he wanted was to become a burden, but they'd started this thing together and Molly was sure they were going to finish it together.

"Guys?" Molly called to the others. "I think we need to stop. Take a break."

Shortly after leaving the grounds of Fairfield Prison, Molly had given Tommy her gun, hanging back to help Colton while Tommy and Alex led the group on their journey back to town. The two of them had already traversed the empty roads once—they knew what to expect—but she was beginning to regret handing it over. She'd felt safer with the gun, even though she'd been praying she wouldn't ever have to use it again, and she'd felt safer when she was the one up front.

Molly tried again. "Guys, we have to stop. Colton needs a break."

"We can't," Erik Banks looked over his shoulder and shouted at her. Too loud. Walking faster instead of slower. "Our mom could be...." He trailed off, glancing at his sister Scarlett, then returning his gaze to the horizon.

An hour ago, as they trudged up the hill away from the prison, they'd witnessed a plume of thick black smoke mushrooming up into the sky and had heard what sounded unmistakably like an explosion. It had come from the south side of town, but whether it was from the Bankses' neighborhood or the less affluent area on the other side of the train tracks, it was impossible to tell.

Either way, Erik and Scarlett Banks had immediately started running. Until their father Alex pointed out there was no way they could run all the way back home and that they needed to stick together until they figured out what was going on; it wouldn't do anyone any good—especially their mother—to charge into danger.

While the Banks twins had looked almost sick with worry, the others in the group—Zack and his brother Tommy, Jenna, and Lucky—had remained quiet. All four of them came from Southside. All four of them were probably worrying about their own parents, but Erik and Scarlett were the only ones who let it show.

"I'm sorry, Erik, but Colton needs to rest for a moment." Molly glanced at Colton and noticed his jaw twitch. "We *all* do," she added.

Lingering between her classmates and her brother, as if she wasn't sure whether she should charge ahead with Erik or listen to Molly, her teacher, Scarlett braced her hands behind her neck and shook her head. "Miss O'Neil, maybe you and the others should slow down? Wait with Colton? Me, Erik, and Dad will go look for Mom."

Up ahead, Alex Banks stopped and turned around. He'd been pushing his bike and continued holding it with one hand while gesticulating with the other. "We're not separating from the group, Scarlett," he said gruffly. "We already decided we're stronger together." Alex rubbed his beard and swallowed hard. Ever since they'd witnessed the smoke and heard that deep, unsettling rumble that made the ground vibrate, Alex's face had been ashen. Gray around the edges. Etched with worry.

He was worried about his wife, of course, but Molly could tell there was something else he wasn't saying. He was extremely keen for them not to separate, despite the fact that he had a bike and could have traveled much more quickly if he'd used it.

This reluctance was troubling, and Molly was willing to bet it had to do with what he'd seen in town when he left home yesterday. While Molly and the kids had been stuck in Fairfield Prison, Alex had traveled through Fairfield to reach them. He'd met up with Tommy and they'd seen what the EMP had done. The start of it, anyway.

"Molly...." Colton tugged at her elbow, and she turned to look at him. "I'm slowing you down." He met her gaze and held it.

"Then *we'll* slow down," she said. "We are *not* leaving you." Putting her hands on her hips, Molly looked at the others. "He just needs a few minutes, that's all."

Alex looked at Tommy, who was also in possession of a bike. "It's your call, man," Tommy said. "If you want to take the bikes, we can catch up with you but…." He lowered his voice and said something to Alex that Molly couldn't catch.

After glancing at the skyline and the whispers of smoke that were filling it, finally Alex said, "Five minutes." When Erik began to protest, Alex held up his hand and told his son bluntly, "Five minutes, Erik."

Molly didn't realize she'd been holding her breath, but as she released it, she smiled at Colton. From the backpack Lucky had given her, she took a bottle of water. "Here," she said.

Colton took it, staggered to a nearby tree, leaned against it and took a long slow drink. "Thanks."

"You'll be fine when you've had a chance to rest."

Colton raised his eyebrows at her. "Oh, yeah? And when do you foresee that happening?"

Molly bristled. Nearby, Lucky and Jenna were talking with Erik and Scarlett in hushed whispers, pointing toward the town and to the Bankses' neighborhood. Between them, they'd decided the smoke was something to do with the trainline, but Molly was trying not to hear what they were saying. She was trying to focus on one thing at a time; escape the prison, get the kids home to their families, and then... well, she hadn't quite figured out the next part.

"I don't know," she admitted, chewing her lower lip. "I have no idea, Colton. All I know is that we've got a better chance if we stick together." She looked back in the direction of the prison. "We survived the jail. We made it out. None of us could have done it alone."

Colton nodded and took another sip from his water bottle. "I hear you," he said, pushing himself away from the tree and allowing the cane to support his weight once again. "In which case, we better get moving."

"You've barely rested for a second." Molly folded her arms in front of her chest and gave Colton her best teacher-stare.

"I'll be fine."

As Colton straightened himself up, Molly put her hands on her hips. Her fingers brushed against her back pocket, and she sucked in her breath as she remembered what was hidden there. Angling herself away from the group, she took out the pills she'd found when she was locked in that dark, awful cell and nudged Colton's elbow.

"I found these," she said quietly. "I don't know what they are but I kept them in case we needed something to bargain with. Perhaps you could…?" She shrugged and her eyes widened as Colton stared at the pills.

After a long moment, he closed his eyes and shook his head. Reaching out, he pressed Molly's fingers back against her palm, hiding the pills from view, and said, "No, thank you. I'll be all right."

"Are you sure?"

"You should get rid of those," he replied gruffly. "Ditch them."

"You don't think they could be useful? They could be prescription pills. Painkillers? I'm sure we can find someone who could tell us…."

Colton's hand was still pressed against her fingers. As he spoke, he held her gaze. "Prescription or not, I don't mess with pills, and neither should you. Get rid of them, Molly."

Molly pressed her lips together and swallowed hard. She was trying to interpret the look in Colton's eyes—a dark, watery look she hadn't seen before—when she heard Jenna's voice behind her.

"Miss O'Neil, I'll hang back with Colton for a while if you want to head up front with Alex and Tommy." Jenna was standing with her hands in her pockets. She looked tired. Her short hair was tucked behind her ears, and she smiled as Molly looked at her.

"Sure. Thanks, Jenna." Molly smiled back and patted Jenna's shoulder with one hand as she slipped the pills back into her pocket with the other. The girl clearly wanted a change of pace, and Molly was happy to take the lead for a while.

Casting a quick glance at Colton, Molly nodded to tell him she'd understood what he'd told her. As soon as she had chance to ditch the pills safely, so they wouldn't be found by a child or an animal who could be harmed by them, she would.

As the group started moving, they formed a cluster with Alex and Tommy up front, the Banks twins with Zack and Lucky in the middle, and Jenna and Colton at the back. Molly wove through them until she was standing between Alex and Tommy.

"Do you really think it's your neighborhood?" she asked Alex.

He nodded solemnly. "Looks like it. But it could be Southside. It's rough. The other side of the train tracks."

Molly cast a quick glance at Tommy. Like Jenna and Lucky, Tommy and Zack were from Southside. She remembered the address from

Zack's school records and thought Tommy might take offense at what Alex had said. Instead, he was nodding.

"You can say that again." Tommy shrugged his shoulders and looked away from the horizon as if he didn't want to think about what might be happening in his neighborhood.

Lowering her voice, Molly leaned a little closer to Alex. "When you left home yesterday...." She pursed her lips, unsure how to ask what she needed to. "What was it like? The town? Is there anything we should be prepared for?"

Alex looked at her. Beneath his beard, his top lip curled into a sad sort of smile. "It was okay," he said bluntly. "But it'll be worse by now."

"The calm before the storm," Tommy added. "Yesterday, some folks would still have been convinced the power was coming back. Some of them were probably kicking back, relaxing, pleased to have a few days off work, waiting for everything to get back to normal."

"And today they'll be realizing that it won't," Molly finished solemnly.

Tommy nodded. He patted the gun Molly had given him. "It'd help if we had a few more of these."

"I'll add 'guns' to the grocery list, shall I?" she quipped.

"Guns and coffee," Tommy replied. "I'd give my back teeth for some coffee about now."

Molly tried to laugh. Even Alex looked a little amused. But as they settled back into the rhythm of their own footsteps, Alex said, "So, what's your plan, Miss O'Neil? When we get to town?" He flexed his fingers on the handlebars of his bike. "Because my plan is to go home, fetch my wife, and get our family to a safe place. Are we doing that together?" He looked back at the others. "Are we collecting these kids' families and heading off in search of safe ground? Or...."

"Or?" Molly asked.

Alex shrugged. "I don't know," he said. "That's why I'm asking."

"I think we should stick together. At least until everyone's found their families," Molly said, trying not to listen to the voice in her head that was whispering, *What about your family, Molly? Aren't you worried about them?*

On the other side of her, Tommy was quiet. Every now and then he looked back at his younger brother Zack, but seemed happy to let him walk alongside his classmates. Perhaps because he sensed that Zack wasn't used to being thought of as one of a group and that he was, despite the circumstances, enjoying this newfound sense of camaraderie.

"Tommy? What about you and Zack? I know Jenna and Lucky want to find their folks." Molly looked away as she asked the question, focusing on the road beneath her feet; she'd heard what people said about Zack and Tommy's mother, and she wouldn't blame them if they didn't give two hoots what became of her now.

"We'll check on her," Tommy said, clearing his throat. "But I doubt she'll want to leave the house. The only time she's left the house in ten years was to go around the corner to the liquor store or to try to score a fix from her dealer, and with everything closed, I don't see her going anywhere now." As he spoke, Molly noticed Tommy's hand go to his jacket pocket as if he was confirming something was still there. When he saw her watching him, he stopped and repositioned his fingers around the handlebars of his bike.

As she might have when she saw a note being passed around the tables in the classroom, or a cell phone being turned on beneath the desk, Molly's instinct was to question Tommy about what he was hiding, but she shook it off; gone were the days when she'd be required to keep an eye out for students who were hiding contraband or causing distractions in class. And, besides, Tommy had never been one of her students. He was a grown man. A grown man with his own complicated history. If he was hiding something, it was none of her business.

She glanced at the group of kids trudging along behind them, then back at Tommy.

Unless whatever he was hiding affected her kids. *Then* it was her business... it was very much her business.

2

MOLLY

Even as the sun inched higher in the sky, it remained painfully dull. The smoke that had started as wisps had turned into clouds, and now the entire skyline seemed black with it.

"Is it spreading?" Jenna had once again swapped places with Molly and was walking beside Lucky.

"How would I know?" Lucky replied, his face a little pale.

"You're our resident pyromaniac," Zack butted in. "I thought you knew all there was to know about fires and stuff?"

Lucky rolled his eyes but smiled at the same time. "I know how to light fires. I don't pay much attention to what happens once they're in action." Lucky tilted his head from side to side and put on a professor-like voice, masking whatever worry he might be feeling for his own family with humor. "If I had to guess, I'd say it's still burning and, yeah, probably spreading." Dropping the voice, he laughed a little. "I mean, I'm guessing there's as much chance of the firefighters turning up to help as there was the cops back there." Lucky tipped his head in the direction of the prison.

Following Lucky's gaze, Molly shuddered. It wasn't particularly cold out. Early summer in Maine was always pretty temperate, even at night. But suddenly Molly wished she had a cardigan or a jacket to wrap around herself. Even though they were miles away, she could still feel the looming presence of Fairfield Prison. While the road they were on was quiet, unnervingly quiet, back there at the prison she imagined all hell was breaking loose. Dougie had wanted to keep the prison as a castle—its generator providing a haven of light in a world where light was now a hot commodity. Thanks to Molly, however, Dougie was gone now. Whoever took his place as the prison's leader might decide on a different plan; they might decide to leave the prison. Storm the town. After all, what chance would a bunch of ordinary townsfolk have against an entire prison's worth of felons? Any second now, a gang of inmates could come charging after them. She and the kids had escaped twice. Would they be so lucky a third time?

"Boys," Molly warned, shoving aside her nerves and directing Zack and Lucky's attention toward Scarlett and Erik. "Give it a rest, okay?"

Zack pressed his lips together, then nodded briefly and stepped away to go talk to his brother. Lucky, on the other hand, muttered, "Sorry," and folded his arms in front of his chest.

Ignoring the two of them, Erik asked loudly, "How much farther do we have to walk on this road? How long did it take you to reach the prison, from our house, Dad?"

"I had the bike," Alex replied, patting the handlebars of his bicycle as if he felt guilty for mentioning it.

"Right." Erik gritted his teeth.

"It'll take a few more hours," Alex added. "But we can only move as quickly as we can move, Erik."

"Tommy said we could take the bikes. Go on ahead. Scarlett and I could share. We could…." When his father shook his head, Erik trailed off and let out a loud groan. His fear for his mother was making him more than impatient—it was making him angry—and even Scarlett was struggling to calm him down.

As Alex opened his mouth to reply, Erik practically growled at him and stalked off ahead. Scarlett jogged to catch up but stumbled as she reached him. She was tired. They all were. For more than twenty-four hours, they hadn't slept, or rested, or eaten properly. They'd survived the prison on adrenaline and their wits. Now they were flagging. But thinking as far ahead as nightfall, wondering where they'd end up by the time it came, made Molly's temples start to throb. So she pushed the thought away.

Thankfully, after a few more minutes' walking, the road they were on sloped downwards, easing their journey a little. The trees on either side began to thin, and Molly spotted unmoving cars up ahead.

"We must almost be at the outskirts of town," she said to Colton. "Look. Vehicles."

Colton nodded in agreement but didn't look pleased. "Which means we'll soon come across people too," he said gruffly.

"Looks like these have been looted already," Jenna called as she peered into the open back seat of an old sedan.

"This one hasn't." Lucky was standing beside a large, almost brand-new truck. "Might be something useful inside?" He wiggled his eyebrows at the others.

"Definitely not." Molly left Colton's side and quickened her pace to catch up with Lucky and Jenna. "We've done enough damage to private property for one day, wouldn't you say, you two?"

Jenna and Lucky, who until a few hours ago had barely even spoken to each other before, exchanged a conspiratorial look and started to laugh.

With a wistful look in his eyes, probably remembering the explosive display that he and Jenna had created to try and attract the cops to the prison, Lucky sighed. "Ah, man. I bet I won't *ever* see anything that cool ever again."

"It was pretty cool," Jenna added, looking at Molly.

As they continued walking, Molly chuckled. "I'm sure it was. Unfortunately, all we got from inside was the noise. None of the pyrotechnics."

"The pyro *what?*" Lucky frowned at her.

"Fireworks," Zack, who was nearby, cut in. "She means fireworks."

"Hey guys—" Tommy had been up front with Alex and the Banks twins but now jogged back toward them. "There's a gas station ahead. We can avoid it, but it'll add to the distance."

Molly was about to suggest that she wait with the kids and Colton while Alex and Tommy checked out the situation—there could be useful things inside, but she didn't want to walk the kids into something dangerous—when a commotion broke out behind them.

"Miss O'Neil!"

She turned to see Jenna and Lucky rushing over to Colton, who was barely managing to stand up.

"Damn thing!" He cursed at his leg as if it might answer him back. When he looked up and saw Molly hurrying over, he allowed himself to drop to the ground and leaned over to rub at his knee. "Just gave out from under me," he groaned.

"Dad... we can't do this. We need to get *home*." Erik Banks was gesticulating wildly, close to panic at the idea of his mother somehow being caught up in whatever was causing the ever-blackening smoke that was filling the sky. Molly couldn't blame him. The twins had come perilously close to losing their mother once before, five years ago when she was in a car accident that almost killed her. After that, they knew all too well what it felt like to believe she'd been taken from them.

Firmly, Alex put his hands on Eric's shoulders. "Your mother can take care of herself, Erik. She has Argent for company. He won't let anything happen to her. He'd drag her out of a burning building if he had to, you know that."

As Molly pictured Laura Banks' assistance dog Argent, she breathed in and told herself Alex was right. Dogs like Argent were trained to protect their owners. The twins' mom would be okay.

Erik swallowed hard, but Scarlett squeezed his arm. "Dad's right, and besides, Colton helped us when we needed him. We can't leave him, Erik."

Molly was watching Colton's face. He winced as Scarlett spoke, but she'd be willing to bet it wasn't because of the pain in his leg; it was because he was mortified that he was slowing them down. No matter how much he wanted to shrug off the pain he was feeling, he couldn't. This was not a case of mind over matter. He'd injured himself and he simply wasn't able to move as fast as they needed him to.

"A splint," Molly said loudly. "We need to make a splint to support his leg."

"Molly." Colton's voice was almost a growl. "Please. Just leave me here. Go with the kids. Come back for me when they're all safe." He looked up and down the road and lowered his voice. "We've been lucky so far, but sooner or later we'll come across another group and it might not be a friendly one."

"You know what's a waste of time?" Molly folded her arms and for the second time that morning gave Colton her most withering stare. "This conversation. I've told you we're not leaving you. So the more you repeat yourself, the more time you're wasting."

For a moment, Molly thought Colton was going to yell at her. His cheeks were flushed and there was a narrowness to his eyes that she hadn't seen before. But he didn't. "Fine," he said. "Then what do you suggest?"

"Get on the bike." Molly gestured to Alex's bike—the larger of the two—but Colton shook his head.

"I can't ride it. My leg…."

"We'll push you," Molly said, gesturing for Jenna to help her pull Colton to his feet.

"Push me?" Colton looked horrified.

"Only over to the gas station." Molly put her arm around Colton's waist and motioned for Alex to bring the bike over. "There'll be something there we can use to splint your leg."

Before Erik could butt in and tell them there wasn't time, Alex nodded in agreement and said, "And we're running low on water. Food. There's a good chance the place has already been ransacked, but it's worth a shot." Turning to Erik, he added, "Son, we'll be no use to your mother if we arrive home dehydrated and half-dead from exhaustion. I want to get back as badly as you do, but we've got to keep our heads. That's what's going to make the difference here, okay?"

“Dad’s right.” Scarlett put her hand on Erik’s forearm. She smiled at him and tucked her long dark hair behind her ear. Her clothes were rumpled. The black eyeliner she’d so expertly applied on the bus yesterday morning was now smudged and nothing more than a shadow. Without it, she looked more like her brother.

As Molly, Jenna, and Tommy helped Colton onto the bike, Erik muttered, “Okay. Okay,” and let Alex put his arm around his shoulders.

“Me and Zack will push him,” Tommy said, offering his bike to Molly.

Molly took it. “I’ll go ahead and make sure the coast is clear.”

Before she could ask, Tommy handed her back the gun he’d been keeping in the band of his jeans. “Be careful,” he said. Then, nodding at Alex, “We’ll wait over behind those cars until you give us a signal.”

As Molly made the short journey across the road, past the extinguished traffic lights and the abandoned cars, toward the gas station, she glanced back. Tommy had pushed Colton forward a few feet and they were now waiting, with the others, behind two cars that had clearly careened into each other when their engines cut out.

She stopped on the concrete. The usually lit-up fuel pumps were dark, the windows of the store had been smashed and the automatic doors had been wedged open with a large red trash can. Molly got off the bike and rested it against one of the pumps. Straining her ears, she walked slowly forward. It was quiet. Very quiet.

Awkwardly, she climbed over the trash can and winced as her boots clacked against the tiled floor inside. She walked along the aisles, peering down each one with her fingers flexed and ready to reach for the gun. Most of the shelves were empty and the store seemed vacant of both goods and people. There was no one there.

When she reached the far end of the store, Molly sighed and leaned back against an abandoned checkout. For a moment, just one small moment, she allowed herself to close her eyes and pretend she was alone in her cabin. In the middle of the woods, looking out at nothing but trees and sunshine, gently swaying back and forth in the porch swing that had belonged to her grandmother. When she opened her eyes, she bit her lower lip, shook her head, and marched back to the exit.

Climbing back over the trashcan, she waved for the others. Tommy waved back, indicating they'd seen her, and she watched as they started to file across the road. Tommy and Colton were slow—pushing a guy Colton's size on a bike wasn't easy and, under any other circumstances, it would have been comical. To an outsider, it looked almost like Zack and Tommy were teaching him to ride, and Molly fought the urge to reach for the cell phone that would usually have been nestled in her back pocket and take a picture of it.

While the kids hurried over, clearly eager to get their hands on any leftover candy or soda, Alex Banks stopped in the middle of the road. He was looking into the ditch at an old, upturned truck. Eventually he tore himself away but when he reached the gas station, Molly was almost certain she saw him wiping moisture from his eyes.

"Can we go in, Miss O'Neil?" Lucky had paused at the doorway and was looking at her for approval.

"It seems like the coast is clear, but be careful," Molly said sternly. "Take anything useful that'll fit in your backpacks, although I'm not sure what's left, to be honest. It's a bit of a mess in there."

Lucky nodded, then grinned at the others. "First to find a can of Moxie wins my everlasting gratitude."

As the kids rushed inside, Molly smiled at them. She was glad they had Lucky to keep them upbeat, and she was glad Lucky and Jenna seemed to have formed a more solid friendship since their escapades with the fireworks and the ammo; if things continued to go the way she was expecting them to, these kids would need each other. *Really* need each other.

3

LAURA

When she woke, Laura expected it to be dark. She felt like she had been unconscious for hours, but the air still hummed with an early-morning freshness, which told her it wasn't long after sunrise.

She wasn't sure why she'd passed out. Exhaustion. Shock. Pain. It could have been any one of those things. But she knew she had because Argent hadn't been there when she'd last had her eyes open, and now he was. He was lying beside her, nose against her hand, staring at her as if he could will her to be okay.

"I'm all right, boy," she said, trying to ease herself up onto her elbows so she could assess the damage to her lower half. "Don't worry."

Looking herself up and down, however, she fought a rising sense of panic in her chest; her lower half was trapped. Whatever had exploded in the distance had caused the old dying tree in the middle of their backyard to finally fall down, and it had landed smack-dab on top of her.

She couldn't feel it, of course, which was probably the only blessing so far in the fact that she had no real sensation in her legs. She could, however, feel it in her back. Already, the spot at the base of her spine was throbbing. Just propping herself up had caused shockwaves to shoot up and down her torso, and the pain was making her eyes water.

"Okay," she breathed shakily. "Think, Laura. How are you going to get out of this one?"

As she stared at her trapped legs, memories of the car accident that had left her in a wheelchair began to careen through her head. Except then it had been Alex who was trapped. She'd pulled him free. She'd risked her own safety to save him, but this time there was no one here to save her. She was on her own.

Laura looked at Argent. She wasn't completely alone. Argent would do anything for her, but even he wasn't strong enough to move an entire tree on his own.

Out of breath and unsure whether it was because she'd injured herself or because she was beginning to panic, Laura allowed herself to flop gently back onto the grass. It was damp and cold. Early-morning dew had begun to seep through her sweater, making her shiver.

Turning her head, she caught sight of the covered patio furniture on the lawn and tried to slow her breathing as she remembered what was beneath it. *Who* was beneath it.

"Think, Laura, think…."

She was about to start yelling for help when she heard a voice.

"Laura? It's Jerry. Are you all right? Me and Barb heard a crash."

"Jerry, thank God," Laura whispered, trying not to start crying. As loudly as she could, she called back, "Jerry! I'm trapped! If you reach over the gate, you can unlock it from the top."

She couldn't see what was happening because the gate was behind her, but she heard a fumbling sound and then the thick clunk of the lock being slid open.

Argent sat up, ears pricked, tail wagging, but unsure whether he should welcome their visitor or protect Laura at all costs.

"Dear Lord, child, what happened?" Laura's seventy-something-year-old neighbor crouched down beside her and reached out as if he was going to check her over, then thought better of it. "I'll call an ambulance," he said, then shook his head at himself. "What am I saying? Of course I won't." He tried to smile, but when he took in the tree branch and Laura's legs, his face paled.

"You can't move?"

Laura grimaced. "I'm afraid not."

"Okay, okay, I'll go find help." Jerry stood up. His face was pale and sweaty, and he looked more than mildly panicked.

Laura nodded. She couldn't think of anything else to suggest. A few hours ago, she might have told Jerry not to worry, that Alex would be home soon with the kids, but now she was beginning to doubt it. He'd been gone such a long time, and she had no idea where the explosion that had rocked the tree had come from. What if Alex and the twins had been close to it? What if they were hurt? What if he'd never even made it to the prison in the first place?

Pushing aside the thoughts, because they terrified her, Laura smiled encouragingly at Jerry. "Perhaps try Mr. Higgins? He lifts weights," she laughed. "He might be able to help."

Jerry nodded. "Mick Higgins. Right. I'll be back!" As he hurried away, Laura bit her lower lip. Despite trying her best not to, again and again, she was picturing whoever came to help her pointing at the table. Suggesting they use the tarp for something. Pulling it loose…

and discovering Dave's bloodied dead body wrapped in a carpet from her husband's office.

She was once again trying to stop her breath quickening into a white-hot panic when she heard the gate. Argent's ears pricked up but this time he simply tilted his head.

"She's over here," Jerry was saying.

"Jesus." Mick Higgins from across the street stepped into Laura's line of sight, put his hands on his hips and surveyed the situation as if he was calculating how much he was going to bench at the gym that day. "Got yourself in a mess here, Laura."

"Sure did, Mick." Laura had never liked Michael Higgins. He was the kind of guy whose nose was pushed out of joint if you drove a fancier car than him, who liked parading his latest thin, blonde girlfriend in front of the neighbors, who invited them over for barbeques so he could brag about how much money he'd made that month. But he was strong and, right now, she needed strong more than she needed nice.

"Jerry, you think you can give me a hand here?" Mick gestured to the tree and Jerry's face paled.

"I can try, Mick."

"If you can lift it, just a little, I can get free," Laura said. "Argent will help me."

Mick looked skeptical—he'd never had much time for Argent—but nodded. "Okay, we'll count to three then go for it. Ready?"

Laura nodded. "Argent, boy."

Without her even needing to show him what to do, Argent dipped his head so she could put her arm around his neck.

"One..." Mick shouted. "Two..." Laura braced herself. "Three!"

As Mick and Jerry—mainly Mick—heaved the tree branch up by a couple of inches, Argent began to pull.

"I'm losing it!" Jerry shouted.

"She's almost there. Hold it!" Mick replied.

"I can't! I'm slipping!" Jerry let out a loud cry and Laura heard the branch thwack back down to the ground.

She winced, breathless, still hanging onto Argent, then dared to look down at her legs. By some miracle, she was free.

"Oh, thank you," she breathed, almost laughing with relief as she nuzzled into Argent's fur. "Thank you."

Jerry was rubbing the back of his neck, looking completely traumatized by almost crushing Laura's feet when he dropped his end of the branch, but Mick was grinning. If he'd had a working cell phone, he probably would have videoed the whole thing and uploaded it to YouTube.

"Second hero mission of the day," he said, clapping his hands together to indicate, *job done*.

"Second?" Laura had managed to sit up, but her head was spinning.

"Didn't you hear the explosion? Must have had to do with something up on the train tracks. Debris came flying through our window, and I pulled Carmel out of the way just in time."

Laura was struggling to keep up with what Mick was saying. Carmel? A train?

"My girlfriend," Mick added. "You guys haven't met. We'll do a barbeque next week."

Laura exchanged a look with Jerry, but didn't bother to tell Mick that barbeques were likely to be off for a while. Unless they were barbecuing over a campfire, that is.

"You all good here?" Mick asked, already moving back toward the gate.

"I just need my chair." Laura peered around the yard. "It should be here."

Jerry cleared his throat and pointed shakily toward the tree. "I'm sorry, Laura. I'm not sure it'll be any use to you now."

She followed his gaze and almost buried her head in her hands; her chair had been crushed under the weight of the main tree trunk. Unsalvageable. Unusable.

"Crap," she said quietly, even though a voice in her head was telling her to be grateful she'd been thrown from it rather than being crushed herself. "Argh! What am I going to do?"

Laura expected Mick to shrug and walk away but instead he headed back into the yard. Bending down beside her, he began to scoop her up.

"Mick! What are you doing?"

Argent began to growl.

"Ah, quiet down, Benji." Mick waved his hand at Argent. "I have a spare chair over at my place. It was my ma's. She died a few years ago and I kept it just in case."

In case? Laura tried to smile and patted Mick's shoulders. "Okay, great. Maybe you could bring it over? My back's not great."

Mick shrugged. "Sure." Then, looking around, he started to move toward the outdoor table and chairs.

"Mick!" Laura's heart was thundering in her chest. "Would you mind taking me inside?" Her mouth had suddenly become extremely dry and her tongue felt too big. Even Mick would notice a dead body if he came across one.

He paused for a moment, casting a glance at Jerry that implied, *Jeez, women. Never happy, are they?* "Sure," he said tightly. "No problem, Laura."

"Thank you," she breathed. "Thanks."

Half an hour later, after Mick and Carmel had made as big a scene as possible of delivering the wheelchair, making sure any neighbors who were around had seen their act of kindness, Laura breathed a sigh of relief. As they closed the door behind them, Jerry laughed. "Quite a pair, those two."

"They are," Laura replied, taking a sip from the bottle of water Jerry had given her. "Listen, Jerry, you should get back to Barb. She'll be worried about you."

Jerry looked at her for a moment, then looked away. Were his shoulders trembling?

"Jerry?" A heavy sense of dread had settled in the pit of Laura's stomach. "Is Barb okay?"

Screwing his eyes shut, Jerry shook his head and sniffed loudly. "I don't know what I'm going to do," he said. "She'll never cope with this, Laura." He waved his hands around the room. "With all this. She just won't. She's too fragile. Someone said they're helping people up at the high school, setting up some kind of emergency center. I thought about taking her there, so she's with other people, but I'm not sure she'll come."

Laura sat up straighter in her chair, already missing the more comfortable back of her own, expensive version. "The school?"

Jerry nodded. "A triage center, I think. Advice. Help." He shrugged. "Maybe it's a bad idea. I just thought it might be better than sitting around here waiting to be robbed."

Laura pressed her lips together. "No, Jerry. It's not a bad idea. It's a great idea. In fact, I'll bet that's where Alex and the kids have headed. They were on a school trip. He went to find them."

"Makes sense they'd go back to the school," Jerry said tentatively.

"It does." Laura was looking around for a pen and a piece of paper, uncertain whether she truly believed Alex would have headed for the school or whether she was convincing herself of it because she was pretty sure she'd go mad if she had to stay in close proximity to the dead body in the backyard. Locating the notepad they kept by the barely ever used house phone, she scrawled: *Alex, I've gone to the school. They're setting up a walk-in center. I'm okay. I'll wait for you there.*

"Right," she said, slapping the note down on the table. "Let's see about convincing Barb to take a little walk with us."

4

MOLLY

As Alex headed inside with the kids, Tommy and Molly helped Colton over the trashcan and into the store.

"Sit over here," Molly said, indicating an upturned chair near the checkouts.

As Colton limped over to it, Tommy set it up the right way and handed him back his cane. "Will you two be okay alone?" Tommy asked, glancing back at the wedged-open doors.

Molly nodded. "I have the gun. I'll keep watch on the front of the store. You and Zack catch up with the others, and if you find any aspirin…."

"You bet," Tommy replied, patting Zack on the shoulder. "Let's go, bud. Aspirin and *food*. Let's see what we can find."

As the brothers sped off down the nearest aisle, stepping over empty packets and broken jars, Molly turned back to Colton. "Right… let's sort out this leg of yours."

"Go find yourself something to eat first," he said. "You look tired, Molly."

"First, your leg. Then food. The kids will find something, I'm sure." She stood up and looked up and down the store, then handed him the gun. "Stay here. I'll be back."

Toward the back, among a small section of cheap clothing, Molly found what she'd been looking for—a shelf of discounted scarves.

"You're going to use those to tie a splint?" Jenna was beside her and was gesturing to the scarves.

"Yes," Molly said, taking one of the scarves and wrapping it around Jenna's neck. "But I also think we should take these."

Jenna frowned at her. Over the next few weeks, the temperature would continue to climb until it reached the mid-seventies on a good day; they'd have little need for winter clothing. Turning around and taking a bunch of hoodies from a second discount rack, Molly handed them to Jenna. "Why d'you think these are still here, Jenna, when the rest of the store is practically empty?"

Again, Jenna frowned.

"Because everyone's thinking about *now.* Tomorrow. Maybe next week. They're not thinking about next month or a few months from now when it's freezing outside. Wet and cold, and with no central heating."

Jenna swallowed hard. "Right. I get it."

"We'll hand these out to the others." Molly grabbed as much as she could carry from the reduced-price winter goods section, then started back to the front of the store. "Did you find any food?"

"Not much. I'll keep looking." Jenna was about to break away and head back toward the food aisles when she stopped abruptly. Molly bumped into her and peered around her stack of hoodies and hats. Jenna was staring at something on the floor.

Molly followed the girl's gaze, and instinctively stepped back when she saw what Jenna had seen; a pool of dark red blood and a series of drips that led in the direction of the exit.

"We shouldn't stay here long," Jenna whispered.

"No," Molly replied, stepping around the blood. "We shouldn't. Go tell the others to hurry up."

As Jenna scurried away, looking horribly pale, Molly returned to Colton and set her stack of clothes down on the empty checkout beside him.

"Smart," he said, nodding at the hoodies.

Tilting her head, but not bothering to say 'thanks', Molly waved a scarf at him. "And this should help with your leg."

She gestured for him to stand up. "Sorry. I need your chair."

Colton did as he was told and leaned back on the checkout as Molly turned his chair upside down and unscrewed two of the cylindrical plastic legs. When she'd finished, Colton *almost* smiled at her.

"Smart?" she asked, bending down and examining his leg.

"Smart," he replied.

Gently touching Colton's swollen knee, Molly looked up at him. "Shall I splint the whole leg or just the lower half?"

"Whole thing, I think. It'll make it hard to walk but it'll stop me flexing the knee and give it a chance to heal."

"In that case, we'll need four chair legs." Molly set to work unscrewing the other two legs and had only just finished tying them in place at the back and sides of Colton's knee and calf when the kids re-emerged from the aisles.

Erik and Scarlett were tucking into an already half-empty bag of potato chips, and Lucky had managed to find a stack of soda, but none of them seemed to be carrying any water.

Alex Banks gestured to Colton's knee. "I looked for something frozen to take down the swelling, but it's all either gone or melted."

"Thanks." Colton stood up, reached for his cane, and tested the splint. "This should help. I'll be walking like a robot for a while, but it'll take the pressure off."

"Did you find any water?" Molly asked.

Tommy gestured to his backpack. "Not much. A few bottles. We've stashed all we could find." He reached into his pocket and handed her a can of diet soda and a chocolate bar. "No coffee, though," he said, grimacing. "Or aspirin."

Barely blinking, Molly opened the soda and took several huge gulps; then she opened up the chocolate bar. Next to her, Colton was doing the same. When they'd finished, she nodded at the group. "Okay, everyone grab a hoodie, hat, gloves, and scarf from this pile. I know I sound ridiculous, but…" She was about to explain, but the kids were already doing as they were told. Alex and Tommy did the same.

"We do have hoodies at home," Erik muttered to his father as he crammed the items into his backpack.

"Yeah, we do. But someone else might need them, so…." Alex widened his eyes to indicate, *just do it, Erik.*

Molly looked at each of them in turn. They were ready. Not rested, but refueled at least.

"Alex, what's the quickest way back to your house from here?" she asked as they made their way back outside.

Alex rubbed the back of his neck, then pointed left of the gas station. "Toward the bridge. But…" he trailed off, sucking in his cheeks. "It was pretty chaotic down there when I left."

"Miss O'Neil?" Jenna tentatively interrupted.

Molly turned to her. "Yes?"

"I have an idea." Jenna's hands were laced together behind her back, and she was swaying nervously from foot to foot.

Molly waited for her to continue.

"Not far from here, there's a section of woodland. There's a clearing. I go there sometimes. It's a quicker route back to town and I have a few more supplies there that we could grab. A first-aid kit. Some food."

Alex's eyes brightened. "Quicker?"

Jenna nodded.

"Why didn't you say so before?" Erik asked her, stepping up beside his father, already bouncing on the balls of his feet, eager to get going.

"I guess 'cos I haven't told anyone about it before. I go there when I want to be alone. Not many people know about it. Maybe no one." Jenna's cheeks flushed. She looked embarrassed.

As Erik rolled his eyes, Scarlett elbowed him in the ribs and said, "Well, thanks, Jenna. We appreciate it."

"Yes," Molly said brightly, finally feeling the smallest sense of relief. "Thank you, Jenna. Quicker is good, and quiet is even better."

"How confident are you that you can get us back to town this way?" Colton was leaning on his cane, but with the aid of the splint seemed a little more like his old self again.

"If we can get to the clearing, one hundred percent," Jenna said confidently.

Colton studied Jenna's face, then looked at Molly for confirmation. When she nodded at him, he said, "Okay. Then lead the way, Miss Cruz."

Molly had expected to feel safer away from the abandoned cars and the anticipation of being discovered by other people. However, as soon as they stepped off the main road and into the trees, her skin started to crawl with uneasiness. Out in the open, the usual morning brightness had been muted by the smoke coming from town, but it had unmistakably been daylight. Beneath the canopy of the trees, the air was thick with shadows, and Molly was fighting a familiar twinge of panic in her chest.

"Okay?" Colton asked as she helped him navigate a fallen tree trunk.

"Shouldn't I be asking you that?" she replied, pushing loose hair from her face.

Colton smiled thinly, wincing as he lowered his weight onto his bad leg; the splint was helping, but it was no substitute for proper rest and medical attention.

"This way." Up ahead, Jenna was weaving effortlessly through the trees, pushing branches out of her way, navigating the woods as if she knew them by heart.

"You know," Molly said, trying not to keep looking at Colton's leg as he walked awkwardly next to her. "I have a cabin in a place like this."

"A dark wood?" he asked. "Sounds idyllic."

Frowning, because she couldn't tell whether he was being sarcastic or sincere, Molly replied. "Yes. A dark, quiet, middle-of-nowhere wood."

Colton leaned heavily on his cane as they followed Jenna and the others down an uneven slope covered in leaves and twigs.

"But, more importantly, a dark *secluded* wood. Off the beaten track. The kind of place people wouldn't easily come across."

When Colton didn't reply, Molly chewed the inside of her cheek. She couldn't figure out why she was telling Colton this. Was she hoping he'd ask where it was and suggest joining her there? Or was she hoping he'd tell her things in town would get better and she wouldn't need to worry about the cabin at all? Except for her usual summer and weekend visits.

Before Colton could say anything, Jenna's voice drifted through the trees. "Here! It's here!" Jenna was out of sight but Lucky appeared in front of them, as if from nowhere, waving at her through the darkness.

"Not far now, Miss O'Neil," Lucky said politely. As he spoke, Molly couldn't help but smile at him. Just twenty-four hours ago, he'd been the irritating class clown who she'd assumed would probably never get his act together and behave sensibly. Today he was different. Perhaps it was because she'd trusted him with the responsibility of escorting the prison guard, Fox, back to the bus. Or because she'd allowed him to keep his lighter. Or just because the whole world had changed, so he had too. Whatever the reason, Molly was grateful.

"Over here." Lucky pointed up ahead.

As they stumbled through a thick cluster of trees, they emerged into a small clearing. Somehow, Alex and Tommy had maneuvered their bicycles through the woods and had leaned them up against a nearby tree.

In the center of the clearing someone, presumably Jenna, had positioned four large logs. Perfect for sitting on. The kids lingered in the middle. Despite the gas station hiatus, they still looked exhausted.

“Can I suggest that we take a break?” Tommy beat Molly to it and looked around the group. “I know you want to get home.” He was speaking to the Bankses. “But it’s going to be a long day. When we get free of these woods, we’ll need our wits about us. If we take half an hour, rest, eat, and plan….” He trailed off. Alex Banks was nodding in agreement; he could see his kids were struggling, and he was probably running on reserves himself.

Molly expected Erik to protest, but for once, he didn’t. Sitting down on a log next to his sister, he swung his backpack from his shoulders and opened it. “Guess we shouldn’t eat too much, though, huh?” he asked, looking to the others for confirmation.

“I have these too.” Jenna had fetched an old ammo can from behind a tree and was prying open the lid. “Just chips and candy bars, but there’s enough for one each.” Dishing out the snacks, so they could save their gas station spoils for later, Jenna smiled. “Knew there was a reason I kept these up here.”

“What else do you keep up here?” Lucky asked, looking around at what seemed to be a makeshift camp; a ratty tarpaulin hung between two trees, giving a small amount of shelter, some old plywood boards beneath it for flooring, and a dirty-looking sleeping bag. “Do you sleep up here?” he continued.

As Jenna blushed and muttered a reply none of them could make out, the rest of the group settled into silence. The woods were humming with quiet. There were barely even any bird sounds, just the occasional rustling of the leaves and the kids’ candy wrappers.

Eventually Alex spoke up. "I should tell you all that what I saw on the way to the prison wasn't pretty." His tone was grave, and his eyes dark. He swallowed hard. "A lot of people aren't thinking clearly. A lot of people have guns, and they're willing to use them."

Tommy was nodding in agreement. "We hooked up when I saved Alex from someone willing to beat him up for his bike," he said, trying to keep his tone light but not quite managing it.

"Should we ditch them, then?" Zack asked bluntly. "We don't want to draw attention to ourselves."

"No, I think we keep them. Just be willing to give them up if we need to—they could be useful if we need bargaining power," Tommy replied.

Molly's fingers went instinctively to her jeans pocket. In prison, the pills she'd found squirreled away in the ceiling had felt like a valuable bargaining chip. Now, however, after what Colton had said, they made her skin twitch. Having them on her person felt risky. Too risky. Yet she didn't want to leave them somewhere where they might be picked up and end up hurting someone.

As the kids tucked into the snacks Jenna had given them, Molly pulled her to one side. "Jenna, is it okay if I leave something here?"

Jenna tilted her head.

For a moment, Molly wondered whether she was doing the right thing; should she be trusting a student with something like this? As she looked at Jenna, however, she realized that she was no longer simply a student. They'd been through something together. They trusted each other.

Reaching into her back pocket, Molly showed Jenna the pills. "I decided to keep these in case they came in handy, but since we don't know what they are I think it's best if I hide them somewhere safe."

Jenna narrowed her eyes at the pills and nodded. She gestured to the tarpaulin. "Bury them under there, Miss O'Neil. They'll be safe."

Molly smiled. "Thank you, Jenna."

When she returned to the group, she picked up a bottle of water and sat down next to Lucky. Releasing a long *pfffft* sound, he scraped his fingers through his light brown hair. "Crap." He looked up at the twisted branches above their head and glanced at Molly. "This is really happening, isn't it? The end of the world?"

"Only going to get worse," Zack answered.

"Don't say that." Scarlett had wrapped her arms around herself and looked like she might start crying.

"You bet it's going to get worse," Molly said loudly, putting down her half-empty soda can.

The others stared at her, surprised by the outburst, but she was fighting back a smile.

"Let's pretend it's Tuesday, and remember, I *always* do pop quizzes on Tuesdays."

For a moment, no one said anything, but as she started to laugh, the teens groaned in unison and both Lucky and Jenna grumbled about not having to take tests on Sundays.

"You all should have studied *Uncle Tom's Cabin* at some point. So, tell me—I'll start with an easy one—who actually *is* Uncle Tom?"

All at the same time, Lucky, Zack, Scarlett and Erik answered her.

"Well done! Okay, next question…."

"Miss O'Neil, that's not fair. I've never read it," Jenna whined.

"Have you read *any* book?" Erik asked sarcastically, reminding everyone that this time yesterday he and Jenna had been about to get into a fist fight on the bus. "In fact, *can* you read?"

While the others bit back sniggers, Molly was about to reprimand Erik when Alex said sternly, "Erik. Apologize. Right now. What would your mother say if she heard you making comments like that?"

"I was just joking around, Dad," Erik answered sheepishly, but when Alex glared at him, he muttered, "Sorry, Jenna."

"Okay, maybe the quiz was a bad idea." Molly laughed and brushed down her jeans.

On the log beside her, Colton whispered, "Worth a try."

She rolled her eyes, looking down at her shirt, which had come untucked from her waistband. She knew there were specks of blood on it. From the prisoner whose keys she'd stolen, and probably from Dougie too. She hadn't thought about it until now, but suddenly couldn't bear to look at it. Despite the fact it was warm, she took the gas station hoodie from her bag and pulled it over her head.

Colton watched her but didn't say anything; when he looked at her like that, she was almost certain that he could tell what she was thinking.

"I have some other stuff, too." Jenna had stood up, perhaps trying to redeem herself, and was walking over to her makeshift shelter. Pulling aside a plank of plywood, she pulled out a plastic bag, then walked back to the circle and emptied it onto the ground. "A first-aid kid, matches, candles, and a knife," she said triumphantly.

"This is great, Jenna." Molly indicated for her to put them into her bag but didn't object when Jenna tucked the knife into her pocket instead. "Perhaps we should take half and leave half? Just in case…"

Molly trailed off. She wasn't sure what the 'in case' was, but Jenna seemed to understand.

"Hey, there's something else in here...." Lucky was crouched beneath Jenna's tarpaulin, pulling aside the remainder of the plywood boards.

"That's nothing!" Jenna rushed over and tried to tug him away, but Lucky was holding something.

Jenna grabbed hold of his wrist; she was stronger than Lucky and easily pried free the stolen object.

"Why are you being weird? It's only a book." Lucky stalked back to his log and sat down, rubbing his wrist.

"Because it's mine and I didn't say you could touch it," Jenna bit back.

Molly tilted her head and examined the book's cover. "*Swiss Family Robinson*?" It looked extremely well-thumbed, and Molly's heart skipped with the sense of excitement she always felt when she discovered that a student had found a book they loved.

"Yeah, so?" Jenna shoved the book into her bag and folded her arms in front of her.

"Isn't that book about a family that builds a treehouse? Is that why you like it?" Lucky waved at the clearing. "You know, Jenna, you've got a ways to go if you're trying to build a treehouse. Considering that treehouses are supposed to be, you know...." He looked at the branches above their heads. "In the trees."

Molly stood up. Jenna's face had turned a deep shade of red, and she looked like she was ready to punch something... or someone. Clearly, whatever Jenna's connection was to the book, she did not want to talk about it.

“Well, I guess you all must be feeling plenty rested if you’re ready to start ragging on each other again?” she asked, hands on hips.

Before anyone could answer, Molly wrinkled her nose and looked up at the canopy above them. Barely any light was making it through, and she couldn’t tell what color the sky was, but she was certain the smell of smoke was getting worse. “Does anyone else feel like….”

“Like the smoke smell is worse?” Lucky was nodding at her. “Yeah. It’s worse than when we got here.”

“In that case we better—” Molly stopped mid-sentence. Something had moved. Behind Jenna’s tarpaulin, something had moved.

She narrowed her eyes.

Not something—some*one*.

5

MOLLY

As fast as she could manage, Molly pulled the gun from her jeans and pointed it at the face in the dark.

"Come out with your hands in the air," she shouted.

Suddenly realizing what was happening, the others jumped up from their seats and crowded together behind Molly. Jenna was holding out her knife. Lucky had picked up a branch.

Molly's heart was beating so fast she felt like it was going to break right through her rib cage, and her fingers were trembling. "I said, come out! Don't make us come in there after you," she yelled.

Beside her, Colton whispered, "Take it easy."

Finally, the leaves behind Jenna's tarp rustled. Three women stepped out into the clearing. They had a child with them. A boy, no more than six or seven. When he saw the gun, he started to cry.

"Oh no," Molly muttered, lowering it and shoving it back into her jeans.

Alex Banks had stepped forward. "Can we help you?" he asked. "Are you lost?"

The woman holding the boy's hand shook her head. She had long blonde hair. Shiny. Straight. The kind that was probably highlighted at a fancy salon once a month. But her clothes were dirty, and she had dark shadows around her eyes.

"We're not lost. We were trying to escape the fire," she said shakily. "It's spreading. They can't stop it. Anyone sensible is evacuating."

"Are you alone?" Molly asked, unsure whether she wanted to know in case a group of men with guns were following behind or because she was concerned for the women's welfare.

"My husband...." The woman looked down at the boy and lowered her voice. "We got separated."

The other two had, until now, been silent, but the one with curly red hair finally spoke up. "I'm not sure where you all were headed, but you can't go that way. You need to turn around."

Molly closed her eyes and pinched the bridge of her nose. She could feel Erik's anger from where she was standing. Then she heard Jenna's voice. "That way? The fire's that way?"

When Molly opened her eyes, she saw Jenna pointing to the spot the women had been standing in. The three of them nodded.

"That leads to town," Jenna said, turning to Molly. "To my street. The back of my house. That's how I get up here."

As Jenna spoke, her face drained of color. She looked back at the blonde mother.

"I'm sorry," she said. "The area around Fifth and Sixth is the worst hit."

Jenna wavered for a moment. Then, before Molly could ask, *hit by what?* the girl took off. Running full speed, she raced off in the direction the women had come from.

"Jenna, wait!" Lucky yelled as he grabbed both his and Jenna's backpacks and started after her.

"Lucky, no!" Molly lunged forward and grabbed his wrist, but he pulled it free.

"My house is only a couple of blocks from Jenna's!" he yelled. "If she's going, I'm going!"

Molly looked back at the others. There was no way Colton could run, and they had just been told specifically not to go that way.

"I'm going after them," she announced. "But I'm not leaving Colton behind."

Tommy and Zack looked at each other, then nodded. "We're with you."

"No way." Erik tugged on his dad's arm. "We need to get back to Mom. Now! If the fire's spreading it could already be at our house."

Alex looked at Molly and she met his eyes. "Erik's right, Alex. I think it's time you guys went your own way."

"Take the bikes." Tommy gestured to the bicycles. "If Scarlett and Erik share, you'll be home in no time."

The Bankses didn't need telling twice. Grabbing the bikes, they headed off into the woods.

The three women and the boy were still standing there, just watching them, clearly unsure whether to make a run for it or stay put in case

Molly drew her gun again. “Thank you,” Molly said, “thanks for the warning.”

The blonde woman nodded. “Be careful,” she said. “It’s not good back there.”

Without Jenna to lead them, they had no idea which direction to go. Molly desperately wanted to run but she was worried about Colton; with the splint, he was moving like a robotic soldier, trying to keep up with them but stumbling every now and again.

She could tell he was fighting the urge to simply sit down and refuse to go any farther, to tell them to go on without him, but he was resisting—for now.

Finally, the trees started to thin out. The smoke smell was worsening and, although it made Molly want to cover her mouth and head a different way, she knew it was a sign they were almost there.

“Do you have much experience with fires?” she asked Colton as she stopped to help him over a fallen tree trunk.

“Almost none,” he replied. “But I know I don’t like ’em, and I know once they get started, it’s hellishly hard to put them out. Especially if the town’s firefighters are too busy looking after themselves.”

Molly pursed her lips. She wanted to say that, surely, the firefighters wouldn’t ignore something like this. But the cops had ignored the prison, so why would this be any different?

“Up ahead, I see a bunch of backyards.” Zack was pointing through the trees. Sure enough, the woods ran behind a row of houses, backing onto their yards and separated by a long line of fences.

“You know which one is Jenna’s?” Colton asked.

“Number four-fifty-five,” Molly replied quickly, picturing Jenna’s records on her computer screen. “I’ve never visited it, though, and from back here, I can’t tell the numbers.”

“We’ll go around the front.” Tommy was leading the way.

Following along the scrap of grass between the trees and the fences, they kept going until they found a narrow passageway that led between two properties. It was dark between the houses, but they soon emerged onto a narrow sidewalk.

“Shoot!” Molly looked up and down the street. “This isn’t Jenna’s street. I know this street. It’s near my apartment block.” She looked back at the woods. “We must have gone the wrong way.”

“Do you know how to get to Jenna’s?” Colton asked, rubbing at his leg.

Molly tried to slow down her thoughts. Whenever she tried to go somewhere new, she used GPS. It had been years since she’d had to map out an area using her own brain. Even her own town. Closing her eyes, she pictured her apartment block and the streets surrounding it. “I think if we go past my apartment, then take a left on Third, and another left, we’ll get there.”

She sucked in her breath, almost instantly regretting it because of the smoke in the air. As they started to walk, she shuddered. The women said the fire was worse in Jenna’s neighborhood. If it had spread all the way here….

As they moved down the street, past stores and cafés that a few days ago had been quiet, picturesque… pleasant, Molly gritted her teeth. The place where she’d sat, just last week, having coffee and reading instead of grading the papers she was supposed to be grading, had been turned upside down. Tables and chairs were overturned. The storefront was smashed, and there was glass everywhere.

Eventually, as they rounded the corner, Molly braced herself for the relief of seeing her apartment. Even if it was just in passing.

She didn't realize it was her who'd let out a cry until Colton put his hands on her shoulders and said, "Molly? What is it?"

Tearing her eyes away from the apartment block, she looked at him, then screwed her eyes shut. "Nothing," she said quietly. "I'm sorry. It's nothing. This way…."

Colton didn't buy it. "Molly?" He was struggling to keep up with her. "Is that where you live?" He was pointing at a burning apartment block.

"Miss O'Neil? That's your place, isn't it?" Zack was looking at her, examining her face as if he could read her thoughts.

Molly nodded slowly. Everything she owned had been in that apartment. Every single thing. Pictures of her parents, of her brother—who she barely spoke to and now probably wouldn't ever see again—and of her college friends. Her teaching certificates. Her books. If it all went up in smoke, the only thing she'd have left would be the cabin.

Biting her lower lip, she straightened her shoulders and kept moving; her grief would have to wait. At least until they'd found Jenna and Lucky.

After what felt like forever, they reached Southside. Jenna's street was nearby, and the black smoke was even thicker than before.

Molly began to cough. Tommy and Zack did too.

"Cover your mouths and stay low, like we did with the tear gas." Colton gestured for them to use their shirts to shield their mouths and noses, and they followed suit.

The street was in chaos. What looked like debris was scattered up and down the middle of the road and on the sidewalk, smoldering, hot. Molly could feel the heat from where they were standing. And it was noisy.

People were screaming. Running. Some were helping injured friends. Others were just sitting on the sidewalk cradling wounds on their heads or their arms. "What happened?" Molly breathed.

"The train tracks." Tommy pointed into the distance. "They go right past here. There's the curve. A train must have…."

Molly screwed her eyes shut. She didn't understand the mechanics, but she was pretty certain it would be bad news if a train was running at full speed when the EMP hit. If the track was straight, it might have just slowed down. But it wasn't. Molly shuddered at the thought.

"We should go find Mom," Zack said quietly to his brother.

Once again, Tommy patted his pocket. For a moment he simply looked at the devastation around them, but then he turned his gaze to his brother and nodded. When he looked at Molly, he said, "Okay if we split off? Or do you want us to stay?"

"We're fine," Molly said quickly. "Go find your mom." As the brothers headed off, she called after them, "We'll meet back at the school. When you've found her, head for the school." But she wasn't sure Tommy heard her.

"The school?" Colton asked, as if she'd forgotten that the high school was now nothing more than a big empty building that *used* to be full of kids and teachers.

"When they drew up the town's emergency plans a few years ago, the school was dedicated as a Community Response Hub. If there's help to be found, it'll be at the school."

Colton narrowed his eyes a little. He looked skeptical.

"But first, we need to find Jenna and Lucky."

"Yeah," Colton said gravely. "We do." Looking down at his leg, he grimaced, then bent down and ripped free the scarves Molly had tied. The plastic chair legs she'd used clattered to the ground.

"Colton…."

"It's slowing me down. And I'd rather have a sore leg than end up as charcoal because I can't outrun a fire," he said, tipping his head in the direction of the houses at the far end of the street.

Huge orange flames licked up into the sky, engulfing the end of the street. As they moved forward, Molly spotted some firefighters, but no trucks. They were yelling at each other, desperately trying to coordinate volunteers with buckets, but it was no use. The fire was spreading.

"Lucky's house is number four-thirty-three. Jenna's is four-fifty-five." Molly was examining the house numbers.

"Four-sixty-three… the numbers are going down." Colton pointed at one of them.

"Which means Jenna's is down there…." Molly looked at the fire and felt like her legs might fall out from under her.

Colton squeezed her arm. "We'll find her. Don't worry. We'll find both of them."

Molly nodded, but as they started to move, a voice in her head asked, *How will you live with yourself if you don't?*

6

COLTON

"Tommy was right." Colton stopped and braced his hands on his lower back. The pain in his leg was vibrating right up into his spine now, and he was sick of it. He wanted to shake it off. He wanted to *will* it to be gone, but it was no use. He'd tried that when he was first invalided out of the Marine Corps all those years ago. It didn't work then. It wouldn't work now. "About the train," he added, gesturing to the tracks up ahead that ran right past the end of the street.

Colton couldn't imagine how noisy it must be to live beneath a railroad bridge. He'd thought once that he might end up in a place like this, when Debs left him, before he got the job with the school driving the bus. Somehow he'd managed to avoid it. Now, for perhaps the first time, he was grateful for the small mercy of a regular job. Even if it was one that made his skin itch with embarrassment when he thought about his fellow Marines finding out about it.

"Shoot." Molly O'Neil stopped walking and pushed her strawberry blonde hair from her face. Yesterday morning, it had been tied neatly back. Now it was snaking free, but he kind of liked it that way. "What happened?" Molly was staring at the bridge.

Dangling off the side of it was a train car. Below it, another two—maybe three—had derailed, flipped over the side of the bridge and plummeted to the ground, long before they arrived on the scene. Debris littered the street. It was everywhere. Indistinguishable pieces of train. The houses closer to the bridge were the worst hit. One had its entire roof missing. The others were engulfed in flames.

"I hope to God that was only a freight train," Colton muttered, shuddering at the thought of what would have happened to any people caught inside it.

"Looks like the fire's spreading in all directions," Molly said, rubbing at her temples and starting to cough again.

Colton was about to tell her, for the tenth time, to keep her mouth covered when he heard shouts coming from the group of firefighters farther down the street.

"Hey! Come back! We need you!" One of them was yelling as a group of what looked like civilian volunteers peeled away and ran in Colton and Molly's direction.

As they passed, a man yelled, "There's no point. Get out of here, man!"

Colton watched Molly's mouth set into a determined line. "We are not leaving until we've got Lucky and Jenna with us."

"Understood," he replied, but as they neared the firefighters—and the heat of the fire grew hotter on their faces—Colton found himself stopping and watching them.

They were working with nothing more than buckets. One had fixed a manual pump to a fire hydrant, but he looked ready to collapse from the effort of pushing it. Glancing at Molly, Colton ground his teeth. He wanted to stick with her. Help the kids. Do what he'd promised. But if someone didn't help the guy on the pump, they wouldn't have a chance of beating back the fire and Lucky and Jenna wouldn't have a chance of making it out.

In a split second, the decision was made. Colton broke away from the sidewalk and headed, as quickly as he could, for the firefighters. When he reached them, he realized that some of them were cops.

"Here," he said, joining the man on the pump and adding his own upper-body strength to the effort of pushing it. "Let me help."

The man stared at him for a long moment, clearly both shocked and relieved, then said, "You a firefighter, son?"

"No, sir. A Marine." Colton gritted his teeth as he continued to push the pump. Across the street, Molly had noticed he was missing and was staring at him.

"Police Chief Richard Bailey," the man replied, stopping short of offering a handshake.

"Colton. Colton King."

"We sure could use a man like you on our side." The chief looked at the fire, then back in the direction the volunteers had run. "There's not enough of us. Simply not enough. We need any able-bodied person we can find."

Able-bodied. Colton bit back an ironic laugh. Then he looked up at Molly. Her face was a mixture of emotions. Running over to him, she pulled on his arm. "Colton, you promised you'd help me find the kids."

Colton resisted her and kept on pushing the pump. “I know,” he said through gritted teeth. “But I’m more use here.” Using all his strength to push free another jet of water, he added, “*This* I can do. Running into a burning building?” He looked down at his leg. “Not so much.”

“But Jenna and Lucky *need* us.”

“They need you.” Colton didn’t want to let her go. He didn’t want to watch her run into a burning building alone, but he could be of the most use here, putting out the fire. He knew that and, more than anything else, he’d always prided himself on doing what was right, not what he wanted. “Jenna and Lucky need you to find them while I hold off the fire.”

“Jenna?” the cop beside him interrupted. “Jenna Cruz?”

Colton watched Molly’s eyes widened. “Yes. That’s her. Do you know her?”

“Diego Cruz is a volunteer firefighter.” He pointed down the street to where a group of people were desperately trying to save a burning house. “And that there’s the Cruzes’ house.”

Molly lingered for a split second, then met Colton’s eyes, nodded at him, brushed down her hoodie, and ran toward the fire.

7

MOLLY

Tearing herself away from Colton, Molly raced in the direction of the Cruz house. Close to the tracks, its roof had already been consumed by fire. Molly could feel the heat humming in the air, could see the flames licking the windows, and knew instantly that there was no way the house would be saved.

"Shouldn't we tell them to stop?" A woman with long black hair, whose hands were knitted together in front of her stomach, and whose face was streaked with charcoal gray smudges, had stopped a few feet behind the group. She looked at Molly as she stepped up beside her, her eyes wide. "Shouldn't we be evacuating? It's hopeless. Isn't it? They'll never save it."

Molly looked back down the street. The woman was right; almost everyone she could see was giving up, retreating, dragging what possessions they could carry out of their houses before the fire spread further.

"Even with the Chief pumping out water, they'd need a fleet of fire trucks to stop the blaze," the woman said. Looking at Molly, she bit her lower lip, unlaced her hands, and shook them at her sides. "That's it. I'm not waiting any longer. Neither should you."

Molly opened her mouth to ask the woman to wait, to ask if she'd seen Jenna or knew Diego, but before she could say anything her lips spread into a smile. There she was. Jenna. As the group parted, running to tackle a burst of flame from one of the downstairs windows, Molly saw Jenna's unmistakably broad shoulders and cropped hair. She almost cheered.

Standing in the middle of the sidewalk, next to a short, stocky man with a dark beard and a stony expression, Jenna was hurriedly handing out buckets and pointing in the direction of Colton's water pump. When Molly reached her, pushing against the tide of volunteers who all seemed to be moving in the opposite direction, she tapped Jenna's shoulder.

"Jenna?" As Molly spoke, her voice was swallowed by a loud creak and a snap from within the Cruz house.

"Faster!" The man Molly assumed was Jenna's father shouted and waved his arms. "We need to move faster!"

Jenna swallowed hard but didn't seem to be able to tear her eyes away from her house. Assuming Molly was waiting in line for a bucket, Jenna reached down to hand her one, but then realized she'd run out. She was looking around, clearly wondering what to do, when Molly stepped into her line of sight.

"Jenna…"

"Miss O'Neil?" Jenna's pupils grew visibly larger. "You followed me?"

"Of course we followed you. Are you all right?" Molly took hold of Jenna's shoulders and ducked to meet her eyes.

Jenna nodded. She seemed surprised that Molly was concerned about her. "I'm fine." Looking past Molly, at the house, she added, "I'm fine but our house isn't. My dad's trying to save it. I don't think he will, though."

Molly stifled a deep, rattly cough and cast a glance at Diego Cruz, then back at Jenna. Something was niggling at the back of Molly's brain. Jenna was clearly upset, and her father was practically ignoring her. Yes, he was trying to save their home, but he didn't seem at all concerned for Jenna's feelings about it or, for that matter, relieved that she'd made her way back to him from the prison.

Molly knew very little about Jenna's father, she'd never even spoken to the man, but she'd heard about him from the other teachers—about his refusal to attend parent-teacher conferences and his old-fashioned 'hard work over schooling' attitude. Now, seeing him in the flesh, something about the man's body language made Molly's stomach tighten when she looked at him. He reminded her of Mick Higgins, except with an edge of unpleasantness that Mick had never possessed.

"You said 'we'?" Jenna was frowning. "Where are the others?"

Forcing herself to look away from Diego, Molly gestured toward where Chief Bailey and Colton were manning the pump. "Colton's back there, but I haven't found Lucky yet. Have you seen him?"

"Lucky?" Jenna's cheeks flushed a little. "He's not with you?"

"He ran after you. I hoped he'd caught up with you."

Jenna shook her head and turned to look at a house a few doors down from hers. "No, but..." she trailed off and pointed.

When Molly turned to follow the gesture, her breath caught in her chest. The movement made her cough again, and she clapped her hand over her mouth as she tried to bite it back. "That's Lucky's house?"

Jenna nodded.

The house they were looking at was also on fire, except—unlike the Cruz house—no one was trying to save it.

"Will you be okay with your dad, Jenna? I need to...." Molly was already moving in the direction of Lucky's house.

"I'll come with you." Jenna looked briefly at her father, then wrapped her arms around herself and nodded. "I'll come and help."

"No, Jenna, you should stay here." Molly waved at her to stay put. Her legs were twitching with the urge to run. "Stay here. I'll be back."

Jenna rubbed the back of her neck. She looked like she was about to say something else when a loud voice from behind her bellowed, "Jenna! Don't just stand there talking. Make yourself useful and find more buckets!"

"Dad, my friend's in trouble." Again, Jenna pointed at Lucky's house.

A few feet away, her father narrowed his eyes at her and waved at their own house. "Your friend's in trouble? Well, so are we! Now, get over here and get me more buckets!"

Molly lingered for a moment. Jenna's face had paled, and she was nodding quickly at her father.

"Sorry, Dad. Sure thing. Right away." Looking at Molly, she said, "I have to go. Please find Lucky."

Molly nodded and stepped away. The fire had spread to the roof of Lucky's house, which meant the whole building would soon be engulfed by it. If he was in there, she had to get him, quickly. "You're sure you'll be all right?"

"I'll be fine. Go find Lucky."

Molly turned and broke into a run, but the effort of it was making her take deeper breaths, which were making her lungs hurt, so she reluctantly slowed into a fast walk. On either side of the street, it seemed like pretty much every home close to the tracks had been abandoned. Diego Cruz and his friends were working to save his house, a few volunteers were throwing buckets of water at the houses nearby, but everyone else was either standing and staring—paralyzed by what they were witnessing—or hurrying in the other direction. In Southside, with the houses so close together, once one went up, the next wasn't far behind; despite the Chief and Colton's efforts, the dark-haired woman was right; it wouldn't be long before the entire street was gone.

Forcing her eyes away from whatever else was happening, when she reached Lucky's front door, Molly stopped and looked up. Debris from the train must have hit the roof and blown a hole in it. Plumes of black smoke were wafting up into the sky and orange flames were dancing in one of the top windows. If Lucky had gone inside looking for his parents, she might be too late.

With shaking hands, Molly tried the front door. "Lucky? Mr. and Mrs. Morton? Are you in there? Can anyone hear me?"

As she shouted, the door refused to budge. It was locked but the handle wasn't warm, which meant the fire hadn't yet spread downstairs. Moving to the small window to the right of the door, Molly pushed the edge of the frame. It too was sealed tight.

Trying to ignore the rising throb of panic in her chest, Molly stood back and looked around her, as if a spare key might be sitting right there on the mat. Seeing nothing of use, she turned, raced down the small alleyway beside the house and around the back instead. The backyard was small and overgrown with weeds. An unused swing set with no swing had toppled over and was almost completely covered by grass. A dying tree stood wearily near the back gate and, although it was only mid-morning, the smoke in the sky was making everything seem too dark.

The backdoor was locked too. Molly swept her eyes over the house, desperately searching for an open window she could crawl through. She'd spotted a small hole in the glass of one of the first-floor windows, which looked like it might have belonged to the bathroom, and was about to bend down and locate a stone she could use to make it larger when a figure stepped out of the shadows in front of her. Molly froze. Her limbs stiffened, but then she smiled.

It was Lucky. He was moving slowly, staring up at the house, his hands loose and floppy at his sides. When Molly approached him, holding out her palms as if she was approaching a wild animal, he didn't even blink.

"Lucky?" She put her hand lightly on his shoulder. "It's Miss O'Neil. Are you okay?"

As Lucky stepped back onto the lawn, the reflection of the flames at the top of the house flickered in his wide, frightened eyes. He didn't reply.

"Lucky? Have you been inside? Do you have a key?"

Finally, he shook his head. "No. No key." He paused and swept his hand over his face. "My parents…."

Molly looked up. The house was sealed up. No one was evacuating. No one was trying to get their belongings out. No one was shouting for help.

For a long moment, neither of them spoke. Then, beside her, Lucky gasped. "Upstairs! Miss O'Neil! I saw someone… I saw someone move."

Without thinking, Lucky lunged forward, but Molly grabbed his arm. "I'll go," she said, ducking to meet his watery eyes.

"Let go of me! They're my *parents!*" Lucky tried to tug himself free, but Molly held firm.

"Lucky, listen to me. Jenna's out front with her dad. He's a firefighter. There are people who can help. Go tell him your parents are trapped. Make him listen to you." As Molly spoke, she prayed that Diego Cruz would take action—that he wouldn't turn Lucky away because his own house was still burning.

Lucky lingered, looking from Molly to the house and back again. Then finally he nodded and took off down the side of the house.

When he was out of sight, Molly ditched her backpack, located a large stone, pulled her hood up, tying it tight so it covered her mouth, then threw the stone at the window with the broken glass and watched as it shattered inward.

With her sleeves tugged down over her hands, Molly knocked the remaining shards of glass from the frame, then levered herself up through the window. Her stomach scraped against the sill, but she didn't have time to wonder whether the hoodie was thick enough to protect her.

She was inside, and she was already struggling to breathe.

Keeping as low as she could, Molly exited the bathroom and found herself in a small, narrow hallway. The entire house was full of thick black smoke. Instantly, her eyes began to water, reminding her of the tear gas back at the prison. Above, snapping and crackling on the other side of the ceiling indicated that the top of the house was still furiously burning, and Molly had to stop herself from imagining the bedroom floors melting down on top of her. Surely there was no one up there? Surely Lucky had been mistaken?

"Hello?!" she shouted, feeling her way through the darkness. "If there's anyone there, please shout, please let me know where you are."

Taking a door on the left, Molly swept through the kitchen and the small square living room. The rooms were empty.

Stopping in the center of the living room, breathing slow shallow breaths through the fabric of her hoodie, Molly looked at the wall behind the sideboard. At least ten small square patches of brighter-than-the-rest wallpaper indicated that someone had very recently removed the pictures that hung there. Had the Mortons left? Packed up their things, locked up their house, and run away without thinking about their son?

Shaking her head, Molly forced herself to return to the hallway. Here too, the walls were empty. No coats hung on the hooks near the door. No shoes on the rack. She'd reached the stairs and was looking up, wondering whether it would even be possible to make it up there, when—just as she'd feared—something went POP behind her. It was followed by a creak and a crash and, as she turned around, a huge piece of ceiling collapsed into the end of the hall, blocking the doors to both the kitchen and the living room.

Almost as soon as the debris hit the floor, it caught fire. Molly spun around as flames snaked up the doorframe and met with the fire above. She was trapped. There was no way out.

Moving toward the front door, she started to yell, but she couldn't be sure she was heading in the right direction. She was certain there had been a window next to the door, but was it on this side? Or the living room side? It was too dark to tell. Thick smoke clouded her vision and began to choke her throat and her nostrils.

Dark. It was dark. Too dark. She hated the dark.

Her chest tightened. Her breath quickened, sucking in too much smoke and making her cough. Feeling her way along the wall, she tried to see past the smoke and the tears in her eyes. Her skin was hot. The air was quivering with heat. It was on her face and her hands. Finally she saw the ghostly outline of the window. She rushed toward it, but before she could get there something smashed through the glass.

Molly heard herself scream. Her hands went to her head and she ducked to the floor, but as she looked up, she saw an ax, and a person. Diego Cruz. He was reaching out his hand yelling, "This way!"

Crawling along the floor, Molly reached up. When she got to Diego, and her fingertips touched his, he pulled her free.

On the sidewalk, Molly scrambled to her feet.

"Thank you. Oh my God, thank you." Her voice came out as nothing more than a whisper.

When she looked up, Jenna and her father were staring at her. Jenna looked like she was about to cry, but Diego had folded his arms in front of his chest. Before Molly could even catch her breath, he began to yell at her. Telling her that she was crazy for charging into a burning building, that she could have got herself—or someone else—killed. That she must be some kind of idiot if she thought she could tackle a burning building alone with no experience fighting fires.

As Diego yelled, Molly leaned forward onto her knees, pulling her hood away from her face and coughing again and again and again. Her lungs were sore. Her throat felt like it had been scratched raw with sandpaper. Her skin and clothes were black with soot, but she could feel air on her face. She was alive.

"Miss O'Neil? Did you find my mom and dad?" Lucky pushed past Diego and stared at her, moving nervously from one foot to the other.

With the heat of the fire still on her back, Molly opened her mouth to reply, but before she could speak, the ground beneath her rattled, moved, shifted. Something exploded, and she was knocked to the ground.

8

MOLLY

Molly had never experienced a bomb going off, but she imagined this was what it would have felt like. The ground vibrated. The houses shook. Something flew through the air and crashed into a house across the street. Molly was trying to heave herself up, reaching for Lucky and Jenna to check they were okay, but she couldn't take her eyes off the house that had been hit. As she watched, her hands flew to her mouth. The already burning structure creaked and groaned before caving in on itself. The entire thing crumpled like a house of cards. Just like that. Nothing but dust and flames.

Behind her, Lucky's house was still burning. Jenna's too, and the fire was spreading.

Still struggling to catch her breath, Molly wavered and fell back to the ground. Jenna's father shouted something and she moved away before

Molly could stop her, but Lucky stayed and reached down to help her up.

"Give me a second," she managed to pant. "I need a second, Lucky."

Molly swept her fingers through her hair and tried to kick her body back into action. *Come on, Molly, get up. Get up.* A few yards away, in the middle of the street, her eyes found Colton. He was saying something to Chief Bailey. Waving his arms. The Chief was shaking his head, looking at the pump. Burning debris had careened into the houses on either side of them, setting alight anything that wasn't already on fire. They were losing the street. It was time to run. Finally, Bailey nodded.

"That was worse than the last one!" someone shouted, running past Molly and Lucky.

"We've got to go!" Someone else grabbed Molly and yanked her to her feet. Her head was swimming. She couldn't tell who it was. "It's the train," they said. "The entire street's going to go."

Whoever had helped her up disappeared, and Molly was left wavering on her unsteady feet. Next to her, Lucky looked like he had no idea what he was supposed to be doing. Torn between looking at the devastation around him and at his own house as it was consumed by flames, he was shaking from head to toe. Still trembling herself, Molly grabbed his hand and pulled him along with her as she followed the crowd of people heading away from the train tracks.

The entire group of firefighters, volunteers, cops and civilians—everyone who'd been trying to hold back the fire—was now running. Molly's boots slapped hard against the sidewalk and she had the fleeting thought that she'd left her backpack in Lucky's garden and that what she had on her person was now all she had in the world.

"Can you see Jenna?" she asked Lucky, peering around the people on either side of her. "Or her dad?"

“No. I can’t see her, Miss O’Neil.” Lucky was holding tight onto Molly’s hand, as if he was terrified of being lost.

“It’s okay,” she said hoarsely. “We’ll find her.”

As they reached the end of the street, the crowd slowed down and Molly stopped running. Leaning back against a nearby tree, she gestured for Lucky to stand beside her and shook her arms in an attempt to loosen the tight, creeping sensation in her chest.

“I’ll go look for Jenna,” Lucky said, moving away from her.

“No.” Molly grabbed his elbow. “We stick together. Just give me a minute.”

She was looking around, trying to locate anyone who looked like they might have some water to spare, when she spotted Colton. Through the crowd, his eyes found her too and he raised his hand.

Looping her arm through Lucky’s, Molly wove through the group and stepped up beside Colton. Almost everyone was staring at the street. Colton’s face was ashen, and Molly was certain she’d seen his hands trembling before he shoved them into his pockets.

“Are you all right?” he asked, taking in her smoke-smudged face.

“I’m fine,” Molly coughed. “At least, I will be.”

Colton glanced at Lucky and nodded. “Did you find Jenna?”

“She’s with her father,” Molly answered, trying to ignore the twinge in her chest as she once again failed to locate Jenna in the crowd.

Colton nodded slowly and looked back toward the train tracks. The part of the train that had been hanging off the bridge was gone.

“It came loose,” Colton said. “Whole thing went up and it fell.”

Molly wrapped her arms around herself; the train itself was barely visible now, and from where they were standing it looked almost as if the entire world was on fire. Looking up, Molly spotted Jenna's father and asked Colton to follow her.

"It must have hit a gas line," Diego Cruz was saying to the police chief, who was shaking his head gravely as he told Diego that there was now very little they could do to save the street.

At Diego's side, Jenna was standing with her hands in her pockets, listening and barely moving.

"We can't abandon the neighborhood," Diego said, his neck muscles twitching. "These are people's homes."

Colton glanced at Molly as the police chief nodded sympathetically and repeated, "I'm sorry, Diego. There's nothing we can do now. The fire's out of control and it's simply too dangerous. Our resources are best spent stopping the fire from spreading to other parts of town."

Molly reached up and tugged her hair loose from its tie. Her entire head was aching. She shook it, but it didn't help. As Diego practically growled and stalked away from the police chief, Jenna ran after him and put her hand on his back as if she was about to offer him a hug. "It's okay, Dad, you did your best," she said softly.

"Jenna, not now," Diego snapped at her and ripped his arm away. As he moved, Jenna flinched before hanging back.

Molly sucked in her cheeks; what kind of father wouldn't hug his daughter after witnessing something like that? What kind of father spoke to a child that way? Showed so little compassion? Visions of her own father and his contorted, angry face danced through her mind. She watched them for a moment, then shoved them back into the dark where they belonged.

"Diego?" One of the other volunteer firefighters had called Jenna's dad, and he moved quickly away, not even checking to see where his daughter was or what she was doing. For a moment Molly thought

Jenna was going to follow him, but then she spotted Lucky, nodded at him and walked quietly over.

"You okay?" Jenna asked, but Lucky didn't seem able to answer. "I'm sure your folks weren't inside," she said softly. "A bunch of people left before the fire got really bad."

Lucky dipped his head and stared at his feet. The way his shoulders drooped made Molly's heart hurt. What could be worse than imagining your parents perishing in a fire and having no way to know whether they had or not?

As Jenna and Lucky settled into a companionable silence, Molly saw that Colton was standing next to the police chief and that the two of them were deep in conversation.

"Okay, Chief, so what do we do now?" Molly asked loudly, stepping up beside them and putting her hands on her hips. "What do all these people do?"

"That's what we were discussing," Colton said, clearly hoping she'd lower her voice because it was making others turn and stare.

"There's a walk-in center up at the school," the police chief said softly. "Colton says you were a teacher there? Perhaps you can lead these people up there while we—" The Chief was mid-sentence when Diego Cruz appeared from nowhere, barging through the crowd, and looking at Molly as if she had no right to do or ask anything because it was *his* neighborhood on fire.

"If anyone's going to lead people to the school, I will do it," he said, raising his voice above the chatter around them.

"I'm not going anywhere," someone shouted in reply.

"There's nothing we can do," said someone else.

"There must be something!" a woman nearby cried out. "We can't just abandon our homes!"

To Molly's surprise, Diego raised his hands for quiet. "Everyone, please. Chief Bailey is right. The best we can do is head to the neighborhood evacuation point."

"Oh yeah, where's that?" an elderly man asked sarcastically.

"The town's emergency plan has three designated points. The nearest for us is the high school," Diego replied, looking to the police chief for confirmation.

Nodding, the Chief added, "Mr. Cruz is correct. All residents of Southside should evacuate the area. This street and the adjacent ones. Don't go back for your belongings. There will be help for you at the school."

Molly frowned. She didn't like Diego Cruz. Something about him made her decidedly uneasy: the way he spoke to Jenna, the way he'd just done a complete one-eighty and was acting as if going up to the school had been his idea.

"Miss O'Neil?" Lucky's smaller than normal voice cut through the crying and shouting that was escalating around them.

"Lucky?"

"My parents? When you were in the house, did you…?" He suddenly looked very, very young. And very, very scared.

Putting her arm around him, Molly squeezed his shoulders. "There was no one inside, Lucky," she said. "I checked."

As his eyes widened and his entire face brightened, Lucky whispered, "You're sure?"

Molly smiled at him, forcing herself to meet his eyes. "Yes, I'm sure."

But as they turned away from the carnage, her stomach twisted violently. Lucky's parents could have been upstairs. She didn't make it that far. They could have burned to death, and he'd never know for sure what had happened.

No. She would think positively. His parents were probably at the high school already. Jenna said lots of people had evacuated and the Mortons had always seemed like sensible people. As soon as the fire started, they probably packed their things and left. Headed off to find Lucky. She'd find them at the school. She was certain of it.

"Colton?" As the crowd started to dissipate, moving off in the direction of the high school, Molly paused and lightly touched Colton's elbow. He was still standing next to the police chief and didn't look as if he was ready to move. "Are you coming? To the school?"

Looking down at his leg, then up at Molly, Colton pushed back his shoulders, his fists tightening at his sides.

"I—"

"You're staying, aren't you?" Molly took back her hand and tucked a loose strand of hair behind her ear.

"I'll catch up with you." Colton caught her gaze and held it. "I *will* catch up with you, Molly. But, right now, I need to do whatever I can to help. If we don't stop the fire from spreading…."

Molly nodded, even though her gut was telling her to object. Their small group was already splintered. Tommy and Zack had gone to look for their mother. Erik, Alex, and Scarlett had gone home too. Molly's instinct was to keep them all together, that it was *safer* together. Her head, however, knew it wasn't that simple. There was no way she could have stopped the Bankses from going home and, from Colton's expression, she could see there was no way she could stop him either. Trying to convince him to leave with her was futile; at his core, he believed in doing what was right for the greater good and, right now, battling the fire and saving the town was the greater good.

"Take this." Colton was handing her back the gun, pressing it firmly into her hand. "Look after yourself, Molly. If you need me, come find me."

"You take care too," she said. "Goodbye, Colton. I'll see you soon."

9

MOLLY

Approaching the high school, Molly almost forgot that they were living in a completely different world from the one they'd inhabited the last time she set foot through its gates.

The yellow buses were lined up in the parking lot. The sky behind it was blue, reflecting only a whisper of the smoke that stained the sky behind them as they walked away from the destruction the train had caused.

As the throng of Southside residents, and people from neighboring streets, filtered through the school gates, Molly felt a hand on her arm and stopped, instinctively reaching for her gun.

When she turned and saw a face she recognized, she shook the tension from her arm and exhaled loudly. "Tommy? Zack?" Without thinking, she pulled them both into a quick hug and patted their shoulders. "I'm so glad you're okay."

"We barely made it to the house. The surrounding streets have gone up in flames." Zack was rubbing his neck. His dark hair was masking a small cut on his forehead.

"You're all right, though?" As Molly examined Zack's face, someone behind her grumbled at them to keep moving. Checking that Lucky was still beside her, Molly gestured for Zack and Tommy to follow and inched forward.

"Fine," Tommy answered on behalf of his brother. "We're fine."

"Your mom?" Molly asked quietly. "The house? Is it okay?"

Casting a quick glance at Zack, Tommy said, "Mom wasn't home. The house is okay, though, for now. The fire hasn't reached our street yet."

Next to Tommy, Zack pressed his lips together and shoved his hands into his pockets.

"Zack wanted to stay and wait but I thought it was best to get out of there," Tommy explained quietly.

Molly nodded. "You did the right thing."

Just inside the gates, to try and lighten the mood, Molly gestured to her small blue Honda, which was sitting in the exact same spot as always, miraculously untouched. "Hey, well at least my car's still in one piece," she said. "If worst comes to worst, we can camp out in there."

"Anything good in the glove box?" Tommy asked. "Snacks? Whiskey?"

Molly laughed. "Boy, I wish there was. Afraid not, though."

"I'm not sure now's the time for laughing." Diego Cruz had stepped up beside them and was gesturing to the others up ahead. "These people have lost their homes."

Molly's jaw tensed. How dare he presume she was being insensitive? This was a man who'd refused his own daughter a hug when she needed one!

"I'm aware of that," she said under her breath.

As if she sensed that she needed to ease the tension, Jenna—who was walking next to her father—said, "Miss O'Neil's my teacher, Dad. She got us out of the prison."

Diego looked at Molly, then at Jenna, the pieces finally slotting together. Nodding slightly, he said, "I see," but didn't bother to add, 'thank you'.

Stalking off ahead, Diego raised his voice. "This way, everyone," he called, waving his arms in the air. "Follow me. We're heading for the gym."

"Wow," Molly muttered, making sure she was out of earshot of Jenna, who'd hung behind with Lucky instead of trying to keep up with her dad. "He's charming, isn't he?"

"A ray of sunshine," Tommy replied.

"He's a jerk," Zack muttered, glancing up at Molly. "Everyone at school knows to avoid Jenna's dad. Ever since he kicked off at one of her wrestling matches."

"He kicked off?" Tommy asked.

"I wasn't there." Zack tilted his head from one side to the other. "But apparently he flipped out at the ref when he penalized Jenna for a super aggressive takedown. Diego *encourages* aggressive takedowns. So…." Zack trailed off as Tommy shook his head at him.

"Dude, if you weren't there, you shouldn't be spreading rumors like that."

"Seriously? Since when were you such a teacher's pet?" Zack rolled his eyes at his brother and, before the tension could rise any further, Molly stepped between them.

"Listen, guys, I don't know anything much about Diego, but I know he wouldn't like it if he overheard us talking like this, so let's drop it, okay?"

As Tommy and Zack grumbled and stopped talking, Molly tried not to allow herself to keep thinking about Colton, and to focus on the task at hand instead—finding out what was going on and who was in charge. Folding her arms in front of her chest, she followed the group into the gymnasium, looking back every now and then to keep track of Lucky's bobbing head and Jenna's stocky frame as they moved through the doors.

As soon as they entered it was clear that, actually, no one was really in charge. The entire gym was in chaos. Some tables had been pushed back against the far wall. To the right of the room, people who looked like volunteers were applying slapdash first aid to anyone with cuts or bruises. One woman was handing out bottles of water.

Stepping to the side of the main throng, Molly watched as Diego strode up to a group of adults who were arguing. "What's going on here?" he demanded. "I have a group of people with me who've lost their homes. A train derailed. It's taken out almost the entire neighborhood. We need food, water!"

"We're trying to get the emergency generator working," replied one of the adults, a man who Molly thought she recognized as one of the school's janitors.

"And I keep telling him it won't work!" shouted another, who looked as if he was sick of repeating himself.

After listening to them bicker for a few more moments, Molly gestured for Tommy and Zack to follow her and stepped forward.

"What have you tried?" she asked, trying to remember what Erik had said about generators.

Before she could receive an answer, however, Diego noisily grabbed hold of a nearby table and dragged it into the middle of the room. Jumping on top of it, he clapped his hands. "Everyone! Listen to me!"

Molly glanced at Tommy as the entire room fell unfathomably quiet.

"We need order. We need a plan." Diego looked around at the people below him and widened his eyes. "What I have just witnessed was a travesty. Your local government let you down. The police let you down. The firefighters—we were the only ones left trying to help and we had no backup."

Picturing Colton and the police chief, who'd almost killed themselves trying to put out the blaze, Molly muttered, "No one to help? Is he serious?"

"People are dead! People are missing!" Diego was waving his arms now, as if he was expecting a series of boos and cheers from the crowd. "I gave them solutions. I offered them ideas, but they laughed it off and ignored me. I'm just a *volunteer* firefighter. What do I know?"

"A volunteer?" Molly glanced at Tommy. "He's not even a real fire-fighter?"

"Well, I know this… I know we need action. A strong leader. Someone to protect the people of this town."

"I'm sorry but it's unfair of you to blame the police." Before she could stop herself, Molly had raised her voice and interrupted. Ignoring the worried look on Lucky's face, she clenched her fists at her side and said loudly, "I saw the cops trying to help you back there. They were doing their best. They have limited resources. They—"

"You think that matters? Limited resources? They should have prepared for this! We all knew an EMP was a possibility. We've all watched the movies. Yet they did nothing." Diego looked away from her and patted his chest. "Luckily, *I* have thought about it. *I* have a plan to make sure everyone is safe."

Seeming not to care that no one had asked what his plan was, Diego continued.

"We scavenge all the diesel we can find to help power the generators."

Molly rolled her eyes and bit her lower lip. "We don't even know it's lack of diesel that's causing them not to work," she whispered to Tommy.

"There are two commercial-sized fridges in the school's kitchen. With the generators working, we can preserve food and medicines. We can also rig up lighting and heat. In a few days, this school will become a safe haven for everyone in need. A place where we can look after each other and work together to keep the town safe." Diego paused, letting his words sink in. Around the sides of the room, Molly noticed that some of the volunteers who'd been working alongside Diego back on Southside were congregating, staring, whispering. "We will scavenge supplies from abandoned homes, too. Anything we can find. We'll bring it here and we'll set up camp."

"We steal?" Molly interrupted, raising her voice and looking around the room. "You want us to go steal from people? That's your plan?"

Nearby, Diego's friends puffed out their chests and glowered at her.

"Do you have a better one?" Diego bit back, almost laughing at her.

"I—"

"Exactly!" he shouted. "Besides, we are not stealing. We are coming together as a community. Every single person should be giving to the community effort. No excuses."

Molly waited for someone else to protest, for someone else to see through what Diego was saying, but no one moved. When she looked at Tommy, he shrugged as if to say, *What can we do about it?*

Clapping his hands, Diego jumped down from the table. There was a moment's silence until he said loudly, "Carry on with what you were doing. You'll soon be assigned a new job."

Toward the front of the crowd, Jenna was studying her father's every move. Molly watched as Diego walked over to her and put his arm around her shoulders. Loudly, so everyone could hear him, he said, "Well done, Jenna. I'm so proud of the way you helped out back there."

Jenna's cheeks flushed at the praise. She glanced back at Molly, but her dad's arm was still around her shoulders. Ignoring Lucky, Diego guided Jenna away from her friend.

"I have a very special job for you," he said, pulling her with him. "Very special."

Molly gritted her teeth and turned away. She was about to ask Tommy why he wasn't as furious as she was, perhaps even demand that he help her challenge Diego, when she spotted someone familiar through the crowd. A dark-haired woman in a wheelchair. A woman with a dog at her side.

"Zack," she said, tugging on Zack's arm. "Is that Erik and Scarlett's mom? Is that Mrs. Banks?"

10

LAURA
TWO HOURS EARLIER

"It'll all work out okay, Barb," Jerry was saying softly to his wife, who'd barely uttered a word since they left their street. "Look at all these people. All heading to the same place. Someone at the school will know what to do."

Laura cast a quick glance at Jerry but tried not to catch his eye; she didn't want him to see that she was having doubts, wondering whether she should have stayed home, wondering how in the world all these people were going to be helped.

As they entered the high school parking lot through the large open gates, Laura saw a woman nearby stumble. She was dragging a large suitcase, but one of the wheels was broken. No one stopped to help her.

Heading over, Laura reached out a hand and helped the woman to her feet. "Thanks," she said. Her voice was thin and reedy, and she looked terrified. "Do you know where we're supposed to go?"

"My kids go here," Laura said, ignoring the voice in her head that whispered: *Went here. Your kids went here.* "I think everyone's going to the gym."

The woman nodded and, without asking if it was okay, stepped in line beside Laura.

"Your case looks in as about as good a state as this chair," Laura said, patting the arms of the wheelchair Mick and Carmel had so generously allowed her to borrow. When the woman blinked at her, clearly unsure whether she was supposed to laugh or not, Laura added, "I usually have a sportier model. This one's on loan and I think it's seen better days." She shuffled uncomfortably—the plastic back rest was already causing her shoulders to sweat and the chair was offering little support for her throbbing lower back.

"I dragged this down from the attic," the woman said, looking at her case. "It got caught on the hatch and now the wheel…." She gave it a tug, as if it was a reluctant toddler who'd decided not to cooperate. When she looked up, she put her hand over her chest and said, "I'm Rebecca. Becky. I was a teacher here."

Laura introduced herself, Jerry and Barb, but didn't offer Becky a handshake; her arms were stinging with the effort of navigating the crowded sidewalks and people-thronged roads, between home and the high school, in Mick's dead mother's wheelchair.

"You taught here?" Laura said warmly. "What did you teach?"

Before Becky could answer, Jerry put a hand on Laura's shoulder. "Well, it sure looks like we're in the right place," he said, pointing at a handwritten sign that had been tacked to a notice board outside the gymnasium.

ALL WELCOME. FOOD AND SHELTER INSIDE.

As Barb let out a sigh of relief, Laura fought the urge to tell her not to get too excited. There was definitely *not* going to be enough food and shelter to match the number of people who were turning up.

Just inside the door, a man Laura recognized as the kids' math teacher stopped her and asked if she had any injuries that needed attending to. He was wearing a high-vis jacket and holding a clipboard. As he spoke, he looked her up and down. His eyes faltered when they met with the shotgun slung across her chest and, again, when they took in the scrapes on her arms.

"I'm fine," she said. "I'm looking for my husband. Alex Banks? And my children. Scarlett and Erik Banks. They're students here. They were on a school trip and—"

The man held up his palm. It was so close to Laura's face that she could see the beads of sweat in the crease between his thumb and index finger. She saw him cast a look at Argent and tightened her grip on her dog's leash.

After a short pause, the man nodded at her. "If you don't need medical assistance, head inside to the tables on the left. You'll be given food and water shortly."

"Thank you," Laura said tightly. Turning to Jerry, she asked, "Are you coming?"

"I'm going to see if I can get Barb checked out," Jerry replied quietly. "We're low on her medication and I'm hoping there will be a doc here somewhere. Good luck finding your husband."

Laura nodded and peered past Jerry to look at Becky. She didn't particularly want to get caught up with another person but—despite having taught at the school—Becky seemed so overwhelmed by the situation that Laura was reluctant to simply leave her behind.

"Becky," she said as they reached the line of tables where most people were congregating. "I need to try to find my family. Will you be all right?"

"Oh sure." The woman wrapped her arms around her waist, nodding. "I'll be fine. I'll just wait here. Thank you for your help."

Next to Laura, Argent whined, and Laura reached instinctively down to pat his head. "Okay, boy," she said, trying to see through the sea of people in front of her. "Let's go find Alex and the kids."

At first, when she'd seen the math teacher with the clipboard, Laura had felt relieved—certain that, inside, there would be someone with a plan, someone taking charge, someone who knew what to do. She'd barely been inside the gymnasium for five minutes when it became very clear this was *not* the case.

All around her, dazed-looking people were clustered in small groups, either talking far too loudly or not at all. Several people were coughing and had soot-covered faces that told Laura they'd been close to the fire that had started in the Southside area. Thinking about it, not for the first time, she thanked God that it had happened on the other side of the tracks; it had been bad enough being stuck beneath a tree. Being stuck beneath a burning tree would have been a whole different ball game.

Nearby, an elderly woman was handing out bottles of water but with seemingly no rhyme or reason to who she was choosing. Wheeling over to her, Laura gently touched the woman's arm. "Excuse me, I'm looking for my husband."

"Oh, I'm sorry, dear," the woman replied.

"He's tall, slim, has a beard. He should be with two kids, teenagers."

The woman shrugged and offered Laura a bottle of water, as if it might somehow compensate for her missing family.

“Who’s in charge?” Laura asked, scanning the room for someone—anyone—who looked in any way official.

“I’m not sure, to be honest, dear. There are some doctors and nurses over there.” She waved toward the right of the gym. “They’ve been patching people up. Maybe they’ve seen your husband?”

Biting back a sigh, Laura shoved the bottle down the side of her chair and made her way to the opposite end of the room. It was a short distance but took far longer than necessary because she had to keep raising her voice and asking people to part and let her through.

By the time she reached the untidy collection of chairs, which seemed to have been allocated as a triage center, she was beginning to sweat. The sheer number of bodies in the gym was making it hot and stuffy, airless. Like the closet had been….

Tugging her mind away from the memory of being locked in her bedroom closet while Dave ransacked the house, Laura took a long drink of water, then held out the bottle for Argent. He was remarkably good at drinking from a bottle; Laura would tip it up so the water slowly trickled out, and he’d lick at it like he was licking a tap or water fountain. Sharing with Argent had never bothered her—he was so much a part of her that it seemed completely natural—but it was something the kids always pulled faces at. “Eeew, Mom! He’s a *dog*. Don’t let him lick the thing you’re going to drink from!”

“Can I help you? Are you hurt?” A voice interrupted her train of thought and she looked up. A young man with a stethoscope around his neck was studying her face. “Ma’am?” He asked, glancing at Argent and taking in Laura’s wheelchair as if he was trying to work out if she was newly incapacitated or if it was a long-term situation. “I’m Doctor Chase. Are you all right?”

"I'm fine." Laura replaced the lid on her bottle. "I'm looking for my husband and my kids. Have you seen a man with a beard accompanied by two dark-haired teenagers?"

"We've seen a lot of people," Chase said. "Have you got a photograph?"

Reaching into her pocket, Laura took out a crumpled photograph of Alex, Erik, and Scarlett. She'd removed it from the frame on her sideboard before leaving the house.

When she handed it to the doctor, he took hold of it and shook his head. "I'm afraid not."

"Is anyone setting up a missing persons list?" Laura knew the answer before she'd even asked the question. "There must be hundreds of people who've been separated from their families."

"No, but that's a great idea." Chase patted Laura's shoulder then turned to shout at a colleague, "Suzanne, this lady wants to set up a missing persons list."

"Great!" Suzanne, a middle-aged woman wearing a nurse's uniform, shouted back. "Tell her to set up over there."

"Oh, no, I didn't mean that *I*..." Laura stopped herself mid-sentence. Why shouldn't it be her? Back when she was on the school's PTA, she'd organized the parent action committee, including setting up the rotation for volunteers. She could do this. She'd go mad if she sat around waiting, hoping that Alex would show up with the kids. Plus, if she was the one organizing the list, when he did come, she'd be the first to know about it.

"All right," she said. "Over there? Can you just pull that table out from the wall for me?"

Chase nodded, swiftly dragged the table out so there was room behind it for Laura and Argent, then reached into his pocket and handed her a notebook and a pen. "So you can take people's details."

Laura nodded, hanging her shotgun on the back of a chair that Chase had positioned behind the table, and then telling Argent to go sit beside it.

As Chase returned hurriedly to the disorganized triage area, Laura turned her family's photograph over in her hand and scrawled on the back their names, ages, and address. Then she placed it dead center in the middle of the table. When she turned around, Chase was directing a young man over to her.

"They said you could help me find my wife?" The man was wringing his hands together in front of his stomach. "She works in the bank downtown. I haven't heard from her since yesterday."

"Do you have a photograph?" Laura asked, pen poised over her notebook.

The man nodded and took a small passport-sized picture from his wallet.

"Great." Laura took it, wrote a number on the back, then scribbled the corresponding number in her notebook. "What's your wife's name?"

She'd only just finished writing when a second person stepped up in front of her, followed by a third, a fourth, and then a line she couldn't even see the end of. She was about to go back to the far side of the gym and ask Becky to come help her when a firm hand landed on her shoulder. "Excuse me, I'm looking for my wife. I was told you could help?"

The voice made every single muscle in her body tense up. She was imagining it; she had to be imagining it.

"Alex?"

Before she could turn around, her husband's handsome, bearded face appeared in front of her. Not once in the past five years had she wished she could jump out of her chair more than she did in this very moment. Slinging her arms around his neck, she let him pull her close, even though it caused a twinge in her lower back.

"You smell dreadful," she laughed, pulling back. "Where are the kids? Did you get them out? Are they…?"

"I'm happy to see you too," Alex said softly, stepping aside and allowing Erik and Scarlett to throw themselves at her.

As Laura wrapped her arms around the twins, she saw Argent leave his post and pad over to them, eyes bright, tail wagging, clearly over the moon that his family was back together.

For a long moment, Laura allowed herself to feel elated, but when Alex asked her if she was all right, her smile faltered. She wasn't all right, not really, but telling him that would mean telling him *why*. Telling Alex about the dead body in their garden would mean telling him why Dave was there in the first place. It would mean admitting the truth about the pills she'd hidden from him.

"I'm fine," she said quickly, squeezing Alex's hand. "Did you go to the house?"

"We found your note," Erik said quickly. "We came straight here."

Laura nodded, aware of the line of people building up behind her. She was about to ask the three of them to pitch in and help her when a dark-haired man with a beard climbed onto a table in the middle of the room and clapped his hands. "Everyone! Listen to me!"

11

LAURA

When the man who called himself Diego jumped down from the table, Alex put his hand on Laura's shoulder. She knew her husband's features by heart and his expression was one that said, *this isn't good.*

"What does he mean? Everyone should be giving to the community?" Laura asked, frowning.

"He means he's going to steal our stuff," Scarlett replied, folding her arms in front of her chest.

Laura squeezed her daughter's hand and tried not to let herself become fixated on her beautiful, tired-looking face; a face she'd feared she might never see again.

"Then we need to leave." Erik was looking from Alex to Laura. "We need to secure the house… don't we? We can't let them take *our* stuff."

As Laura fought back the urge to tell them she didn't want them anywhere near the place after what had happened, Alex began to nod.

"I think we do, Erik, yes. Your mom did a great job getting supplies together and, while I'm all for helping others, I get the feeling this guy," he jerked his thumb toward Diego, "is only out for himself."

As the crowd of people waiting to register loved ones continued to grow behind her, Laura handed Scarlett her notebook and asked her to take her place. Scarlett hesitated but Laura nodded at her pleadingly. "Scarlett, it's just while I talk to your dad."

"Okay." Scarlett glanced at the line of mostly crying or upset people and breathed in deeply. "What do I do?"

"Take their names, addresses, and number each photo. Erik, help your sister, please."

Erik opened his mouth to object, but then changed his mind and miraculously did as he was told. Putting his hand on Laura's shoulder, he nodded. "Okay, Mom."

Laura reached up and brushed her fingers against her son's. She wanted to pull him into the tightest embrace. She wanted to hide away with her family and forget all of this, and she most definitely did *not* want them to return to the house.

If they found Dave... If they discovered his body, Laura would have two choices; lie and tell them she had no idea how he'd gotten there or admit that she had killed him. She didn't doubt that Alex would understand what she'd done, but she knew that confessing to him about the shooting would lead her to confess other things too. He loved her, and he'd stuck by her through everything, but would he continue to do that when he found out she'd lied to him? Kept drugs in the house all that time?

With the twins out of earshot, Laura was about to tell Alex she really didn't like the idea of them all heading back across town when she realized someone was standing next to her. "My daughter's taking missing persons' details," Laura said, barely looking up.

"Sorry, I'm not lost, I'm—"

"Molly?" Alex was smiling. "You're safe. Thank God. How are the kids?" Turning to Laura, he added. "Sweetheart, meet Miss O'Neil, the twins' teacher. She's the one who got them safely out of Fairfield Prison. Molly, this is my wife."

Clasping her hands to her chest, Laura's entire body swelled with gratitude as she took in the tall, smoke-covered woman in front of her. Wearing a white shirt that had seen better days, and her hair hanging in a disarray around her shoulders, Molly O'Neil smiled and patted Alex on the shoulder.

"I'm so glad you found your wife. With the fire spreading, I was worried."

"The fire's spreading?" Laura asked, glancing furtively at the rapidly increasing number of coughing patients in the triage area.

Molly nodded. "I'm afraid so. The police chief and a few others stayed behind to try and stop it but…."

"Then we need to get back home as quickly as possible and retrieve our supplies before…" Alex lowered his voice, casting a glance in Diego's direction.

"Before Diego and his men start raiding the neighborhood," Molly finished his sentence for him.

Alex nodded gravely. "If the neighborhood's being deserted, Diego won't waste any time taking advantage of it."

Pressing her lips together, Laura shook her head. "Alex, I think you should stay here. It's too risky. Besides, it took me forever to make it across town in this chair *and* I'm needed here." She gestured to where Scarlett and Erik were trying to comfort an elderly woman. "I promised I'd help reunite people with their families. It's not right for me to leave as soon as I've found mine."

"Then I'll take the kids," Alex said gruffly. "If it looks like the fire's holding off, we'll secure the house and we won't let Diego in."

Laura's stomach twisted violently. If Alex set foot in the study, he'd see the blood. If he decided to move the tarp from the table outside, he'd see Dave. As her skin became both hot and cold at the same time, Laura searched desperately for something she could say to make Alex stay with her.

"Mom, I agree with Dad." Erik had left Scarlett with the lost and found people and was standing with his hands on his hips. "I've got stuff at the house that could be useful." He lowered his voice and ducked his head. "Stuff that could help fix a generator. Some batteries that might work." He paused then added, as if he was a little embarrassed to admit it, "I put them aside in a steel box a while back after I watched this awesome EMP documentary on YouTube."

"Erik…." Laura was already shaking her head.

"That's settled, then," Alex interrupted, putting his hand on Erik's shoulder. "I'll take the kids back to the house. If it's safe to stay, we'll stay and secure the barracks." He was trying to smile, to make her smile back, but it wasn't working. "If not, we'll bring what we can carry back here to the school and then we'll decide what to do next."

Alex crouched down in front of Laura and put his hands on her knees. In the immediate aftermath of the accident, she had hated it when he did that. It had made her feel small, like a child, like he was patronizing her. Looking at him now, however, all she felt was a tsunami of love and fear, mixed together in a concoction that was making her seasick. "I know you're scared. I am too. I don't want to be separated from you ever again, Laura. But there are things at the house we need. Plus…" Alex grinned cheekily, "I think I can fix your chair situation." He cast a withering look at Laura's geriatric transport.

"My chair's broken, Alex. Crushed. There's no way you can."

"Ah." Alex put his finger to her lips and shook his head. "That's where you're wrong. You know that sporty model you wanted?"

Laura frowned, then widened her eyes. "The one with the orange trim? The one that costs three thousand dollars?"

"That's the one." Alex rubbed the back of his neck. "Well, I bought it for you. For our anniversary."

Laura stifled a laugh as she reminded herself that money was pretty much meaningless now, so it was pointless asking Alex why he'd spent so much or whether they could afford it. "Our anniversary was last month."

"Yeah, well, I chickened out. I wasn't sure it was a romantic enough gift. Wasn't sure if you'd…" he trailed off.

"Be mad at you?" Laura pursed her lips; she had a habit of accusing Alex of being insensitive but, really, it was her own sensitivity that was the issue.

Shrugging, he replied, "It's in the garage in the trunk of my car." Again, Alex patted the arm of Laura's temporary transport. "You'll make it across town in record time if you've got that baby to drive."

This time, Laura couldn't stop herself from laughing. Pressing her forehead against Alex's, she inhaled slowly and absorbed the familiar feel of his heart beating close to hers. "All right." When she sat back, she folded her arms in front of her stomach and nodded firmly. "All right, take the kids. But Alex?"

“Mmm hmm?” Alex began to stand up, but Laura caught his hand.

As he stared at her, she almost said it. *I have something to tell you.* It would have been so easy, but instead she found herself whispering, “I love you.”

Alex’s mouth twitched into a smile. “I love you too, Laura.”

12

COLTON

Colton woke with a start. His neck was stiff from where he'd slept propped up beneath the bridge and, despite the cardboard he'd been sitting on, the backs of his legs were damp. After working until well past midnight, trying to create a firebreak that would stop the blaze spreading from Southside to the surrounding neighborhoods, he'd followed the police chief's instructions to get some rest.

Looking up at the belly of the bridge that arched above his head, the irony of the situation was not lost on him; leaving the Marines, he'd been determined not to end up where so many injured veterans ended up—on the streets, sleeping rough—and now look where he was. Doing exactly that.

He was rubbing his knee, trying to ease it back into being moveable, when the young police officer next to him—a slim, wide-faced guy by the name of Hicks—said, "You get any sleep?"

"Not much." Colton left his knee alone and tried to focus on building the energy to stand up.

"Me neither," Hicks replied. "Still, at least we're out of the way of that smoke."

Colton winced as he flexed his leg.

"Want some?" Hicks was holding out a small metal flask. "Whiskey," he said. "Seeing as we're still technically off shift."

"Not sure I was ever *on* shift," Colton said, accepting the flask and allowing himself to take a larger than normal swig from its neck. When Hicks raised his eyebrows, Colton added, "I'm not a cop."

Taking back his flask, Hicks screwed the lid back on and tilted his head. "I didn't think I recognized you… but I gotta say you're pretty handy for a guy who's not a cop."

"Marine," Colton said, scratching his palm over the bristly shadow that had formed on his chin. It was more than forty-eight hours since he last shaved, the longest he'd gone since the dark days when he first returned home from the Middle East and had found himself unable to coax himself out of bed. The days when Debs had become increasingly frustrated with him. The days when, more than once, he'd wondered what the point of it all was.

"My brother's a Marine." Hicks' voice interrupted Colton's train of thought before it could run away with itself. He sounded hoarse, from the smoke. So did Colton.

"Oh yeah?" Colton tried to sound interested. Hicks was proud of his brother. He wanted to talk about him. Colton *should* ask what unit he was a part of, where he was serving, when they last saw one another. Ever since he left the Corps, however, he'd found these kinds of conversations difficult. Inevitably, they would lead to the question: so, what happened to you? Why'd you come home? And he hated answering that question.

"Yeah, he's—" Hicks' eyes had lit up but before he could say any more, the two men were interrupted by a tall, bulky shadow, which blocked out the hazy morning light beyond the bridge.

"Nap time's over, gentlemen." It was Dukes. A sergeant who'd spent most of yesterday getting on Colton's last nerve; the kind of guy Colton had come across far too many times—a sycophant. A guy with contacts who'd been promoted way above his capability threshold and whose core plan of attack was to make others look bad, so he looked good.

Hicks rose quickly to his feet and brushed down his uniform. "Sir," he said, straightening his shoulders.

"Hicks," Dukes replied tightly, looking down at Colton instead of meeting Hicks' eyes.

Trying to keep his expression as pain-free as possible, Colton braced himself on the cool bricks beside him and creaked into an upright position.

Flexing his leg, an involuntary wince crossed his face, and Dukes spotted it immediately.

"You injured, old man? Need to bow out?"

Colton's jaw twitched. "It's an old injury. Nothing to be concerned about, Sergeant."

"If you're not fit, you should head to the Community Relief Center." Dukes' hands were on his hips, his fingers twitching next to his holster as if he wanted to remind Colton that he had a gun and that Colton—not being a cop—did not. As he finished speaking, Dukes' tongue darted out to moisten his lower lip. The gesture made Colton shudder. “Volunteers are only useful if they don’t get in people’s way.” Dukes emphasized the world *volunteer*.

“Understood,” Colton growled.

“He’s not in the way, sir. Colton has been very helpful. Chief Bailey—”

Again, Dukes cut Hicks’ sentence short. “Good. Make sure it stays that way.”

As the three of them headed back toward the road, Dukes walked quickly. Every now and then, he glanced back at Colton as if he was hoping to catch him stumble.

“This guy always been a jerk?” Colton muttered under his breath.

“Pretty much,” Hicks answered quickly and quietly, clearly worried about being overheard.

Although Colton didn’t want to cause any trouble, part of him—the part that simmered just beneath the surface and which he managed, most of the time, to keep at bay—thought it might not be such a bad thing if Dukes did overhear them. Gun aside, even with his injury, Colton knew he could take him, and Dukes was the kind of guy who needed to be shown the right way to treat people.

“Not today,” Colton whispered to himself. “Not today.”

As they ascended the bank up toward the road, each footstep caused Colton to bite the inside of his cheek as a lightning rod of pain shot from his knee to his hip and then down into his ankle. Hicks reached out to offer him a hand but Colton shook his head. “I can manage,” he said gruffly.

Finally on steady ground, Dukes tipped his head toward the train tracks that ran over the bridge. “The track seems to be working as a firebreak. Now that we've cleared this section of combustibles it's unlikely the fire will continue to spread."

"Good," Hicks said. "So, what's next?"

Looking Colton up and down, Dukes folded his arms in front of his chest. "Our next job is to get the roads clear. When the power comes back on, we need emergency vehicles to have good access to all areas." Waving at the cars and trucks that had been abandoned up and down the street, Dukes added, "This lot won't be a problem, but there's a crane a few blocks over that needs shifting."

"Let's take a look," Colton said, moving off in the direction Dukes had indicated.

Dukes quickened his pace, easily passing Colton, and strode off ahead. "This way."

When he was out of earshot, Hicks tugged Colton's arm and passed him something. "Here," he said. "For the leg."

Colton opened his palm. Hicks had given him two small white tablets.

"Ibuprofen," Hicks said. "Had a bottle on me when the power went out."

"These will be like gold dust soon," Colton said, inhaling deeply through his nostrils as he ran his thumb over the tablets. "Are you sure you want to share them?"

Hicks winked and patted Colton's shoulder. "Just don't go spreading it around that I've got 'em."

Colton nodded, still staring at the pills. Since his injury, he'd avoided even the most innocent of painkillers. Becoming dependent on pills terrified him more than losing his life, more than losing his career, more than anything. Despite the pain, sober, he had his wits about him. He had his brain, his mind, control of his actions. He'd known too many injured vets who'd lost those things through no fault of their own; a prescription for Vicodin, a desperation to escape the torment caused by their injuries.

Before, though, he'd been able to rest. He'd taken time to do physical therapy. He'd applied for the job driving the school bus because it allowed him not to strain himself too much. Now, resting and PT weren't possible. For the foreseeable future, he'd be on the move. And if he wanted to be useful, he needed at least a modicum of relief from the pain.

Before they rounded the corner up ahead, Colton paused, closed his eyes, and knocked back both tablets. He'd contemplated spacing them out, but he needed relief *now*, not later.

Hurrying after Hicks and Dukes, Colton gritted his teeth and told himself that in twenty minutes, when the medication entered his bloodstream, he'd feel better.

"Colton, good. Are you rested?" Police Chief Bailey was standing on the sidewalk in front of a boarded-up liquor store. He glanced at Colton's knee.

Colton instinctively straightened his shoulders. "Yes, sir. Thank you, sir."

With dark shadows beneath his eyes, and deep creases at their corners, the Chief himself looked anything but rested, but Colton wasn't going to tell him that. "Good," Bailey said, as if he really meant it. "Now, what do you think about this?" The Chief stepped aside and gestured to a large orange crane that had been abandoned in the middle of a crossroads. It was blocking the intersection in all four directions.

"If we have enough men, we could—" Dukes had barely finished his sentence when Bailey waved at him to be quiet.

"Just a moment, Dukes, I wanted Colton's opinion."

As Dukes quietly fumed, Colton avoided his gaze and stepped a little closer to the crane. "We'll never move it with manpower alone. We need to be clever about this."

"Oh yeah, and what do you suggest? Marine?" Dukes' eyes had darkened, and his mouth was set in a thin angry line. Colton half expected Bailey to tell him to be quiet, but he didn't.

"There's a lumberyard not far from here. I passed it on the bus route every day. If we take some men, we can grab a bunch of logs or posts, use them to roll the crane out of the way."

Almost spitting as he laughed, Dukes tipped back his head. "Ha! Nice try, but that'll never—"

"How d'you think they built the pyramids? Stonehenge?" Colton widened his eyes. "You *have* heard of Stonehenge, haven't you, Dukes?"

A pinkish heat began to creep up Dukes' neck. Hicks bit back a smirk.

"Do you have a piece of paper, sir?" Colton asked.

Bailey turned to Dukes and waggled his fingers at him. "Dukes… your notebook?"

Looking like he might explode, Dukes handed over his notebook and Colton leaned on the top of the fire hydrant in front of them. After quickly sketching out what he'd pictured, he handed the notebook to Bailey.

The Chief examined it for a moment before a slow smile spread across his face. "Very good." He thumped Colton's shoulder. "Very good indeed."

Three long hours later, Colton lowered himself onto a bench while Hicks and the others finished the task of moving the crane. Just as he'd planned, the logs had done the trick, but he was paying for his enthusiasm.

The trek to the lumberyard hadn't been a long journey but it had been a difficult one. Determined not to lag behind, every step had felt like a thousand miles for Colton and his knee. If it hadn't been for the fact that no one would have taken him seriously if he was wearing it, he'd have longed for Molly's makeshift splint. As it was, he'd made do with the two ibuprofen he'd taken, which had made little to no difference.

Every now and then, as they had made their way to the outskirts of town, he had allowed himself to pause between strides, take a breath, brace himself for the pain he knew would come when he returned his foot to the ground. Sensing that Colton was struggling, Hicks had walked alongside him. When they'd reached the lumberyard, he'd snuck him another swig of whiskey.

"Pills not helped?" Hicks had asked quietly.

Colton had been unable to reply. Shaking his head, he had allowed himself another gulp of whiskey and closed his eyes. Ten years without booze or pills—one power outage and it had all gone to hell.

Now, as he watched Dukes shouting orders at his fellow cops as if it had been his idea to use the logs in the first place, Colton felt nauseated with exhaustion. It had been years since he'd exerted himself like this, and he couldn't remember a time when his pain was as bad as it was now.

"You're pushing yourself too hard," Debs would have said. "Why do you always have to think about other people before yourself? Are you really so desperate to fit in that you'll put your own health at risk? What about me, Colton? What about *us*?"

Colton pushed her voice from his mind. He tried to remember the last time he saw her, but he couldn't. Was it when she loaded the car and moved out? Or was it when they met for coffee in that depressing little diner to sign their divorce papers? It was all so long ago now that he couldn't even remember what order it had happened in.

"Excellent idea, Colton." Chief Bailey sat down next to him and handed him a bottle of water.

"I'm just sorry I couldn't do more, sir." Colton took a long drink, felt the liquid soothe his smoke-scratched throat, and straightened his shoulders.

"Nonsense, you've done plenty." The Chief glanced at him and gestured to Colton's leg. "That an old injury or a new one?"

"A little of both," Colton replied.

"You're doing well, son." Bailey patted Colton's shoulder. The contact surprised him, but he didn't move away.

"Thank you, sir." Colton paused, cradling the water between his hands. "You should make sure you rest, too, sir. The town needs you."

Removing his hand, Bailey nodded slowly, watching as the cops who'd been moving the crane began to whoop and congratulate one another for a job well done. "The town needs a lot of things. Electricity mainly." Bailey let out a soft chuckle. "And some coffee wouldn't be amiss."

Colton laughed and laced his fingers together behind his neck. "I hear you on that one, sir." He was about to suggest that he take a walk to try and locate some in one of the nearby stores when he noticed Bailey sit up a little straighter.

Following Bailey's gaze, Colton spotted what he'd spotted; a young female officer, out of breath, hair coming loose from its neatly tied braid, waving her arms at Dukes.

Without speaking, Bailey got up and gestured for Colton to follow him. As they approached, they could hear Dukes telling her to calm down.

"Take it easy, Miranda, and tell me again. What's happened?"

"We…." The female cop—Miranda—sucked in a deep shaky breath. "We were assessing the next section of the train tracks, like you asked, but there are people on board."

"People?"

"Looters, sir." Miranda turned to Chief Bailey and put her hands on her hips as she continued to struggle for breath.

"Did you approach them?" Bailey asked.

"No, sir. They're armed. I left Manning and Pratt on surveillance and came straight back here. I wasn't sure what our policy is?"

"Policy?" Dukes echoed her as if she was asking a ridiculous question.

"On looters, sir." Miranda looked nervously from Dukes to Bailey. "Do we try to stop them? Do we have the power to stop them?"

As everyone waited for Bailey to reply, the Chief's lower jaw twitched. Colton could almost see his mind faltering. He was exhausted. For more than forty-eight hours, the man had barely sat down let alone slept. Cautiously, Colton said, "Sir, I think it's pertinent to assess the situation before making that decision. Don't you?"

"Yes." Bailey snapped out of his frozen thoughts, shook his upper body like a dog shaking off river water, and motioned for Miranda to show them the way. As she hurried in front with Dukes, Bailey nodded at Colton. "Thank you."

"No problem, sir. Looks like you could do with that coffee."

"I sure could, Marine. I sure could."

"After this next crisis is averted, we'll schedule a pit stop at Starbucks." Colton laughed and braced his hands on his lower back because, somehow, the pressure eased what was happening to his knee.

"Now that's a plan I can get on board with," Bailey replied.

Colton glanced at him. Something about the Chief reminded Colton of his father, except he was softer than Colton's father. More congenial. More empathetic. "If you don't mind me asking, sir, what *is* the policy with looters?"

Bailey clenched his jaw. "Under normal circumstances, it would not be tolerated. But now? In all honesty, son, I have no idea."

13

COLTON

"It'll be looters from Southside, sir. Their homes have gone up in flames, so they think it's okay to steal what they need." Dukes' fingers were twitching at his belt as if he was ready to draw his gun and start shooting.

From the shelter of a nearby apartment block, Colton, Hicks, and the others were staring at a partly derailed train car. On its side, but still whole, its doors were open to the sky. A hole had been cut in the wire fence nearby, and they could hear movement inside.

Pacing up and down in front of it, two armed men were guarding the entrance, and Dukes was practically simmering with the urge to confront them.

"Sir," Colton interrupted. "We don't know what that train car was carrying. We've only just secured the eastern side of the tracks. If it were to go up because someone's messing about up there, all the progress we've made will be lost, but—" he looked purposefully at Dukes, "if we want to keep the townsfolk on our side, we need to avoid any civilians getting hurt."

"Quite right." Bailey rubbed his chin, then put his hands into his pockets. "Dukes, take Hicks and Colton. Try to move them on." Glancing at Dukes' gun, the Chief added, "Be friendly. *Reason* with them. Explain to them that we need to secure the tracks in order to prevent any more outbreaks like the one on Southside."

"Sir? You don't want to accompany us?" Colton could think of no one worse equipped to negotiate with volatile thugs than Dukes.

Bailey shook his head. "Seeing the Chief of Police barging in is likely to escalate the situation. I'll hang back with these three." He gestured to Miranda, Pratt, and Manning. "We'll back you up if you need assistance."

"Colton can stay with you, sir. Hicks and I can handle this," Dukes' shoulders had stiffened, and he was purposefully avoiding eye contact with Colton, "alone."

"Colton's a Marine, Dukes." Bailey's patience for Dukes' bitterness seemed to be wearing thin. "Take him with you."

Dukes' neck muscles twitched. His jaw was clenched so tightly he looked as if his veneer might crack. "Yes, sir."

As they approached the train, Colton allowed Dukes to walk ahead and whispered to Hicks, "We need to keep this low-key. The last thing we want is for Dukes to kick off." He was looking at Dukes' gun as he spoke.

Hicks nodded. "Agreed."

When they reached the open train car, however, before Colton or Hicks could speak, Dukes took out his weapon and began to yell.

"Police! Stop what you're doing. You two, lower your weapons. Those inside, come out with your hands in the air."

The guards looked at one another but did not lower their weapons.

No one emerged.

On the ground in front of the train, boxes had been piled up, clearly ready to be carried away. Nearby, beyond the wire fence, a horse and cart was waiting.

Dukes moved closer. "I said lower your weapons." He looked back at Hicks, who reluctantly moved his hand to his holster.

Glancing at one another, the guards finally did as they were told, put their weapons on the ground, kicked them away, and put their hands in the air.

"You'll regret this," one of them said loudly.

"Shut up!" Dukes ducked through the hole in the fence, gestured for Hicks to take the guns, then moved closer to the train car. "Fairfield Police! You are surrounded. Come out now and put your hands in the air!"

Colton bit back the urge to intervene, but when a frightened-looking woman emerged from the body of the car with her hands in the air, he muttered to Dukes, "She doesn't look like a criminal, and these guys did what you asked. Perhaps calm it down, okay?"

"I'll handle this, Marine." Dukes gestured for the woman to climb down and stand in line next to the two, now unarmed, guards. Lowering his gun, he raised his voice and said, "Ma'am, we know you're not alone. Tell whoever's left inside to come out now with their hands in the air."

"We only want to talk," Colton said, finally unable to take Dukes' incompetence.

“We’re not doing anything wrong,” the woman shouted back, putting her hands on her hips and trying to look as if she wasn’t fazed by Dukes and his gun.

Stepping in, Hicks moved closer and gestured to a warning sign on the side of a tank car. “Listen, guys, there’s flammable liquids on board this train, and I’m sure you’re aware there have been fires in the area. It’s not safe for civilians to be here.”

For a moment, the woman examined Hicks’ face as if she was trying to work out how old he was. Then she turned and shouted back into the train car, “Diego, you better get out here! It’s the cops!”

As Colton, Hicks, and Dukes lined up beside one another, people started to emerge from the train car. Instead of jumping down, they crowded together, standing on its upturned side.

“Jenna?” Colton narrowed his eyes. Jenna Cruz was in the middle of the group, wide-eyed, clearly not comfortable being involved in whatever was happening. “Jenna? You should come down from there.”

Slowly, Jenna raised her hand, offering a small polite wave. She was cut off by a thick-necked man with dark hair who’d pushed his way to the front of the group. Colton recognized him instantly; he was Jenna’s father, the volunteer firefighter who’d offered to lead everyone from Southside up to the school.

“Diego,” Colton called. “Mr. Cruz… there could be diesel on board, among other potentially dangerous products, and we don’t have a full inventory on what the train was carrying. We have teams securing the train bit by bit. We need you to come down so we can continue to do that.”

For a moment, Diego didn’t move, but then he smiled. “Diesel? Good,” he replied. “We need diesel for our generators. *I* need diesel so I can keep the people of this town safe.”

"Diego, that's not a good idea." Colton moved closer, ignoring the way the apprehended guards were staring at him.

Gesturing to a boy who looked no older than the kids Colton drove to school each day, Diego said loudly, "Mickey, go back inside and tell the others to start on the tank cars next. There's diesel on board." Selecting another boy, he said, "And you… start siphoning fuel from these abandoned vehicles."

"Stop!" Dukes' cheeks were red and his shoulders were shaking. "Stop this, right now. You have no right to be here."

"We have every right to be here." Diego Cruz jumped down from the train and strode toward them. "This train is no one's property. Property and possessions mean nothing now. We are doing what's right for the greater good. We need diesel for the generators at the school and we need supplies for the people of this town. The people cops like *you* have abandoned."

Behind him, up on the exposed, hot metal side of the train, some of Diego's group were nodding but others looked nervous. The guards who'd given up their weapons slowly positioned themselves behind Diego. The woman followed suit. Then three more men jumped down from the train.

As Dukes squared up to them, Colton assessed each in turn. One had a shotgun; the other two and Diego had holsters containing Sigs that looked a bit too new. Old man Petersen's gun store had been raided last night—a coincidence? Colton thought not. Three guns and a shotgun vs. Dukes' and Hicks' one gun each. Five men versus three men. Not to mention whoever else was still inside that car.

"Abandoned? We've been up all night trying to *save* this town!" Dukes was yelling. A vein in his forehead was pulsing.

"Save it?" Diego moved forward, jutting out his chest and releasing a clap of laughter. One of the men behind him was reaching for his holster.

Colton stepped in front of Dukes and lifted his palms. "Mr. Cruz, I know your daughter Jenna. I was with her on the trip to the prison. I helped her escape."

Diego narrowed his eyes. His head ticked, the tiniest bit, to the side.

"Diego, listen, I appreciate what you're trying to do here, but it isn't safe." Colton looked around the group and gestured to everyone's weapons. "I'd also suggest it's not safe for any of us to be waving firearms around when we've been battling gas explosions for the past twelve hours. This is a freight train. We have no manifest. We have no *idea* what it was carrying, but we know it caused one hell of a fire. You were there. You saw it. We don't want a repeat of that, do we?"

"Never mind all that," Dukes cut in. "What you're doing is illegal. What's in that train is private property. Whether it's diesel or donuts, you have no right to take it."

As Diego's lips spread into a grin, the men behind him laughed.

Colton closed his eyes; every time he thought he was getting through to Diego, Dukes opened his big mouth and ruined it.

"What a surprise," Diego drawled. "A cop who's more concerned with protecting the private property of the rich than caring for the people of the community." Pointing to the people up on the train car, who were still gathered nervously, unsure whether to go back inside or climb down, Diego continued. "Many of these people have lost everything. They have no belongings. No way to clothe or feed their children. Are you going to do that for them, officer? Are you going to take care of these people? Because if you're not, then I am."

Nodding at Hicks to get Dukes away from Diego before he exploded, Colton gestured for everyone to calm down.

"Okay, I get what you're trying to do here, Diego, but we still can't risk this train catching fire. So, what I'm going to suggest is that you take what you've got here." Colton gestured to the boxes that had been dragged down from the train. "But no more. Not until we've confirmed it's secure and safe. We'll do what we can to help you, but you've got to help us in return."

Diego sucked in his cheeks and rubbed his beard, clearly weighing up claiming looting rights over the train versus getting blown up if Colton was right about it being a liability.

Behind Colton, Dukes pulled his arm free from Hicks' grasp and spat onto the ground in disgust as the younger officer tried to herd him away.

Ignoring Dukes, Diego assessed Colton. Looking him up and down, he narrowed his eyes then eventually nodded. "All right," he said. "But we *will* be back."

As Diego called for his companions to climb down from the train, Colton realized he'd been holding his breath and exhaled quietly.

"Pick up what you can from the ground out here and load it onto the cart," Diego yelled.

As the others did as they were told, Colton tried to catch Jenna's eye. Was she really okay with this? Was she *safe* being a part of this? And what about Molly? Where was she?

Before Colton could get any closer, however, Diego put his arm firmly around Jenna's shoulders and guided her away.

They were barely out of earshot when Dukes started waving his arms in the air. "What do you think you're doing!? You just let them—"

"Oh, for Pete's sake, Dukes, shut up!" Hicks had had enough. His normally polite, jovial exterior had hardened, and he looked just about ready to knock Dukes out. "If we'd have followed your lead, this whole thing would have ended up in a shootout. You'd have gotten us killed."

Dukes opened his mouth to reply, but then closed it again. "Screw you," he said, turning away from them. "Screw both of you."

As Dukes stalked off, probably to tell tales to the Chief, Hicks and Colton looked up at the train. "What do we do now?" Hicks asked. "Try and secure it somehow? Set up a barrier?"

Colton rubbed the back of his neck. His leg was throbbing. He wanted to sit down. He *needed* to sit down. But there was no time for that; if Diego had already claimed looting rights, law and order was crumbling. Which meant things were about to become much, much worse.

14

MOLLY

While Laura Banks continued to list the names and addresses of people's missing loved ones, Molly enlisted Lucky to help her keep an inventory of the supplies that were being brought into the school.

"If we're going to steal from people, we can at least write down who donated what, so they can be reimbursed when this is all over." As she spoke, she knew how she sounded; she was talking like one of the 'deniers'—a term that had been coined to refer to those who believed that, any second now, the power would be back and life would return to normal. But listing supplies was better than doing nothing, and it was keeping Lucky's mind off the fact that they still had no idea what had happened to his parents. So, she carried on.

"Lucky, find someone to help you pull all the gym equipment out of the storage cupboard. Food and water are being taken to the school kitchen, but we need somewhere to store other essentials. Maybe ask Zack?" Molly looked down her list: rope, firewood, tools, blankets….

She raised her eyes and noticed that Lucky was shuffling his feet uncomfortably.

"Lucky? What is it?"

"It's just…" He paused, then gestured to the side door of the gymnasium. "They left. Last night."

"Who left?"

"Tommy and Zack. They went to look for their mom again."

"Oh, of course." Molly tried to ignore the twinge of nervousness in her stomach; their numbers were dwindling. With Jenna occupied doing her father's bidding, and three-quarters of the Banks family halfway across town, it was just her and Lucky. Just the two of them. And she had to admit she felt a little hurt that Tommy and Zack hadn't told her they were leaving.

As if he could read her mind, Lucky said, "They probably thought you'd try and stop them. They told me to tell you they'll be back."

Molly nodded and focused on her fingernails for a moment. She'd never been the kind of woman to have neatly manicured nails, but she also wasn't used to seeing them quite so dirty. The soot beneath her nails seemed unwilling to budge, so despite changing into some fresh clothes—given out by a woman who'd been put in charge of re-clothing people whose outfits were too smoke-damaged to be washed—she still felt unclean.

When Molly looked up, the crowd at the front of the gym was parting. The room had gone quiet; Diego was back, marching in and waving as if he was a true-to-God hero.

Behind him, the group he'd taken out looting were carrying boxes—which had clearly come from the train—and several cans full of diesel. Diego himself, however, was carrying nothing but a bottle of beer, which he swigged in an exaggerated fashion as he strode toward the back of the room.

"Diego?" Molly stepped in front of him and folded her arms in front of her stomach. "I'm clearing the storage closet so we can keep supplies in there. The kitchen's just down the hall and there's plenty of room for water and canned goods. At some stage, we need to think about setting up a sleeping area for those who can't return to their homes. People have been—"

Diego held his palm up and took another long drink from his beer bottle. After wiping his mouth with the back of his hand, he looked her up and down and said, "Thank you, Miss O'Neil. I'll take that into consideration." Side-stepping around her, he gave a throaty chuckle and gestured for those carrying boxes to gather around.

When Lucky returned, letting her know that the storage closet was ready, Molly put her hand on his shoulder and nodded. "Thanks, Lucky." When she looked at Diego, however, he'd sent only two of his hoard of boxes in the direction Molly had indicated. The rest, he seemed to be siphoning off.

"Where's he taking those?" asked Lucky, frowning as Diego pulled open the doors at the rear of the hall and began to usher people through them.

"I have no idea," Molly replied. "But I don't like it."

As Molly watched, Diego leaned back against the wall and continued to drink. Two other men joined him and they passed the beer between them, while the majority of what they'd scavenged was taken into the bowels of the school by those who'd accompanied them. *It can't all be food*, Molly thought as she tried to make out what was written on the side of one of the boxes. She was tilting her head, examining a printed label that was half obscured by someone's large chubby hand, when she finally caught sight of Jenna.

Carrying a box that was almost as big as she was, Jenna's brow was decorated with beads of sweat and she looked exhausted. She set down the box and, pushing her hair from her face, glanced over her shoulder to where Molly and Lucky were standing.

"Dad? Is it okay if I go hang out with Lucky? He still hasn't found his folks and—"

Before Jenna could finish her sentence, Diego stood up straight and jutted out his chest. He wasn't much taller than Jenna, but he was bigger. As he leaned over her, she almost visibly began to shrivel. The men behind him sniggered.

"Are you done putting away these boxes?" Diego looked at the box Jenna had placed on the floor.

"Not yet, but—"

"You take a break when I say you take a break, got it?" Diego stooped down, picked up the box, and shoved it into Jenna's arms.

Jenna nodded, but lingered for a moment.

Telling Lucky to stay where he was, Molly walked quickly over to them. Usually her boots would echo around the vaulted ceiling. Today there were too many bodies present cushioning the noise.

As Jenna went off with her box, Molly found herself tapping Diego, hard, on the shoulder. "Mister Cruz?"

Slowly, Diego turned around.

"I need Jenna's help in the storeroom."

"You have plenty of *help*." Diego looked past her at Lucky and a few other students who'd gathered to help out. Leaning forward, he narrowed his eyes. "You wouldn't be trying to cut Jenna some slack, would you? Get her doing an *easy* job?"

"She's had a tough few days, Mister Cruz."

"Good!" Diego laughed, exposing his yellowish back teeth. "She needs to toughen up. She's too emotional. Like her mother. She needs to get her priorities straightened out." He paused and passed his beer bottle to one of the men standing behind him. "Isn't that why she was on your Scared Straight trip in the first place?"

"Jenna was an asset on that trip. She was a great help, but it's been my experience that girls like Jenna sometimes respond better to *kindness* and *encouragement* than tough love."

For a long moment, Diego said nothing. Then, without warning, he positioned his face within inches of Molly's and said, "You dare try and tell me how to raise my daughter again, *Miss* O'Neil, and I'll see to it you're no longer welcome here."

Diego's friends had inched closer and were all glowering at Molly. A part of her felt like laughing; twenty-four hours ago, she'd been trapped in a prison with murderers and rapists. Heck, she'd killed one of them. And these three amateurs thought they could get the better of her?

Molly's fingers twitched and almost reached around to the back of her jeans. What would Diego do if she pointed a gun at him? Would he maintain his cocky exterior? Or would he shrivel up and beg for mercy?

Tilting her head at him, she sucked in her cheeks and nodded. Before she could say any more, Diego turned away from her and back to his friends.

How did someone like that end up in charge? Molly looked around the gymnasium. It was becoming more and more full by the hour. Word had spread, and even those who hadn't had their homes damaged by the fire seemed to now be heading to the school for respite and company.

Those who had come from Southside, or other areas neighboring the tracks, were still coughing. To start with, Molly had assumed it was smoke inhalation, but she was beginning to think it was something else. Their coughs weren't easing. If anything, they were getting worse.

Scanning the crowd, she spotted the doctor Laura Banks had introduced her to and jogged over to him.

"Doctor Chase?"

The far-too-young-looking doctor, with floppy blond hair and blue eyes, turned and started gesturing to the waiting area. When he realized she wasn't looking for medical help, he stopped. "I'm sorry, you're Miss O'Neil? The teacher?"

"Yes." Molly stuck out her hand to shake his.

"Is everything all right, Miss O'Neil?"

Molly bit her lower lip. Lowering her voice, she gestured to a woman nearby who'd been coughing solidly for at least five minutes and said, "Is it my imagination, doctor, or are these people's coughs getting worse?"

Chase rubbed at his forehead as if it might erase the crease in it. "Well, they're certainly not getting any better. The problem is, we don't know what was on the train. All kinds of toxins could have been in that smoke."

"Should we try and move people to a hospital?"

"I spoke with Diego and he says the hospital in Ridgeview is overrun already. That's the closest one. The next is in Rockridge and it's just too far to go on foot."

"But we can't just leave them like this, surely?" Molly tried not to let her volume increase.

Chase shook his head. "Diego says our focus right now is securing supplies and getting the generators working. One of his guys is a doctor and he thinks they're fine."

"But you're a doctor," Molly began to protest.

"*Junior* doctor. I'm outranked." Chase grimaced and looked back at the triage area. "I'm sorry. I have to—"

"Sure." Molly breathed in sharply and flicked her index fingers against her thumbs, something she always did when she was feeling frustrated to the point of beginning to yell. "Okay. Let me know if anything changes."

As Chase returned to treating head wounds and minor burns, Molly looked up and spotted Jenna walking slowly through the open doors at the front of the gym. Weaving through the crowd, Molly tried not to lose sight of her, but by the time she walked out into the afternoon sun, Jenna had disappeared.

Molly looked left and right, and finally spotted Jenna leaning against the tall oak tree in the center of the parking lot. As Molly approached, Jenna slid down to the ground and began picking at a hole in her jeans.

"Hey…." Molly sat down beside her. "You okay? I heard you talking with your dad."

Without looking up, Jenna shrugged.

"If you need a break, Jenna, maybe you should tell him? He's being quite hard on you."

Jenna's shoulders tensed. She glanced up at Molly from beneath her thick dark hair and narrowed her eyes. "He cares about me. That's just the way he shows it."

"Jenna," Molly said tentatively, "I hope I'm not overstepping here, but it seems a strange way to show affection. Especially when you've been through so much over the past few days...."

Molly had barely finished speaking when Jenna stood up. "What would you know?" she said angrily. "You haven't even got kids. My dad raised me all on his own. My mom walked out on us. He's helping the *entire* town and what are you doing? Stirring up trouble?"

"Jenna, I...." Molly stumbled to her feet. She reached for Jenna's arm but Jenna pulled it away. "I'm sorry." Molly raised her palms and met Jenna's eyes. "I'm sorry, but I know what it's like to live with a father who's a little too tough sometimes. You start to think that it's normal —the yelling and the raised voices and the lack of affection—but it's not." Molly dipped her head. "It's not, Jenna."

Jenna was chewing the inside of her cheek. Her eyes had filled with tears and she quickly swiped at them with the back of her hand. "You don't know what you're talking about. You know nothing about my dad." Jenna turned and began to walk away. She'd gone just a few paces when she turned back and yelled, "If you don't like the way he's running things around here, then maybe you should just leave! Forget about us—the ones who are trying to help other people—and go run away to your pathetic little cabin!"

For a moment, the two of them just stared at each other. Molly's face twitched into a frown. How did Jenna know about her cabin? The only person she'd told was Colton.

As if she was reading Molly's mind, Jenna folded her arms and sucked in her cheeks. "That's right. Lucky heard you talking about wanting to get out of here. So, why not do us all a favor and just *go* already!"

As Jenna practically ran back inside, Molly rubbed her temples and looked up at the sky. It was pale blue. The smoke from the fire was gone, and the sun was shining. She could leave. She could walk away right now and just keep walking, but she knew she wouldn't.

Instead of running for the woods, and keeping on running, Molly walked. She walked the same route she'd have taken if she'd decided to go home from school on foot instead of by car. Past the park, the river, and the train tracks.

Her legs were throbbing, and her stomach was empty, but she kept walking, unsure what she was looking for until she spotted two police officers climbing out of the blackened carcass of a nearby building.

"Excuse me?" she called.

"Ma'am, this area is pretty dangerous right now. I'd advise that you...."

"Sorry, I'm looking for someone. He was helping the police chief down on Southside yesterday. Name's Colton?"

"Big guy? Bad leg?" the younger of the two officers replied.

Molly nodded. "That's him." *Please say he's okay. Please say he's okay.*

"He's working a couple of blocks over. On Fifth."

"Thanks." Molly allowed herself to breathe out. "Thank you."

When she reached Fifth, her nostrils twitched uncomfortably. Even though the fire was out, the smell of smoke hung heavy in the air and scratched at the back of her throat. Toward the far end of the street, she could see a group of officers and civilian volunteers carrying something out of one of the fire-damaged buildings.

It wasn't until she got closer that she realized it was a body, and that one of the people carrying it was Colton.

Molly stopped and wrapped her arms around herself, watching as Colton and another man carried a flesh-charred corpse into the middle of the road and laid it down. Beside it was another, and beside that another still. She looked away; there must be at least ten of them, laid next to each other in rows, and the men were returning for more.

"Colton?" Molly finally found her voice and held up her arm.

He looked up as if he'd been imagining hearing her voice. When he saw her, he hurried over. "Molly?" A smile twitched across his lips. "Are you all right?"

"I'm fine," she said, swallowing down the nausea that had formed in her throat. "Are you? How's your leg?"

Guiding her away from the road, Colton reached into his back pocket and took out a bottle of water. He took a swig and passed it to Molly, and she did the same. "The leg's okay."

He was lying. It was written all over his face, but Molly didn't call him on it.

"How are things at the school? We came across Diego looting a section of the train earlier. Jenna was with him." Colton looked deeply concerned.

Molly shook her head and smoothed her hand over her hair. She hadn't been able to wash it since the fire and she knew she must look terrible. "Ah," she said, shaking her arms to release some tension, "not great. Diego's taken over. People are listening to him. I don't know why, but they are, and he's the kind of guy who's likely to make a situation like this worse instead of better."

"Yeah, I got the same impression." Colton straightened his shoulders and looked at her, studying her face.

"The stuff they took from the train? It's all under the guise of gathering supplies to help the community, but Diego's siphoning things off for himself. I set up a system to log everything, but he's bypassing it. He's pretty much convinced everyone it's okay to start stealing from people, telling them it's for the 'greater good', but I saw it with my own eyes. Under everyone's noses, he took most of what they'd found and squirreled it away somewhere."

Colton pressed his lips together.

"What happened earlier? Couldn't the police arrest him or something?"

Leaning back against the wall, Colton sighed. "It's complicated, Molly. We have so many other things to do to try and straighten out the town." He looked over at where the others were now loading the dead bodies onto the back of a horse-drawn cart. "The Chief thinks it's best to try and keep the peace with Diego but—"

"But you're not so sure?"

"People like him? Once they take control, it's hard to snatch it back, but I'm hoping he's more arrogant and stupid than dangerous."

"I'm not so sure," Molly said gravely. "I think arrogance and stupidity can quite easily lead to danger."

After a pause, taking in what she'd said, Colton glanced at her, then looked quickly back at the bottle of water he was holding. "So, are you going to stick around? Up at the school? Or are you heading off to that cabin of yours?"

Molly considered the question. It was the second time in as many hours that someone had mentioned the cabin to her, and she was beginning to wonder whether she should take it as a sign. "No, I'm not going anywhere. Not yet. I'm needed at the school." When Colton waited for her to continue, she added, "Lucky still hasn't found his family, and there has to be someone in that place who's not trying to turn all this to their own advantage." She laughed a little. "Don't get me wrong. I'm tempted. I mean, you must be too?" She looked past him and shuddered as the cart began to trundle off down the road.

Colton followed her gaze and nodded solemnly. "Very tempted, but there's been talk of the cops trying to take proper control of the town. If they do, if they decide to fight Diego, I should be here."

"Fight him?" Molly wrapped her arms around herself. Despite the warmth of the late afternoon sun, a violent shiver was creeping down her spine. "I thought you said the cops wanted to keep the peace?"

"We do. But he might not give us a choice."

Molly nodded, then looked back in the direction of the school. "Okay, well, I should go. If things with Diego escalate, you'll need someone to rely on, from inside the school."

"I can count on you?"

"Yes," she said. "You can."

Colton opened his mouth to speak, but then stopped himself.

"What is it?"

"I don't want to ask you this…" He trailed off.

"But it sounds like you're going to."

Colton smiled, the corner of his mouth twitching. "If you hear anything about Diego's movements—anything that could be important—would you—"

Molly put her hand on Colton's arm. "You'll be the first to know."

He looked at her hand. For a moment, she thought he might put his fingers on top of hers, but he didn't.

As Molly watched him walk away, she tried to slow the anxious thud-thud-thud in her chest. He was limping but trying to hide it. He was struggling, and so was she. Yet, for now, their paths remained separate and there was nothing she could do about it.

15

ALEX

When Alex and the kids had first returned to the house, they'd spent just a few minutes inside before spotting Laura's note and leaving for the school. Intent on finding his wife, Alex hadn't taken the time to examine the place. Now, however, as he pushed the door open and stepped inside ahead of the twins, he realized it wasn't quite as undamaged by the fire as he'd remembered.

"Okay, kids, come on," he called over his shoulder after confirming the living room and kitchen seemed empty.

Last time, he'd made Erik and Scarlett wait outside while he ran in. When he'd returned brandishing a note in Laura's handwriting, they hadn't even complained; they'd just taken off jogging in the direction of the school.

This time, they stood stock-still in the center of the living room. "Dad, is this because of the fire?" Scarlett was pointing at the windows in the kitchen, which had shattered and left splinters of glass all over the worktops and the floor.

"Someone said there was an explosion because of a gas line." Alex was tracing his finger along a noticeable crack in the wall behind the dishwasher. "Looks like the kitchen took the worst of it."

"And the tree outside," Erik said, pointing through the open window.

"That thing has been dying for years." Alex stepped up beside Erik but, as he examined the cracked trunk of the ash tree, he inhaled sharply.

"Isn't that Mom's chair?" Scarlett was wide-eyed and pointing to where a branch was splayed out, pinning Laura's wheelchair to the grass beneath it.

"She said she'd damaged it, but she didn't say how." Alex peered at it and flinched.

"What was she even doing out there?" Erik asked, turning away from the window and absentmindedly picking up a protein bar from the counter nearby. As he dusted it free of glass and ripped it open, he shook his head. Mouth half-full, he said, "Okay if I go check out my room?"

Alex nodded, trying not to think about what might have happened if Laura had been trapped instead of the chair and reminding himself to thank Jerry next time he saw him.

"You too, Scarlett—grab anything you want to keep with you. We'll secure the house as best we can, then head back to the school for Mom. It looks like they've stopped the fire from spreading, so I don't think there's any need for us to evacuate the house right away. We might not be able to stay here long-term, but for now, we can take care of ourselves just as well as Diego Cruz can take care of us."

As Scarlett followed Erik through the living room and toward their bedrooms, Alex allowed himself to lean back against the counter and take a breath. When he left home a few days ago, he hadn't allowed himself to think much further ahead than fetching the kids and getting them back here safely. Now, looking at the carnage in his garden and his kitchen, he wasn't even sure where to start.

They'd stayed in the gymnasium with Laura until nightfall. After his announcement, Diego had positioned someone at the door to ask everyone who was coming and going what they were doing, and Alex didn't want anyone to get the impression they had things of value they were trying to hide.

When the sun finally went down, and a hushed quiet fell on the room, Alex had kissed Laura goodbye, reluctantly agreed to take the shotgun from her, and smuggled the kids out of a side exit that Scarlett knew about from her *very* brief time as a cheerleader a couple of semesters ago. As they crept through the parking lot, Alex's heart had thundered in his chest and the sensation had made him angry; escaping a prison, you expected to feel nervous. Leaving a high school? He should have been able to walk out without a care in the world. He shouldn't have been worrying for his safety or the safety of his children.

"Should we board up the windows?" Scarlett's voice interrupted his train of thought and he looked up to see her standing with her arms folded, staring at him. "Is that what people do in these situations?"

Shaking himself out of his lethargy, Alex straightened himself up. "Well, I don't know much about *these* situations, Scar, but it sounds like a good idea. There's some plywood in the garage we can use, and we can fetch Mom's chair while we're there."

"It was nice of you to get her a new one. Why didn't you give it to her?" Scarlett asked as they opened the door that led from the kitchen directly into the garage.

Alex rubbed the back of his neck and shrugged. "I bought it as an anniversary present, but then I wasn't sure whether it was romantic or...."

“Lame?”

He smiled at his daughter. “Is it? Lame?”

Scarlett laughed. “I dunno, it’s not like you bought her a vacuum cleaner. Usually, practical gifts are a no-no, but Mom loves sports, so….” She wrinkled her nose as if she was thinking hard about her verdict. “No, I don’t think it’s lame. I think it’s nice. What did she say when you told her?”

“She seemed pleased. I think.” Alex glanced at his daughter and laughed. “I really should be better at reading her by now, shouldn’t I?”

Scarlett grinned at him. Her complexion was paler than usual and her hair was a little matted, but when she smiled she looked just the same as she had when she was younger—mischievous, like her brother. “Yeah,” she said. “You should.”

Chuckling to himself as if they were completing a little father-daughter DIY project on a weekend, Alex guided Scarlett over to the racks where he kept his tools and supplies. “You take the plywood through to the kitchen. I’ll figure out how to get the chair out of the trunk of my car when we’ve got no working key.”

“Oh, that’s easy.” Erik’s voice made them both turn around. “I saw a video on YouTube once… you got any wire?”

“You saw a video on how to break into cars? On YouTube?” Alex put his hands on his hips and narrowed his eyes at his son.

“If you’d prefer it, we could just throw a brick through the back window and get in that way.” Erik tilted his head. Next to him, Scarlett stifled a giggle.

“No, no. We’ll try the wire.” Despite knowing he’d probably never drive it ever again, Alex couldn’t quite bring himself to damage the car that had cost him more than a year's wages and which, until a few days ago, he'd still been paying off.

As Erik sifted through Alex's toolbox looking for some odd ends of wire he could use to jimmy the trunk open, Alex headed back toward the house. "You two okay here? I'm going to grab some tarps from the shed so we can try to rainproof the windows."

Concentrating deeply on the task at hand, the twins barely answered him.

"I'll be out back if you need me…." Alex raised his voice and Scarlett waved in his direction.

"Okay, Dad. We'll let you know if someone breaks in or tries to shoot us."

Alex opened his mouth to tell Scarlett that joking about break-ins and shootings wasn't really appropriate at a time like this—at any time—but stopped himself. The twins had been through a lot in the past few days; perhaps it was time he started treating them less like kids and more like the almost-adults they were.

Out on the deck, Alex avoided looking at his wife's crumpled wheelchair and the dead tree, and headed for the shed. He was pretty sure he had three large tarps, but couldn't find the third. Scratching his head as he walked back onto the lawn, he stopped and rolled his eyes at himself. Of course, the third had been used to cover up the outdoor furniture when it had rained a few weeks ago. He'd been meaning to remove it, get ready for summer, but hadn't gotten around to it yet.

Leaving the other two tarps on the steps up to the back door, Alex headed across the lawn and began to tug the third free from the table. He was bending down to unfasten one of the loops from the table leg when his fingers met with something solid. What the hell? He tugged the tarp free and lifted it up to peer underneath.

At first, he was confused. What was the carpet from his den doing out here? He frowned at it and tilted his head. Laura had always hated it, but remodeling when he was out trying to rescue their kids from a *prison* in the midst of an EMP seemed unlikely. He gave it a tug. It was heavy, rolled into an almost cylindrical shape. He pulled again and, as the carpet unfurled, he sprang backward so quickly that he smashed his head on the underside of the table.

"Oh crap!" Feet. There were feet, and legs, and a torso. There was a *body* in his garden!

Alex scrambled backward, using his hands to push himself away. For a moment, he didn't move. Just stared breathlessly at the half-unwrapped carpet body bag.

"Dad? We did it! We got the chair out. It's awesome." Erik was standing at the backdoor waving at him.

Alex stood up and waved. "I'll be right there," he said, his voice coming out a little croakier than he'd expected it to.

Heart hammering in his chest, Alex tugged the tarp back into place and glanced back at the house. A dead animal. He'd tell the kids it was a dead animal, but what would Laura think when she found out?

It was only when Alex got to the other side of the lawn and was about to ascend the steps that he stopped and looked back. Laura was in the garden when the tree fell, and she'd been extremely reluctant for any of them to return to the house. But, surely not? Surely she didn't have anything to do with a dead body being hidden in their backyard? That was something she'd have mentioned. Wasn't it?

Mid-afternoon, as the twins flopped on the couch and tucked into their third protein bar of the day, Alex picked up his notepad and scrutinized the lists he'd made. They had a good amount of supplies, but not *infinite* supplies. They'd be able to camp out here for a few weeks, a month maybe, but by that time they'd be out of everything, which meant they needed a plan.

"Hey, Dad, I think I heard someone knocking next door." Erik had stood up and was peering out of the window. "There's some guys. With a clipboard."

"A clipboard?" Alex almost laughed, despite the fact that deep in his stomach he still felt nauseated over what he'd found in the yard. "Not really the time for checking the gas meter."

He'd only just made it to the door when there was a loud rap on the door. "Hello? Is anyone home?"

"Dad, don't answer it. Pretend we're not here." Scarlett tugged at Alex's elbow, but he patted her shoulder and told her to calm down.

"I want them to know we *are* in," Alex said, reaching for the shotgun and slinging it over his chest.

Before he opened the door, he inhaled deeply and counted to ten. He was met by two men who looked to be in their mid-twenties. They reminded him a little of Tommy, except with harder edges.

"Can I help you, gentlemen?"

"I sure hope so, Mister… we're looking for supplies. For the relief effort at the school run by Mr. Cruz."

"Relief effort?" Alex pretended he knew nothing about it.

"To help those who lost their homes and possessions in the fire." The younger of the two was trying to look past Alex into the hallway. He was glad the twins were out of sight.

Stepping forward, making sure to smile, Alex shook his head gravely. "I'm afraid we've already been looted. Cleared out while we were helping our neighbors up at the high school."

"I see." The older guy scribbled something on his clipboard, then jerked his head toward the road. "We'll get out of your hair, then. But, sir, I'd be careful if I were you. Nice house like this? The looters might be back." As he spoke, he met Alex's eyes and smiled a too-broad smile.

"Thank you, thanks for the tip." Alex made a Boy Scout gesture but didn't move from his doorstep until the men had moved on to the next house.

When he finally stepped back inside, he locked the door behind him and looked at the twins. "This isn't good," he said. "Not good at all."

16

COLTON
TWENTY-FOUR HOURS LATER

With the sun on his back, Colton could almost imagine that he was on vacation. Somewhere in Florida, perhaps. Face-down on a lounger at one of the fancy hotels Debs had always wanted him to take her to but which he'd never gotten around to booking.

"Here." Hicks passed him the binoculars they'd been sharing between them ever since they took up their post.

Colton raised them to his face and peered through the lenses. The street below was clear—for now—but Molly had been adamant that Diego's men would be hitting this part of town *tonight*, and Molly O'Neil was rarely wrong. Stubborn, yes. Wrong, no. She had risked her own safety to sneak out of the school at the crack of dawn to warn Colton of what she'd heard. So, he was damn well going to take her seriously.

Glancing at the sky, in a hushed voice, Hicks said, "It'll be dark in an hour or so."

"It will," Colton agreed. "But they'll be here before then."

"How can you be so sure?" Hicks shifted uncomfortably; they'd been lying flat on their stomachs all afternoon. From the rooftop of one of Midtown's shortest apartment blocks, the two of them had watched and waited. Watched and waited.

Colton was used to operations like this—keeping as still as possible for as long as possible, getting the lay of the land before taking action, waiting for a target to show their hand. Except, in his previous life, he'd been unencumbered by an injury. Now, he had his leg to deal with. The effects of the ibuprofen he'd taken earlier had long worn off, and he was beginning to find it hard to stay focused.

Passing the binoculars back to Hicks, Colton allowed himself to rub his knee. Pain was pulsing up and down his leg. Soon it would migrate to his hip, which wasn't good news; if they needed to descend from their hiding place at any speed, he'd struggle to get down the steps, and the entire point of this mission was to prove to Chief Bailey that he was useful. Not to end up in a crumpled heap.

"You haven't had any since this morning, right?" Hicks had removed his bottle of ibuprofen from his pocket and was offering it to Colton.

"I can't. You keep them." Colton shook his head. "Seriously, Hicks, you don't know when you might need them and you've been more than generous." He didn't add that he was trying to tell himself it was about time he learned to cope without them.

"Right now, *you* need them. And I need you to be in top form, so…." Hicks widened his eyes at the bottle. "Take 'em. Keep the bottle."

Colton was about to protest when he sensed something moving down below. Tipping back his head, he swallowed two tablets and shoved the half-empty bottle into his back pocket. Gesturing for the binoculars, he wriggled closer to the edge of the roof, staying as close to the warm concrete floor as possible.

"There, around that corner." Colton pointed and Hicks followed his gaze.

"Shoot, will they see us?" Hicks had started to move back, but Colton took hold of his arm.

"The sun's directly behind us. If they look up, all they'll get is glare and shadows."

"Is it them?" Hicks asked, narrowing his eyes as if it would help him see.

"I don't see Diego, but they've got a wagon." Colton watched closely through the binoculars as a large horse-drawn cart appeared at the end of the street. "We've got two men sitting up front, one holding the reins. Next to the horse, a woman holding…" Colton tilted his head, "looks like a hand-drawn map. Houses crossed off like squares on a Monopoly board."

As Colton lowered the binoculars, Hicks pointed at the wagon, which was piled high with a mixture of boxes and loose objects. "They're definitely looting. And they're being methodical about it."

Colton pursed his lips. Criminal activity was never good. *Organized* criminal activity was worse.

"Looks like they're heading for that one." Hicks pointed to a large house with three garages and brand-new siding. "What do we do? Stop them?"

Colton shook his head. "If we're going to convince Bailey that Diego needs to be stopped, we need evidence. He's a stand-up guy, but he's reluctant to rock the boat. We need to show him this guy's dangerous and, right now, they're not doing anything wrong."

"So, we just wait?" Hicks rubbed his temples.

"We wait." Colton said. "Watch and wait."

As the sun continued to set, Colton watched the people below stop their wagon and walk up to the door of the fancy three-garaged house. The woman knocked. The two men were standing behind her, as if by letting her go first they'd come across as less intimidating. When no one answered, however, they left her. Without even hesitating, the one who'd been driving the wagon smashed his elbow through the large front window, climbed inside, then unlocked the front door for his friends.

Next to Colton, Hicks looked incredibly uncomfortable; as a police officer, his instinct was to run down there and put a stop to whatever was going on.

"I know what you're thinking, kid," Colton said gruffly. "I feel the same, but sometimes you have to let things play out."

Hicks pressed his lips together but didn't object.

A short while later, too short in Colton's opinion, the three intruders reappeared. They made two trips back and forth, loading food and water into the wagon, but on the third trip, they carried out two large hunting rifles and a box of ammo.

Colton took a deep breath. "Hicks, where would you expect the owners of a house like that to keep their guns? Lying around or locked up?"

"I…." Hicks paused. "Locked up."

"Exactly."

"What are you thinking?"

As the wagon pulled away and headed past them, down the street, Colton shuffled back from the edge of the roof and sat up. "I'm thinking that if those folks had left the property, they'd have either taken their guns with them or they'd have locked them up."

"Which means...." Hicks swallowed hard and closed his eyes for a moment. "They could have been home."

Satisfied the wagon and its inhabitants were out of sight, Colton and Hicks descended from their hiding spot. Climbing down the black metal fire escape on the side of the building, Colton had to hold his breath to stop himself from audibly groaning. Each step jolted his knee, and Hicks' ibuprofen hadn't yet taken effect.

By the time they reached the sidewalk, Colton was panting, but stopped when Hicks glanced back at him.

"Okay?" Hicks asked, already halfway across the street.

Colton nodded. "Okay."

The intruders had left the front door of the house unlocked. Reaching for the gun Captain Bailey had given him, Colton went first and pushed the door back on its hinges. With the light quickly fading outside, the hallway was dark. The house itself was silent. No ticking clocks, no hum of electricity, just the sound of their footsteps on the hard wood floors.

"Everything looks in order," Hicks said quietly.

Colton peered into the living room. "They weren't interested in taking random objects," he said. "They've clearly got a list, a plan that they're sticking to."

Ahead of him, Hicks pushed open the kitchen door and released a long whistle. "Well, we know food was on their list."

As if a poltergeist had been playing tricks, every cupboard door was open and the shelves were bare.

"They've taken the knives," Hicks said, gesturing to a wooden block on the countertop.

Colton's jaw twitched. "I'll check upstairs. You finish the rooms down here. See if you can locate a gun safe."

While Hicks moved through to the dining room, Colton used the banister to steady himself as he climbed the stairs. The upper landing was large, with a soft cream carpet on the floor and large family portraits on the walls. He had the urge to remove his shoes but ignored it.

"Hello? Is anyone home? I'm with the police. We're here to check everyone is okay."

No one replied.

Continuing to call out, Colton assessed three guest bedrooms, a children's room, and a bathroom before coming to the master suite. He paused with his palm flat on the door. A familiar twisting sensation in his gut made him want to turn back. Leave. Walk away.

Breathing through it, he pushed the door.

The first thing he saw was the safe. Wide open and completely empty. Not far away, sticking out from the floor on the far side of the bed, was a shoe. A man's shoe.

Colton walked around the foot of the bed, then lowered his gun. A gray-haired man was lying face-down, a large bloodstain on the back of his shirt. Colton was kneeling down and feeling for a pulse when Hicks entered.

"He's dead." Colton stood up and pointed to the man. "Looks like a stab wound."

"Damn." Hicks looked away, bracing his hands on the back of his neck. "Shoot, Colton, if we'd come down here…."

"Then we'd probably be dead too, and there would be no one to inform the Chief about what's going on." Colton was determined not to allow the sickening feeling in his chest to show on his face. Striding toward the door, his leg marginally less painful now the ibuprofen had kicked in, he said, "There's nothing we can do here, Hicks. But we need to take this to Bailey. Let's go."

Along with most other officers in town, Police Chief Bailey had returned to the police station. Colton found him in his office, sitting in his leather-backed chair with his elbows on his desk and his head in his hands.

"Chief?" Colton tapped on the door.

Bailey looked up. His entire face seemed to have aged at least ten years in the last few days. "Colton? Hicks? Where have you been?"

"Sir, we were given some information regarding Diego Cruz."

"The volunteer firefighter? The one who tried to loot the train? I thought we'd made him see sense." Bailey sat back in his chair and instinctively reached for the coffee mug on his desk. Remembering it was empty, he sighed and put it back down.

"It seems Cruz has taken control up at the high school."

"The Community Relief Center? Isn't the principal supposed to be heading up that operation?"

"I have no idea, sir. Cruz was quick to put himself in charge."

Interrupting, Hicks stepped into the room. "Sir, Cruz is instructing his men to steal from people out in the community. The train was just the tip of the iceberg—he's coordinating organized looting under the guise of doing it for the benefit of the townspeople."

"Except my source tells me that Cruz is siphoning off the majority of the goods to keep for himself. Setting up some kind of separate faction. Using his power to control people." Colton glanced at Hicks, then continued, "We spent the afternoon staking out a street in Midtown. We witnessed three people, two men and a woman, accomplices of Cruz, break into a home. When they exited, they took with them food, water, two shotguns, and some ammo. We entered the property after they left and found the owner dead in his bedroom."

Through gritted teeth, Hicks added, "He'd been murdered, sir. A stab wound to the back."

For a long moment, Chief Bailey didn't speak. He simply looked from Colton to Hicks and scraped his fingers through his thick gray hair. Then he muttered, "Damn it."

As Bailey stood up and turned to face the window, folding his arms in front of his chest, Hicks cleared his throat. "Sir? What do you want us to do?"

"Do?" Bailey turned back around. This time, his eyes were different. This time, he meant business. "We take back their weapons and seize control of this town, that's what we do."

"Sir?" Hicks' eyes widened.

"I was hoping to avoid this course of action, but I think it's obvious at this point that the Fairfield police force is on its own. If the Army's coming to back us up, they're not showing up any time soon. So it's up to us to secure the town and keep our people safe. Cruz has to be stopped. A man like him cannot be allowed to take control."

"I agree, sir." Colton stood up straight, his hands knitted together behind his back. "And I think we should move soon. Tonight."

Bailey pursed his lips. "Very well. Tonight. Hicks, gather the officers. Colton, tell me everything you know about the layout of the school."

17

TOMMY

Deep down, Tommy had hoped they wouldn't find their mother. He was pretty sure this made him an asshole. He'd never have admitted it to Zack, but the last thing they needed was to be worrying about her. She was like a child at the best of times—needy, helpless, self-absorbed. Besides, she sure as heck hadn't worried about them. It seemed to him that while he went off looking for his brother, trying to rescue him from Fairfield Prison, their mother had gone searching for a fix. Which was depressingly predictable.

When they'd made it back to the house, fleeing the high school along with anyone else brave or dumb enough to try and make it on their own rather than stay with that tin-pot dictator Diego, it had been empty. Just like the first time.

That time, they hadn't stayed long. The fire on Lucky and Jenna's street, a few blocks over from their own, had been spreading and the entire neighborhood had evacuated. This time they'd taken their time moving from room to room, but had still found nothing to indicate what might have happened to their mother.

Now, twenty-four hours later, they were sitting at their old scratched dining table trying to decide what to do next. It was late afternoon, the sun was almost ready to set, and Tommy was beginning to feel twitchy. The map he'd been carrying with him since he'd started his journey to find Zack was starting to burn a hole in his pocket. Would the Robinsons be worried about him? Would they be wondering why he hadn't turned up yet?

He was about to take out the map and show it to Zack when his brother said, "I don't think I thanked you properly."

"For what?" Tommy's hands were wrapped around a too-warm bottle of beer. He'd been sipping at it for over half an hour.

"For coming to find me. Can't have been easy coming back here." Zack glanced toward the living room where the indent of their mother's scrawny body still showed on the couch. Even before Tommy was locked up, she'd barely had the energy or the will to move from it. Except when she was trying to score—or out earning money so she could score.

"Deciding to come find you? That was the easiest thing in the world," Tommy said, smiling. As Zack looked down at his hands and made an embarrassed clicking noise with his tongue, Tommy finally plucked up the nerve to do it. "Listen, Zack, there's something I've been meaning to talk to you about."

Zack tilted his head and pushed his hair from his face. He was skinny and his face was dirty, but he'd changed into a black T-shirt that was identical to the one he'd been wearing at the prison. "Yeah?"

"I really don't think Mom's going to show up. She's been gone for days."

Zack sucked in his cheeks and shifted his own beer bottle from one hand to the other. “She’s been gone for days before. She always comes back in the end.”

“Yeah, but this time it’s different. This time there’s nothing to come back to. No TV. No radio. No booze.” Tommy tried to shift the note of disgust in his voice; he’d always been much harder on their mother than Zack had, and had never been sure which one of them was right. “You know what she’s like. She’ll have latched onto someone who can get her what she needs.”

“Meth? She stopped—”

“Meth. Crack. Booze. Whatever.”

Zack shook his head. He’d matured a lot since Tommy last lived at home, but deep down he was still a little kid who wanted to believe his mom loved him.

“What I’m saying is we need to come up with a plan. We need to decide if we’re sticking around or—”

“Or what? Where else would we go?” Zack stood up, pushing his chair back across the sticky linoleum floor and leaning against the dish-covered counter.

This was it—the moment he’d been waiting for. After days of almost doing it, Tommy reached into his pocket and spread out the map Beck Robinson had given him. “My old cell mate, Luke… I stayed with him and his family when I was released. They’re a real good bunch of people. A nice family.”

Zack hadn’t moved closer and was ignoring the piece of paper. “So?”

“So, they’re kind of hippie-ish. Preppers. Used to living off grid. They have a cabin. They packed up two wagons’ worth of stuff and….” Tommy pushed the map toward Zack. “They gave me directions to where they’re going. They said we can join them.”

For a moment, Zack didn't move. Thoughts flittered across his face but Tommy was out of practice translating them.

"It's the kind of place we'll be safe. The kind of place we can hole up and *survive* this thing."

Zack sat back down and looked at the piece of paper. When he picked it up, Tommy thought for a moment that he might tear it in two. Instead, he studied it. Then his face brightened. "Okay, as soon as we've found Mom, we'll go."

"Zack, buddy." Tommy grimaced. "We're not gonna find her and, even if we do, I don't think she's the kind of person the Robinsons want around. You know?"

"Oh yeah, and what kind of person is that?" Anger flashed in Zack's eyes as he instinctively came to their mother's defense. Of all the arguments Tommy and Zack had ever had, most were about their mother.

"Listen, Zack… wherever she is, she isn't thinking about us. It's time we thought about ourselves. Fairfield's getting more dangerous by the day. All the towns will be. People fighting each other for supplies, for food and water. If we go now, in a couple of days' time we'll be safe. Away from it all."

"We can't leave. Not without giving her the chance to come with us." Zack folded his arms and stared at Tommy.

Tommy stared back. When Zack was in this kind of mood, he wouldn't back down. "All right. How about we give it one last shot? We go check her usual haunts. If no one has heard from her or knows where she is, we leave."

Eventually, Zack took a slow sip from his beer bottle and said, "Okay. Okay. But we check *everywhere*."

Two hours later, as the sun finally sank below the horizon, Tommy and Zack reached the last place on their list; a derelict warehouse near the train tracks at the end of their street. Luckily, this section hadn't caught fire, but the train had half-derailed and Tommy could see the silhouettes of people—perhaps Diego's people—picking it over for useful scraps.

"Ready?" They were standing in front of a red door. Its paint was peeling off in large messy chunks. When Zack nodded, Tommy pushed it and it creaked loudly.

Directly inside the door they came to a stairwell. Tommy had been here only once before—a memory he'd tried for years to erase from his mind—and the smell brought it all back to him. Urine, smoke, weed, and who knew what else.

Beneath the stairs was a large, stained mattress. It had holes in it, a filthy blanket thrown across it, and twisted-up beer cans all around it.

"Hello?" Tommy called into the darkness. His voice echoed back at him.

"Maybe we should...." Zack looked back at the door. He'd fetched their mother out of bars and alleyways, but never a place like this.

"No," Tommy said firmly. "I said we'd look everywhere. This is the last place."

Zack swallowed hard and put his hand on Tommy's elbow as they moved deeper into the building.

"Mom? It's Tommy and Zack. We're here to take you home." Tommy had begun to ascend the stairs. His footsteps were heavy and made a *thwack* sound as they met with the sticky floor.

At the top of the stairwell, he wrinkled his nose. It was hotter up here and it smelled awful.

"Mom?" Zack called out, his voice a little shaky.

"This way." Tommy motioned for Zack to follow him down a narrow corridor. They could hear movement at the end of it. Armed with only a baseball bat and a knife, Tommy told Zack to hang back, called out again, then pushed open the door in front of them.

The room was darker than the hallway. Tommy blinked into it, willing his eyes to adjust sooner.

"Tommy? Is that you?" A woman's voice—hoarse and barely audible—filtered through the darkness.

Tommy focused on the silhouette. It wasn't his mother. "Aunt Susan?"

"Sweetheart." Susan's lips spread into a wobbly smile. "And Zack too. Come in, honey, come in."

Beside Susan, on another filthy mattress, was an unconscious man with long black hair.

Zack was frozen to the spot, unable to move from the doorway.

"Susan, you seen our mom?" Tommy spoke firmly, gruffly, willing her to pay attention and answer him quickly, so they could leave before he was overwhelmed by the stench of the place.

"Carol?" Their Aunt Susan looked from Tommy to Zack, unable to focus. "You boys are so handsome."

"Susan—we're looking for our mom. Have you seen her?" Tommy had crouched down and was looking Susan in the eyes.

"Right, Carol.... No. I ain't seen her."

"When was the last time you were with her? Before the EMP? After?" Tommy paused and waved around the room. "Has she been here?"

"Oh!" Carol waved her arms as if she was trying to recall a memory. "I remember. Yeah. She came here a few days ago. Maybe a few hours ago…." She frowned and Tommy fought the urge to snap his fingers and drag her attention back to him. Susan's head swayed from side to side. "She was with Terry. He said he knew a guy in Rockridge who had a plan for when something like this went down. A bunker or something." Susan frowned as if the word 'bunker' wasn't the right one.

"She left Fairfield? For Rockridge?" Zack had stepped up behind Tommy and was staring at their aunt.

"Yeah. That's right, honey. Rockridge. With Terry." Susan began to sink back down onto the mattress. She was scratching at her forearm.

"Did she leave us a message?" Zack asked.

Susan looked at him, then looked away. She was distracted. There was no use asking her any more questions.

"Zack, let's go." Tommy stood up and moved back toward the door.

Zack wavered for a moment, then sighed, turned around, and followed Tommy back outside.

At the top of their street, they stopped. The moon was bright, and so were the stars, but their mood wasn't.

"I'm sorry, buddy. I know that was tough."

Zack shook his head quickly. He was twitching his thumb the way he always did when he was trying not to show his emotions. "Nah. It's fine. I've always known what went on in those places."

"Yeah, but you haven't seen it."

"You have?"

Tommy's lower jaw twitched. "Couple of times, yeah. When you were younger. I used to go fetch her if she'd been gone too long."

Zack lowered his gaze. "Right." When he looked up, he glanced at Tommy's pocket. "I guess that's it then. We're out of here?"

"You okay with that?" Tommy asked, putting his hand firmly on his brother's shoulder.

"Yeah. I'm okay with that." Zack looked toward their house. "I guess we should take whatever we can carry for the journey."

Tommy nodded. "Let's go."

But when they reached their front porch, Tommy stopped dead in his tracks. He gestured for Zack to do the same and strained his ears.

"Someone's inside," he whispered before putting his finger to his lips. Slowly, he reached into his pocket and handed Zack his knife, then raised his baseball bat. They were about to enter when they heard a noise from behind them.

Quickly, Tommy grabbed Zack's arm and pulled him down to squat in the bushes beneath the porch.

"It's a wagon," Zack whispered as a horse-drawn cart pulled up in front of their house.

Tommy's heart was hammering hard against his rib cage. A tall guy with broad shoulders jumped down from the cart, consulted a piece of paper he was holding, then strode up to the house and knocked on the front door. What was going on?

After a short pause, the door opened.

"Took your time, didn't you, Jay?"

"Screw you, Marty."

Tommy craned his neck to see what was happening.

The guy who'd answered the door stepped back inside. The other followed him. Less than a minute later, they reappeared with armfuls of stuff.

"Bunch of crap, really, but Diego said to take it all," said Marty, the one who'd been inside.

"Anything *good*?" Jay, the wagon driver, replied. "If I'm right, this is Carol Hargrave's house and that woman *always* has some good stuff around. If you know what I mean."

"Not today," Marty replied. "No one's home and there's nothing exciting. Just two half-empty beer bottles."

Tommy could feel Zack quivering beside him. His rage was so hot it was vibrating on his skin. "They're taking our stuff," Zack spat under his breath. "They're taking our stuff, Tommy."

In jail, Tommy had learned one important lesson: pick your fights. Only get involved in a spat you think you can win and *always* weigh up the consequences. But in that moment, as he watched two scumbags dragging his little brother's blankets and pillows from their house, those rules went out of the window.

"Who are you?" Tommy jumped from the bushes, waving his baseball bat, yelling as loud as he could and as fiercely as he could. "Get out of here! Leave our stuff alone!"

He ran for the shorter of the two—Marty—and realized Zack was behind him.

Marty and Jay exchanged a perplexed look, as if they weren't sure whether to be scared or amused. Then in one swift gesture, Marty knocked the bat from Tommy's hand and smacked him square on the temple while Jay pulled a gun.

"Zack, stop!" Tommy yelled, struggling against the hold Marty had him in.

Zack put both palms in the air. "Don't shoot," he said shakily. "Don't shoot."

"Do we have a problem here?" Marty asked, his lips unnervingly close to Tommy's ear.

Tommy struggled a little, then stopped. "No. No problem."

"Whose stuff is this?" Marty swung Tommy around so he was staring at the wagon.

"Your stuff." Tommy knew what answer the guy wanted but spoke through gritted teeth.

"I'm sorry? Whose stuff?"

"Yours." Tommy spoke louder. "Your stuff."

With so much force that he knocked Tommy to the ground, Marty pushed him away. Zack bent down and put his hand to Tommy's head. It made Tommy flinch.

"That's what I thought." Marty turned and walked toward the wagon.

"Say hi to your mom for me," Jay—who'd been watching from the sidelines—yelled as he climbed back onto the wagon.

"Screw you!" Zack yelled. "Screw both of you."

As the wagon pulled away, they stood up and stumbled back to the house. Lighting a candle, Zack held it up as they moved down the hall and into the kitchen. The entire place had been ransacked. Everything useful was gone. Everything.

What did they do now?

18

LAURA

As darkness fell outside, for the second night in a row, the atmosphere in the gymnasium shifted. With the generators still not working, candles had been lit and a quietness had settled, but it was not a comfortable quiet. People were nervous; Diego and his men were becoming increasingly aggressive, and Laura was beginning to wonder whether she'd done the right thing staying behind.

While Becky Simmons, one of the school's old English teachers, continued to populate the Lost & Found board with help from Lucky and Miss O'Neil, Laura told them she was going to check on Doctor Chase in the triage area. The nurses who had been present a few hours ago were now stationed at the back of the gym, seeing to any members of Diego's supplies team who returned from their excursions with an injury, and Chase was looking increasingly overwhelmed.

"Everything okay?" Laura wheeled over and pushed an empty chair to one side so she could pass. When Chase didn't answer, from beside her, Argent barked loudly. Several people startled at his sudden bark, but Laura didn't care.

"Mrs. Banks." Chase stopped what he was doing and turned around. He'd been applying a dressing to a woman's arm and gestured to her that it was all right to leave.

"You're run off your feet. Do you need a hand?"

"Do you have any first-aid training?" Chase asked, allowing himself to flop down into a nearby chair and take a sip of water from the bottle Laura offered him.

"Basic training, yes, from when I was a personal trainer." Laura nodded in the direction of the chairs nearby. "I can at least assess people for you. Clean up anything that's not serious? Help prioritize the others?"

With a relieved sigh, Chase nodded. "Thank you, yes. That would be immensely helpful." He reached for a clipboard that was balanced on a nearby table. "If anyone needs prescription medication replacements, make a note of it here. Before my nurses were commandeered, we made a list of the supplies."

"Supplies?"

"Diego secured drugs from the nearest pharmacies, so we should be able to replace most medications."

Laura took the clipboard, trying not to think about what drugs they might have secured and how she'd feel when she looked at them. "Okay. I can do that." As she moved, she inhaled sharply when a jolt of pain spread across the entirety of her lower back.

"Are you all right?" Chase asked, his eyes softening. "Do you need something? I can see what pain killers we have...."

"No," Laura said quickly, her mouth becoming instantly dry. "No, thank you. I'm fine."

Chase paused for a moment before bracing his hands on his thighs and standing up. "Okay, well then, if you could start on the left over there and work your way through?"

Laura nodded. As she moved away from Chase, she looked at Argent and told him to go sit by the wall. "Good boy," she said, fondling his ears because he was looking at her as if he couldn't believe she didn't want him within touching distance. "I love you, buddy. But you have big teeth. Some people find that scary."

An hour later, as twilight finally gave way to nightfall, Laura spotted Jerry and Barb in the line for the triage area. When they reached the front, she smiled and took hold of Jerry's hand. "How are you two doing?"

"Sorry, Laura, we've been waiting for a long time."

"You have?" Laura looked at Chase's clipboard. Jerry and Barb weren't listed but, until Laura had stepped in, Chase hadn't been particularly organized. "Are you all right?"

"It's Barb's medication," Jerry said, clasping his wife's hand. "Her blood pressure pills… we were due to collect a new prescription from the pharmacy a few days ago. Never made it."

"Right. Do you have the name of the pills?"

Jerry reached into his pocket and took out a prescription slip.

Laura copied down the name, then told them to take a seat. She now had six people waiting for medication, enough to force her to stop avoiding a trip to the supply closet.

Telling Chase where she was going, Laura accepted the keys from him and set off across the gym with Argent in tow. When she reached the door that led to the hallway out back, she was met by a barrel-chested man with folded arms who said, "Can I help you?"

"I'm with Doctor Chase. We need some medications for our patients." Laura waved the keys at him.

The man assessed her, glanced at her clipboard and at Argent, then moved aside. "First door on the left."

In the hallway, Laura unlocked the door to the supply closet, which had been allocated as the gym's new pharmacy, and pushed it open. Scanning the shelves, she concentrated on the task at hand. After carefully studying her list, she returned her gaze to the shelf in front of her.

"There's barely anything here," she muttered.

Apart from some boxes of aspirin and ibuprofen, some bandages, and sterile wipes, the entire closet was almost empty. Two patients, including Barb, needed the same blood pressure meds, but there was only one bottle.

Laura gritted her teeth. Her fingers tightened on the clipboard. None of the other medications on her list were here.

Back in the gym, the solitary bottle of blood pressure meds squirreled away in her pocket, she approached Chase and pulled him to one side. "Who has access to the drugs closet? Just you?"

Chase narrowed his eyes. "A while ago one of the nurses came back and asked for the key."

"Crap." Laura closed her eyes. When she opened them, she put the clipboard down with a loud clunk on the table beside her, then took the bottle from her pocket and set it on top. "There's barely anything left. My neighbor Barb takes these daily, and so does Mrs. Carter over there, but we only have one bottle."

"One bottle?" Chase shook his head. "That can't be right."

"Come see for yourself."

A few minutes later, standing in the center of the supply closet, Chase looked like he was about to either cry or scream, but went with neither and, instead, punched the wall.

"Hey." Laura put her hand on his arm. "We need your hands in working order. Go steady, Doc."

Chase waved his arms at the shelves. "The portable oxygen's gone," he said. "The strongest pain meds, antibiotics… there's hardly anything left."

"So, what do we do?"

"We can't prove who took it," Chase said, hanging his head.

"And even if we could, who's going to do anything to stop Diego and his cronies?" Laura glanced at Argent, wondering if Diego would be intimidated if she allowed Argent to do his best, most fearsome, bark.

As Chase started sorting through what was left and jotting it down on the clipboard, Laura told him she'd be right back. When she reached Jerry and Barb, she took a small plastic bag from Chase's portable supplies tray and tipped fifteen of the thirty pills into it. "We only have one bottle at the moment, Jerry," she whispered. "There's another lady who needs these too, so I've split it."

"Only one bottle?" Jerry's eyes widened. Next to him, Barb had fallen asleep on his shoulder.

"We'll find more." Laura tried to sound confident. "For now, though, maybe you could space them out. One every other day?"

Jerry breathed in deeply and glanced at his sleeping wife, then nodded. "All right, Laura. Thank you."

After giving Mrs. Carter the other fifteen pills, Laura looked around the triage area and bit back the bubbling rage in her gut. Of the people who weren't sick, many soon would be if they didn't get their medication. Others were in desperate need of antibiotics, and everyone knew the hospital was not a good place to go right now. Yet, Diego had still siphoned things off for himself. So much for *the community*.

She looked over to where Molly O'Neil was consoling a middle-aged man and a little boy. Molly had been the only one to even attempt to stand up to Diego *and* she'd survived twenty-four hours in a high-security prison full of escaped convicts. If anyone could help get Diego in line, surely it was Molly.

19

MOLLY

"Tomorrow morning, I'm going to go look for my parents." Lucky was standing in front of the Lost and Found board with his hands on his hips and a determined look on his face. Molly put down the notebook she was holding and chewed the inside of her lower lip as she studied the scrawny teenage boy in front of her. A week ago, he was no more than a student to her. Now, after what they'd been through, he felt more like a nephew. At least, what she imagined a nephew might feel like. "You can't stop me," he said. "They're my parents."

"I wasn't going to try and stop you, Lucky." Molly leaned against the table and sighed. Her limbs were aching with tiredness, but the people who were looking for lost loved ones just kept coming. Even at night, they didn't stop. One after another after another, they came and told her their stories. Some became separated when the fire spread, others had been in different locations when the EMP hit and hadn't managed to find one another since. All were desperate. "If there's been no news —if they haven't showed up and no one has seen them or heard from them—I'll go with you."

A smile twitched at the corner of Lucky's mouth, but he seemed surprised. "You will?"

Molly nodded. "I will. We'll search every inch of Fairfield until we get some answers."

"Thanks, Miss O'Neil." Lucky grinned at her as if he genuinely expected them to find his mom and dad if they looked hard enough. Despite being concerned for them, it was as though he was picturing them simply lost. Unsure where to go. Wandering the streets because they had no home to return to. What Lucky didn't know, however, was that the cops who'd been removing dead bodies from the burned-out houses were starting to make lists. If they found ID or any distinguishing features, they were writing them down, along with the location in which the victim was found. An hour ago, a youngish officer called Hicks had presented Molly with their first list. It'd had fifteen numbers on it accompanied by fifteen short descriptions and fifteen addresses. None had belonged to Lucky's parents, and Molly was praying that none of the next fifteen would either. She was also praying she never had to find out the answer to the question: what are they *doing* with the bodies, seeing as they have no access to a morgue or somewhere cool?

As Molly had accompanied Hicks back out of the building, slipping the piece of paper he'd given her into her pocket to cross-check it later with the board and Laura's notebook, he had spoken to her under his breath. "Colton convinced the Chief to make a move against Diego. Be on your guard. We're going to try to keep things civil, but Cruz is volatile."

Molly had paused for a moment, her mouth hanging open and her skin prickling as if it had suddenly turned a couple of degrees cooler outside. "You know Colton?"

Hicks had nodded briefly and glanced over Molly's shoulder. In front of the entrance, two of Diego's guards were watching them.

Before she could figure out what to say or ask for more details, Hicks had jogged off toward the parking lot.

Now, looking at Lucky, Molly wondered whether she was doing the right thing by making him wait until morning. Hicks hadn't told her details of what the cops were planning or when they were planning to do it. What if it was tonight? What if it didn't go as they hoped and people got hurt? Shouldn't she be thinking of getting out of there? She wrapped her arms around herself and squeezed to soothe the tension in her belly; Colton would have told her if she needed to get away from the school. He wouldn't leave her and the kids in harm's way.

"Miss O'Neil, you don't think…." Lucky was looking down at his shoes, scraping his toe against the squeaky gymnasium floor. "You don't think my mom and dad left without me, do you? 'Cos the house was all locked up and, I mean, maybe they left before the fire started. Maybe they left as soon as the EMP took out the power—"

Molly breathed in sharply through her nose and ducked her head to meet Lucky's eyes, dropping her hands to her sides. "If they did leave, Lucky, it'd be because they were trying to keep themselves safe so they could be reunited with you."

"But they wouldn't have left town, would they? Not without me? And if they didn't leave town, where are they? Why haven't they turned up yet?" Lucky looked around the gymnasium. People had come and gone over the last two days, but most had stayed and the school was now full to bursting.

Molly watched Lucky carefully as she considered how to answer. In truth, she had no idea where his parents were and she wasn't sure what was worse—for them to have perished in the fire or for them to have left town without thinking about their only son.

"Honestly, Lucky," Molly said firmly, "I don't know, but from what I know about your parents, I know that they're good people and I know that they love you." Her stomach was twisting with the effort of sounding as if she believed what she was saying when, really, she had no idea whether Lucky's parents were good people or not. They didn't have the reputation Diego Cruz had, but that didn't mean they weren't the kind of couple to think only of themselves in a crisis.

Pointing to the board, Molly said, "Why don't you add their names and descriptions? Someone might have seen them."

Lucky nodded but as he turned around, he stopped and furrowed his brow at someone in the crowd. "Zack?"

Molly followed Lucky's gaze. Sure enough, inching through a group of people in the center of the gym were Zack and Tommy. Fighting the urge to rush up to them—because it felt strangely good to have more of her kids where she could see them—Molly waved.

The brothers waved back. "Fancy meeting you here," Tommy said with a grin. "Sure looks cozy." He gestured around the dark gymnasium to where people were huddled together, talking quietly, sharing blankets, occasionally coughing.

"You find your mom?" Lucky asked, bouncing up and down on the soles of his feet as if knowing Zack's mom was safe would imply good news about his own.

Zack shook his head and scraped his fingers through his dark floppy hair. "Nah. She wasn't home. We went all over town looking for her but…." Zack trailed off and looked at his brother.

Tommy had pressed his lips together and was looking at the Lost and Found board. "Why don't you go put her name up there, buddy?" Tommy pointed to the board.

"You think someone might have seen her?" Zack asked, his eyes brightening.

"It's worth a shot."

"We should have brought a photo," Zack said, stepping up to the board.

Tommy opened his mouth to speak but then closed it again. He glanced at Molly and moved a little closer to her. While Zack scrawled their mother's name in the top corner of the board with a brief description beneath, Tommy muttered, "Only photos we've got are from years ago." When Molly didn't reply, he added, "No one would recognize her. When I went home to find Zack after the EMP hit, *I* barely recognized her."

Molly put her hand lightly on Tommy's shoulder. Would she recognize her parents if she saw them now? Her brother? She'd never even found the time—or the motivation—to video call her family, and now she wouldn't have the chance. Not for the first time, she wondered why she wasn't feeling the way Lucky was or the way the Bankses had—desperate to be reunited or for news.

"I'll find us something to eat." Tommy was looking at her. "I assume there's food around here somewhere?"

Taking hold of Tommy's elbow, Molly moved him away from the board and the line of people and tried not to sigh. "You need to register." She tilted her head in the direction of the registration table Diego had set up near the front entrance. "They'll assign you jobs. You work, you eat."

Tommy's eyebrows twitched. "Oh, that's how it is?" He scanned the room, his jaw tense. "Who's in charge? Cruz?"

When Molly pointed discreetly to Diego, who was sitting on a pile of gym mats smoking a cigarette with his cronies, she noticed Tommy narrow his eyes.

"Hey, Zack." He called Zack over and lowered his voice. "Are those the guys? Not Cruz, but the others?"

Zack followed Tommy's gaze and nodded slowly. "Yeah. That's them, all right."

"What guys?" Molly stepped in front of Zack in case Diego looked in their direction.

"The guys who looted our house," Zack replied tightly.

When Molly looked at Tommy, he jutted out his chin in agreement. "They were inside when we got back from searching for Mom. Looking for drugs, food, blankets, whatever they could take. They trashed the place, then attacked us when we tried to stop them." Tommy motioned to a bruise on his forehead.

"Well, crap," Molly muttered, looking up at the ceiling and rubbing the tense muscles at the base of her neck. "I didn't realize things were this bad already."

"No one's standing up to the guy?" Tommy's lip had curled and he was looking around the room as if he was hoping to spot a weapon or a group of people who might join with him and start a fight.

Speaking quietly but quickly, Molly whispered, "Things with Diego are getting a little… out of control, but I've spoken to Colton about it. He's working with the police—"

Tommy tilted his head at her. "Oh yeah?"

"For now, just play along," Molly said, meeting Tommy's eyes so he could see that she was serious about this. "Colton's got a plan. He promised me. So, you two just go register. Diego's crew will assign you a work duty and they should give you some mats and sleeping supplies. We eat late around here so they might even let you have something tonight if you're lucky."

"Sleeping supplies?" Zack laughed darkly and brushed at the dirt on his pants. "Great, maybe I can request to get back the blankets they stole from our house."

Elbowing his brother, Tommy made a *shhh* sound and told him to do as Molly said.

"Seriously? After everything you said, I thought we were going to—"

Tommy shook his head at Zack and the gesture made Molly feel as if something was going on between them.

"We will, but not tonight. Tonight, we need food and shelter."

"Even if that means sleeping under the enemy's roof?" Zack had moved closer to his brother and was clenching his fists at his sides. Unlike Tommy's, Zack's knuckles looked unscathed.

"Yes," Tommy said firmly. "Even if it means that."

20

MOLLY

Half an hour later, after Tommy and Zack had been told that in order to receive their food and bedding supplies, they'd need to sign up for 'unloading duty', they flopped down on their mats and Tommy held onto the paper bag of food they'd been given.

"What did they assign you?" Molly had left Becky at the Lost and Found board and had positioned her own mat next to Tommy's. She'd been on her feet all day and needed a break. Remembering all the times she'd complained about how her feet hurt after a full day teaching classes, she almost laughed at herself; back then, she'd had no idea what true exhaustion felt like.

"Unloading, whatever that means," Tommy replied, tightening his grip on the brown paper bag in his lap.

"It means retrieving stuff from the carts outside—boxes, bags, and crates, whatever else they've looted—and bringing them inside to be sorted," Molly explained. "There's a classroom down the hall behind the gym where they're unpacking it all."

"And then what happens to it?" Tommy asked.

Molly exchanged a look with Lucky, who was opening up his own bag of evening food rations. "Who the heck knows? We don't see it," he replied.

Trying to change the subject, because Diego's men were patrolling up and down and she didn't want any of them to get into trouble, Molly gestured to Tommy's ration bag and smiled as if they were in the school cafeteria. "Anything good?"

Tommy handed the bag to his brother, and Zack reached inside it. He took out a battered looking apple, a protein bar, and a bottle of water, then looked at Tommy. "Where's your stuff?"

"We're sharing tonight, buddy," Tommy said, as if it was no big deal.

"We only got one bag between us?"

"We'll get more tomorrow morning, after we've worked." Tommy's jaw twitched with irritation as he replied, but he was hiding it well in front of his brother. "You eat them. I've lost my appetite."

Molly's bag contained the same, an apple and a protein bar, but with the addition of a candy bar too. She handed it to Tommy. "Never been a fan," she said, tucking into her apple.

She expected him to rib her for that. *Not a fan of candy? Are you even human?* But instead Tommy simply took the candy bar and ripped it open. He did not smile. He was quietly fuming. Molly could feel it vibrating on his skin.

"You okay?" she asked quietly.

"I spent ten years in prison and never got treated as badly as this." Tommy ripped a chunk from the end of the candy bar and chewed it as if it tasted disgusting. "They shouldn't be allowed to get away with it."

"No, they shouldn't," Molly said quietly, willing Tommy to keep his voice down.

After a long pause, Tommy took a long drink from Zack's water bottle and wiped his mouth with the back of his hand. Looking over at the gym mats in the corner, he narrowed his eyes at Diego. "Who is that guy, anyway?"

"He was a volunteer firefighter," Lucky answered through a mouthful of apple. Glancing at Zack, he added, "Jenna's dad. He tried to save my house."

"Yours and Jenna's both went up?" Zack asked, chewing slowly. He must have passed by Lucky's street and seen the burned carcasses of the houses near the tracks.

Lucky nodded. "Not sure if my parents were inside or if they'd already made a run for it."

"Shoot." Zack shook his head. "That sucks."

"My apartment burned down too." Molly spoke up before she'd really had the chance to think about whether it was a good idea or not.

"It did?" Lucky looked at her with wide eyes.

"You live in Southside?" Tommy raised his eyebrows in surprise.

"No, the other side of the tracks. The fire spread."

Zack, who'd been beside her when she'd spotted the fire, hung his head, perhaps remembering the look on her face when she realized that her entire life had gone up in flames.

"Sorry, Miss O'Neil." Lucky looked as if he was about to reach out and pat her shoulder, but didn't.

"Yeah, sorry," Zack added.

After that, for a few long minutes, the four of them remained quiet. They ate their meager suppers in silence, quietly scanning the room and watching others do the same. Some, those who'd helped fetch supplies, had been allocated classrooms to use as dorms. The rest of them had to make do with being in the hub of the action, and it was *not* conducive to a good night's sleep.

Aware there was no point in trying to bed down yet, Molly was preparing herself to head back to the board when she felt movement behind her. She turned to find a wet nose, two big ears, and a furry face staring at her.

"Argent," she smiled, reaching out to pat the dog's neck. "Where's your mom?" Argent sat down and tilted his head. Seconds later, Laura Banks appeared behind him and Molly pushed herself to her feet.

"Laura, are you okay?" Molly was pleased to see her; the more friendly faces the better.

Laura, however, did not look pleased. Her face was ashen and her hands were trembling. "Molly?" She looked behind her and lowered her voice. "We need to talk."

When Laura finished speaking, Molly could practically feel her blood starting to simmer. Doing her best to keep her voice low, so it didn't bounce above the hushed evening tones of the gym, she stalked over to the triage area and—hands on hips—asked Doctor Chase how long the current medical supplies would last.

With dark shadows under his eyes, Chase sighed. "I don't know. Not long."

"Is there any word from the hospitals?"

Chase shook his head. "None, but if this is what we're dealing with, just imagine what the hospitals will be like once folks from all the surrounding towns start showing up."

"So, we need our own medical supplies." Molly looked over to where Diego was still sitting, surrounded by cronies, laughing loudly and shattering the peace of the people who were trying to snatch a few minutes of sleep. There were a ton of classrooms he could be using, and yet he had to flaunt his authority here in the center of everything. He really did make her blood boil.

"What do we do?" Laura was holding a dishcloth and twisting it between her hands. "Diego's hardly going to just hand the drugs over."

Molly began to pace up and down. In the prison, her instincts had taken over. But that had been more to do with *physical* instincts. This was different; if she was going to make Diego see sense, she'd need to be clever.

"He might if he thinks people are going to turn against him," Molly mused. Turning to look at Chase and Laura, she added, "Look at him… sitting on his makeshift throne thinking he's king of the castle, surveying his kingdom. People are playing along because they think he's trying to help them. If they realize he's taking valuable drugs from sick people, it won't be long before the penny drops, and people start to question his authority."

"Agreed, but he's the one with the guns." Chase nodded in the direction of the two men who were patrolling up and down the middle of the room, each holding a hunting rifle and clearly enjoying the look on people's faces as they walked heavy-footed past their mats.

"Not the only one." Molly gestured to where she'd tucked her gun into her jeans, hidden by her shirt so that Diego didn't try and seize it.

"But let's hope it doesn't come to that. He's power-hungry. The thought of losing that power might be enough to make him see sense."

"Do you want me to come with you?" Laura offered.

"No. You're needed here. I'll handle this." Molly sucked in her breath and held it while she counted to ten then, fists clenched at her sides, she strode across the room.

She was about to call Diego's name when she realized that he was deep in conversation. Hesitating, she ducked into the shadow in front of the wall and listened.

"How far have you canvased?"

"We've been out as far as the woods down toward Ridgeview," the man next to Diego replied.

"And?"

"We found some bodies, boss."

"Bodies?" Diego puffed on his cigarette.

"Prisoners. Escaped felons by the looks of it."

"What'd they die of?"

"Looks like they were bludgeoned, Boss."

A smile spread across Diego's lips. "Good. Then it looks like someone's doing our job for us and keeping the woods free from scum." Diego waved his hand. "You can go. If you see signs this vigilante has headed into town, you tell me. I don't care what he does in those woods, but I don't want him here. Understood?"

The men on either side of Diego nodded.

"Go get yourselves some food, then get back out there, yes?"

Again, the men nodded.

As they walked away, Molly stepped out of the shadows. "Diego?" She purposefully raised her voice. "I need to talk to you about our medical supplies."

Rolling his eyes, Diego jumped down from his mat throne and swaggered toward her. "It's always something with you, schoolteacher." Standing close to her, he blew a plume of smoke into her face. "I had a teacher like you once. A meddlesome little shrew with her hand in everything. A bitter, lonely, old woman who'd complain about anything she wasn't in control of because it was the only thing she had in her life."

Molly blinked as the smoke grazed her eyes. Meddlesome? No. She was trying to help. "We need more medicine. Some supplies have been siphoned off. What's in the storeroom doesn't match the lists of what was brought from the pharmacies, and we've got sick people here."

Diego took a step back, dropped his cigarette—not caring that it left a small black mark on the floor—and stamped it out with his foot.

Breathing in slowly, Molly tried to soften her tone. "If there's theft going on, Diego, you need to use your authority to put a stop to it." She turned and gestured to the triage area, where people were still waiting for antibiotics and pain meds. "What will the townsfolk think if you allow them to get sick?"

Diego's jaw twitched. At his sides, he was flexing his fingers. "Are you accusing me of something, schoolteacher?"

"Dad." Behind Diego, Jenna stood up and reached out as if she was about to take her father's arm.

"Not now—"

"Jenna, leave this to me and your father." Molly nodded for Jenna to sit back down.

BANG!

From outside, a gunshot sounded, causing almost everyone inside the gym to duck their heads.

BANG! BANG! BANG!

And then people started screaming.

21

COLTON

"Colton, Hicks, head around back. Take six men with you. Dukes and I will go through the front entrance and see if we can get Cruz to capitulate. I want to keep this as de-escalated as possible. There are civilians inside."

Hicks cast Colton a glance that said, *he wants to de-escalate and he's taking Dukes?* But Colton gave him a brief shake of the head. "Yes, Chief."

Although his most recent ibuprofen had barely touched his leg, adrenaline was beginning to take its place. "This way." They'd stopped outside the school gates, across the road in the shadow of some trees. Colton pointed right, to a path that led around the back of the building. As Hicks selected six men and told them to follow suit, Colton put his hand on his gun. "Molly says they're storing weapons in a classroom behind the gym. If we can breach that room while the Chief talks to Cruz, we can take control of their supply and they won't have the power to fight back."

Hicks nodded. "And if they have men guarding the classroom?"

"I don't doubt they will," Colton replied. "But the Chief's arrival might spook them, make them head out front."

"If it doesn't?"

Colton twitched his jaw from side to side. "Then we use our powers of persuasion to make them see they're on the wrong side."

"You think that'll work?" Hicks took his gun from its holster and checked the safety. "From what I saw when I was up here earlier, Cruz seems to have these guys well and truly under his spell."

"I have no idea if it'll work, but we can try." Colton turned to the others and motioned for them to gather around. "Keep low and keep in the shadows." He looked up, wishing the moon wasn't so bright; if Cruz had men positioned on top of the school building—which was what Colton would have done in his situation—it would be all too easy for them to spot movement down below. "We do *not* want to be spotted."

Walking in a line, their group of eight followed the path that snaked around the outside of the school. They'd barely made it to the back of the gym when gunshots rang out. Everyone stopped.

"That was a hunting rifle, not police issue—" Hicks had barely got his words out when they were swallowed by the Chief and his men returning fire.

"*Those* are police firearms," Colton replied.

Rushing to the edge of the block that joined onto the gymnasium, Colton scanned the area. "There—that window's open." He headed for it and, without needing to be asked, Hicks offered him a leg up. The others quickly followed.

Wincing as he climbed through the window and landed heavily on the floor of the staff toilets, Colton turned to help Hicks and the others through. "This way." Colton paused behind the door and pointed to a fire escape map on the wall. "If we head right, then take a left, we'll come to the rear of the gym. There's a side door. If Cruz and his men are out front, we should be able to enter from there and, if need be, get the civilians out."

Hicks looked braced to run, legs apart, upper body twitching with readiness. Colton nodded at him, then put his finger to his lips to indicate that they should all stay quiet.

Gingerly, he pulled the door open. The hallway was empty. Sticking close to the wall, he waved for the others to follow. They made a right, then a left. The side door of the gym was in sight. Colton pressed his ear to it. Inside the gym, people were screaming. As more gunshots were fired, Colton raised his weapon and reached for the door handle. Silently, he thanked God that Molly still had her gun.

His fingers were millimeters away from the handle when it began to turn.

Colton froze. Every muscle stiffened. He mouthed at Hicks to stop and twitched his fingers, indicating that he and the others should stay back.

Raising his gun, Colton flicked the safety. His finger was hovering above the trigger. Backing away, he kept his eyes trained on the door, but before he could reach the cover of the corner they'd come from, the door opened.

"Stop!" a woman holding a shotgun yelled at him. She was tall, with long blonde hair and a heavily made-up face. She did *not* look like the sort of woman who'd want to be involved in a shootout.

All the same, Colton shouted back, "Lower your weapon, ma'am! We're the police."

"Police don't mean crap anymore!" she replied loudly, moving forward. Then, over her shoulder, she yelled, "Mick! Get out here!"

As she turned, Colton yelled to the others, "Retreat! Fall back! We need to get around the front of the school, now!"

They ran. Back down the hall, into the toilets, and through the window. "Make a right—it'll take you straight to the front of the gym!"

Hicks was running fast but stopped to look back at Colton. As the woman and a man Colton didn't recognize hurled themselves through the open window and began to run, Colton yelled for the others to keep going. "Don't stop!"

The alleyway beside the gym was pitch dark, narrow, and smelled of urine. Colton choked back the smell and kept running. With every slap of his feet against the ground, he wanted to cry out, but he didn't.

Up ahead, a door opened.

"Hicks!" Colton yelled and Hicks stopped, just seconds before a series of shots rang out. One of the other officers, who'd been level with the door when it opened, fell to the ground. Hicks raised his gun and returned fire. The door slammed closed.

When Colton reached Hicks, he was bending down to check on the fallen officer. She'd taken a bullet to her temple. Her eyes were open, but she was dead.

Colton pulled Hicks to his feet. "She's gone."

"How do you know?!" Hicks resisted and put his trembling fingers on the woman's throat. "Come *on*, Miranda."

“She’s *gone*. They need us out front.” Colton heaved until Hicks stumbled upright, pulling him away from his fallen colleague and trying not to allow her bloodied face to burn the backs of his eyes.

When they reached the end of the alleyway, they stopped. Shots were being fired from all directions. The officers who’d accompanied them into the building had disappeared. It was a massacre.

People from the high school—Cruz’s people—were everywhere, brandishing all manner of weapons, firing at anyone in a police uniform. Colton pulled Hicks sideways and pushed him down behind a large granite sign the principal had erected last spring, right ahead of the tri-county athletics tournament the school had so proudly hosted.

As a bullet pinged off the sign, Hicks ducked.

“This is a setup,” Colton said. “They knew we were coming. No way they’d have had all these men armed and ready to shoot if they weren’t expecting us.”

“Your friend?” Hicks asked loudly.

Colton shook his head—there was no way Molly would have betrayed them.

“Can you see the Chief?” Hicks asked.

Colton paused; his heart was hammering so hard in his chest that it was making it hard to breathe. Slowly, he peered out from behind the sign. Illuminated by the light of the moon, the grass in front of the gym was littered with bodies. On the sidewalk, a cop was trying to drag himself to safety, a trail of blood staining the concrete beneath him. Before he could reach shelter, a shot was fired. Then another. After the third, he stopped moving.

Colton closed his eyes. The noise was too familiar to him. His leg was throbbing. His instinct was to run, and yet he was frozen at the same time. When he opened his eyes, they landed immediately on a figure running through the doors. "Chief…" Colton muttered.

"He's okay?" Hicks asked, moving closer and looking up at Colton.

Colton breathed a sigh of relief. "Yeah. He's okay. He's—"

BANG!

Colton gripped the sign. If he'd been standing, he would have wavered, possibly even fallen to his knees. Watching Chief Bailey's body collapse onto the ground, Colton could barely even swallow. "He's…."

"Damn it!" Hicks had seen it too and was punching the ground.

"We have to retreat." Colton ducked back down, struggling to slow his breath and his thoughts. Looking at Hicks, he brushed his palms over his hair. "We're being slaughtered. If we're not careful, there'll be no one left."

"Colton! Hicks!" Someone was calling them. Colton turned, looking for the owner of the voice, and saw Dukes. He was behind a tree, back pressed up against its trunk. "Chief Bailey is gone. I'm in charge now and *no one* is retreating."

Dukes paused, waited for a brief gap in gunfire, then ran the short distance from the tree to their hiding spot. Crouching down in front of them, he growled, "We storm the school. All of us. We can't let Cruz win."

"Storm the school? Are you mad? We'll be slaughtered! We're *being* slaughtered." Colton turned away, completely ignoring the thunderous look on Dukes' face. "When I tell you to, you run," he said to Hicks. "If you can get to the parking lot, you can take cover behind the buses and the cars and get out of here. Make sure the others follow."

Hicks nodded, pressing his lips together. "What about you?"

"I'm going to give you some cover… you have a smoke grenade? The ones the Chief handed out?"

Hicks reached into his pocket and passed his grenade to Colton. From the other side of Hicks, an out-of-breath female officer said, "I have one too."

"Good. I'll throw this one to give you cover. When you get to the parking lot, you turn and throw yours. It'll give you time to get out."

The female officer nodded. "Yes, sir."

Next to Colton, Dukes tried to protest, but no one was listening.

Colton pulled the pin out of his grenade and shuffled closer to the edge of the sign. With his other hand, he motioned for Hicks to wait. Wait. Wait.

For the briefest moment, the shots stopped. Without hesitating, Colton stood up and hurled the grenade as far as he could into the middle of the lawn in front of the gym. "Go!" he yelled.

Hicks and the officer next to him began to run, gathering up others on the way. "Retreat!" Hicks yelled. "Everyone retreat!"

Colton stepped out from behind the sign and fired a shot into the air. Two shots were returned but, through the shield of the smoke, they were shooting blind and missed him by a mile.

Colton glanced back. Dukes was shaking with rage. Eventually he cursed loudly, fired three random shots into the air as if to release the tension in his body, then hurtled after the others just in time to be hidden by the second grenade.

Taking a deep breath, Colton readied himself, then—screaming through the pain because no one could hear him over the sound of the guns—he ran after the others.

22

MOLLY

Molly's first thought when the gunfire started was, *Thank God, the cops are here*. It took just a few seconds for her to realize it wasn't the cops who'd started shooting. Barely missing a beat, Diego pulled his gun, yelled, "Now! Move! Now!" and charged toward the entrance. "Man the exits. Take your positions! Now!"

As people screamed and ran instinctively toward the back of the gym, Molly was pushed this way and that. She was trying to watch Diego; something about this wasn't right. It was almost as if he'd been expecting it.

"Molly, this way…." Somehow, Laura had made it across the room and was pointing to the tables at the side of the room. Those who were able were ducking beneath them, praying they'd provide shelter. Those who weren't—those who were too old, too slow, or too badly injured from the gunfire—were panicking.

"Go." Molly pointed to the tables with one hand and reached to the back of her jeans with the other. When she pulled her gun, Laura's eyes widened.

"Molly, you shouldn't—"

"I could help." Molly was about to charge forward when another three gunshots fired. Except, this time, they weren't outside. They reverberated off the ceiling and someone let out a blood-curdling scream. From the triage area, Chase yelled, "She's been hit! Stop this! Stop this, now!"

But Diego wasn't listening. He was a few feet away from the doors and was still pointing his gun at the ceiling; it was him who'd fired the shots.

Another wave of screams broke out. Some cops had made it past Diego's men and were trying to break through the barrier at the entrance. In the middle of them was Chief Bailey. "Mr. Cruz! Tell your men to stand down and no one has to get hurt!"

Bailey was speaking to Diego, but his eyes were scanning the gym. When they landed on the injured woman, writhing on the floor while Chase tried to drag her to safety, he pointed his gun at Diego. "An innocent woman has been shot, Diego. Stop this. Now."

Molly looked down at the gun in her hand. She could help the Chief. She could sneak up behind Diego and put a gun to his head, but his cohorts were everywhere and all of them were armed.

Laura hadn't moved. She and Argent were waiting by Molly's side, waiting to see what she'd do. "Molly, please. Leave this to the cops. The kids need you." Laura looked over to where Lucky, Zack and Tommy were crouching by the wall, their arms wrapped protectively over their heads.

Finally, Molly returned the gun to her jeans. Laura was right; she could do more for the kids than she could do in a gunfight. Stooping low, she raced across the room, slowing her pace to match Laura's as her arms burned against the resistance of her old-fashioned chair.

When they reached the others, Molly ducked down next to Lucky and put her arm around him. "It's okay," she said, "It'll be over soon."

And it was over soon; far more quickly than she'd expected.

In what seemed like a well-rehearsed maneuver, Diego and his cronies pushed Bailey and the cops away from the entrance and back onto the lawn outside. Once they were through, he yelled for someone to pull the doors shut.

The dark gymnasium quivered as muffled shots continued to echo through the walls. Then, suddenly, they stopped. Someone yelled, "Retreat!" Was it Colton? Was he out there? Surely the cops weren't leaving?

There was a long pause. A minute. Maybe more.

Finally the doors opened again. It was dark outside, but Molly could see the unmistakable mist of grenade smoke in the air.

Diego was the first to appear, grinning and patting a shotgun-holding friend on the back. As his soldiers filed back inside and closed the doors behind them, Molly hung her head and tried not to let her emotions show on her face. Diego had overpowered the cops, and that could *not* be good.

"It's like someone knew the cops were coming," Tommy muttered.

"Yeah," Molly said, "it is."

With most people who'd been inside the gym now positioned toward the back, as far away from the gunfire as they could get, Diego and his men set up camp at the front. If anyone had thoughts of leaving, they'd have had to go through Diego.

"Did you see his face when he realized we were armed?" A skinny guy with a loud voice performed an exaggerated impression of the Police Chief.

"Did you see his face when I shot him?" another shouted, tipping his head back to guffaw with laughter.

As Diego slapped the laughing guy on the back and congratulated him, Molly screwed her eyes shut and stood up, bracing her hands on the back of her neck. It was already obvious that more than a few cops had lost their lives. What if Colton was one of them? She was certain she'd heard his voice and when she saw the grenade smoke, she knew it was Colton who was responsible. So he had to be okay. Didn't he?

Moving sideways, Molly scanned the exits. Every single one was being guarded.

"Warren?" Diego was shouting at someone across the gym. "Go out front and clean up."

Warren hurried over and, without thinking, Molly followed.

"Now, boss? It's the middle of the night." Warren shoved his hands into his pockets and glanced at the closed doors.

Diego tilted his head then slowly stood up. "Are you *questioning* a direct order?"

"No, sir."

"We don't want these nice civilians to see all that mess, now, do we? We don't want to scare them." Diego pulled two more guys to their feet and shoved them into line next to Warren. "So, go do as you're told."

As Warren pulled open the door, Molly inched forward, craning her neck to catch a glimpse of the lawn outside. The smoke had cleared, and it was lit by a bright moon. Bodies were everywhere. She scanned them and didn't see Colton, but it didn't do much to ease the swishing nausea in her gut.

"Miss O'Neil? What do we do?" Lucky had followed her and was staring too.

Quickly, Molly put her hand on Lucky's shoulder and guided him back to the others before anyone noticed them. While Diego and his cronies cracked open some beer, one of them raised their bottle and shouted, "Smells like bacon!" For a brief moment, no one spoke, but then Diego hollered and slapped the guy on the back, and the others started whooping and stamping their feet.

Molly turned away, pulling Lucky with her, and exchanged a worried look with Laura Banks.

"My husband and my kids are still out there," Laura said tightly.

"Diego's not interested in them," Molly replied quickly. "This was about beating the cops."

Laura nodded, but her hand went to her dog's collar and Molly watched her nestle her fingers into his fur.

As Molly and the others huddled together, two guards carrying shotguns marched past them. "Someone here told the police we had weapons," one was muttering.

"Yeah, well, a cop told us what the Chief was planning, so we're even, aren't we?"

"Maybe." The first guard stopped and scratched his chin. "But Diego will want to know who the rat was."

Molly reached for her water bottle and took a long sip. Inside, she was muttering, *stay calm, stay calm,* but it wasn't doing much good; Diego would suspect her. Of course he would. She'd already drawn attention to herself and caused trouble, and she'd made it clear she didn't agree with the way he was running things. She was the obvious candidate for treachery, and if he found out she was hiding a gun on her person....

"Listen up!" In the middle of the room, Diego was—once again—jumping up onto a table. This time, he tapped his beer bottle against the barrel of his gun.

As the room settled into silence, Diego said solemnly, "I'm sure a lot of you are upset about what just happened. We beat back the police, but you might not see that as a good thing. Possibly, you're scared. Frightened about what this means. But I'm here to tell you that this is a victory for all of us."

As a hushed murmur spread through the crowd, the guards near Molly told everyone to settle down.

"The police were not coming here to help you. They were coming to steal our supplies, but I'm drawing a line in the sand. This side of town, and everything down to the train tracks, belongs to us. The Community Action League!"

Molly glanced at Laura.

"Community what?" Tommy muttered.

"The CAL is in charge now. It's clear the power's not coming back on. We need to accept that and we need to find a way, not just to survive, but to thrive." Diego paused and gestured with his beer bottle to the people around the room. "The CAL will take care of you. We will fortify our domain against intruders, we will keep you safe, we will create order!"

From the front of the gym, Diego's crew whooped and hollered as his voice grew louder.

"We will use the supplies we've gathered to fix the generators. We'll build a fence to protect what is ours. And we will not let anyone stop us!"

Another round of cheers, and Molly's stomach turned to lead.

"Which means…." Diego's tone darkened and he weighed his gun up and down in his hand, "you are either *with* the CAL or you're *against* the CAL. If you're with us, you will have our protection. You'll work hard and you'll be rewarded with food, water, shelter… whatever you need. If you're out…." He turned to look in Molly's direction and allowed his eyes to fix on hers. "If you don't *like* the way I run things, then you need to leave. Right now."

"What about the sick people?" Molly shouted before she could stop herself. "Will you return their medicine?"

Nearby, people began to exchange worried glances.

Diego narrowed his eyes, then tilted his head from side to side. "The sick will need to leave," he said bluntly. "We cannot afford to carry people who can't or won't pull their own weight."

"This isn't right!" a voice from the triage area of the gym called out. "What you're talking about is indentured servitude. You can't force people to—"

Next to Molly, Laura Banks whispered, "Jerry, don't."

"You know him?"

"He's my neighbor." Laura went to move forward but Molly put her hand on the back of Laura's chair.

As Jerry continued to shout, Diego snapped his fingers and, seemingly from nowhere, someone with a gun sprang forward and hauled the old man to his feet.

"Get your hands off me!" Jerry shouted.

Next to him, a woman who looked like his wife began to wail. Someone grabbed her too.

"Get them out of here," Diego spat.

"No!" Laura gripped the sides of her chair. Argent whimpered. But Diego didn't move. He just watched; he watched as Jerry was dragged to the front of the gym and thrown outside, followed by his wife. Then he raised his eyebrows and shrugged. "This is what happens if you don't like the way we're doing things." Jumping down from the table, Diego added, "Those who want to leave, you've got thirty minutes. After that, anyone caught disagreeing with the CAL will not be treated so kindly."

As Diego stalked off toward his friends, Molly breathed out heavily and shook her arms to release the tension in them.

"That's it, we're out," Tommy said loudly, pulling Zack to his feet. "We're not sticking around for this crap."

"Tommy…." Molly looked from Tommy to Zack.

"Miss O'Neil," Zack said bluntly, "I didn't leave one prison behind to end up in another one. Besides, Tommy has a plan. We have somewhere safe we can go."

"You do?" Molly asked, torn between feeling relieved and worried.

Tommy nodded. "You should leave too. What possible reason have you got to stay here?"

Molly knitted her fingers together and squeezed. Without answering him, she said, "Be careful, you two."

Watching Tommy and Zack weave toward the front of the gymnasium, Molly bit the inside of her cheek. Maybe she should go with them? Lucky looked undecided too but before she could talk to him, Laura pointed to the triage area. "Looks like Chase is leaving," she said, already moving toward him.

"You're going?" Molly asked when they reached Chase. A nurse next to him nodded.

"We're taking the patients to Ridgeview Hospital."

"I thought you said the hospitals would be overrun?" Laura asked.

Chase gritted his teeth. "They will be, but at least we have a chance of getting medication there. If we stay, Diego will kick most of these people out."

Laura nodded slowly, then turned to Molly. "In that case, I'm going too."

"Laura?" Molly tried not to let the panic in her chest show on her face.

"I've done what I can do here. I need to get back to Alex and the kids."

Molly blinked and held her eyes closed for longer than usual. When she opened them, she tried to smile. "I understand," she said. "But Laura?"

Laura looked up at her.

"Whatever you do, if you come in contact with Diego's men, don't let them know about Erik and Scarlett's talents… if they realize Erik could help fix the generators—"

"I won't." Laura nodded solemnly, then clipped on Argent's leash and turned to Chase. "I'll go with you part of the way," she said.

"Wait..." Molly tugged Chase's arm and glanced behind her to make sure no one was watching. "Here. Take this." She'd removed her gun from her jeans and was offering it to him.

Chase's eyes widened. "Oh, I don't shoot," he said.

"You might have to." Molly looked at him solemnly. "You need to keep these people safe."

"What about you?"

"It's more dangerous for me to be found with it." Molly motioned for Chase to hurry up and hide the weapon. "Please, Chase, just take it."

Reluctantly, Chase agreed. As Molly watched him and Laura go, she braced her hands behind her head and tried to slow her thoughts. Her instinct was to leave. To take Lucky and get out of there. Except Lucky wasn't the only one of her students who needed taking away from this place.

She scanned the room and stopped when her eyes landed on the person she'd been looking for—Jenna. She had been taking boxes into the storeroom when the fight broke out and, for a brief moment, Molly found herself thinking that at least Diego had shown one fatherly instinct; giving Jenna a task that would keep her out of the way of the gunfire.

Now Jenna was standing next to him, but when he growled something at her, she turned and headed over to Lucky. Molly copied her, moving away from the vacated triage zone toward Lucky. They met in the middle of the room and Molly tentatively put her hand on Jenna's shoulder as she stepped into line beside her.

"Jenna? Are you okay?"

Jenna barely glanced at her, just shrugged out from under her touch and said, "Fine." She tugged at her sleeve and the movement caught Molly's attention; a large bruise was splashed across Jenna's forearm.

Molly was certain it was the imprint of someone's hand. "I have a job to do for my dad," Jenna said, still not looking at Molly, the bruise now obscured by her sweater. For a moment, she didn't move. Then she shook her head and stalked away.

As Molly watched her, she knew there was no way she could leave.

Reaching Lucky, she kept her eyes on Jenna and said, "Lucky? You okay if we stay put for a while?"

Lucky followed her gaze. She'd expected him to protest, to demand they get out of there, stick to the plan to find his folks, and then get out of town. Instead, he nodded. "Yeah," he said, his eyes fixed on Jenna. "As long as it's only for a little while."

23

LAURA

As soon as they were beyond the high school's parking lot, Laura felt a strange mixture of relief and nausea. Despite Diego's increasingly worrying behavior, it had been safe back there. At least for a while. Now she'd made the decision to leave, there was no going back, and although she knew she'd done the right thing, the thought of going home was making her hands tremble.

"Will you be okay?" Dr. Chase had asked the group to stop at the crossroads and had stepped to one side to talk to her. He glanced at the road. Left would take them out of town. Right went to Laura's neighborhood. Her family. Her kids and her husband. And Dave.

"We can wait if you want to go collect your family. Or we can come with you." Chase was looking at Laura's hands. She took them away from her wheels and folded them into her lap.

"Alex has a fancy new chair for me back home. It'll make things easier," she said, as if tiredness from traveling in the old chair was the reason her fingers were shaking. "You should get going. Get these people the help they need." She looked past him at the wide-eyed patients who had bravely made the decision to leave.

"All right, but if you need help, Laura, head to the hospital. I'll be there and I'll help you if I can." Chase began to reach for the gun Molly had given him but Laura shook her head at him.

"No. Absolutely not. You need it. You have people to take care of."

Chase paused but didn't object.

Laura smiled. She felt strangely emotional; they'd known each other hardly any time at all, but they had shared something. A common goal. A purpose. A crisis. Saying goodbye was harder than she'd expected. As she spoke, her voice wavered. "Thank you. For everything." She cleared her throat and laughed. "Gosh, sorry. I don't know why I'm so—"

"Because this…" Chase waved his hand at the abandoned vehicles and extinguished streetlights around them, "all of this? It's a lot to handle."

Behind them, someone coughed loudly. It was an elderly woman. She was struggling to catch her breath. "Go on," Laura gestured to the woman, "go help her. If we don't meet again, good luck."

"You too, Laura." Chase smiled and looked at Argent, who was waiting patiently to be told what was happening next. "And Argent, it was a *pleasure* to meet you, buddy."

Without lingering to watch Chase and his patients leave, Laura took a deep breath, tugged Argent's leash, and headed toward home.

Just like the journey to the high school, the journey away from it was proving to be hard work. In her second-hand, second-rate chair, she could feel every bump and dip in the sidewalk. Navigating obstacles was tough, jerky, and caused her back to throb with the effort of it, and none of it was helped by the fact that the only light she had to guide her came when the moon stuck its head out from behind a cloud.

Her only consolation was the fact that because she was trying so hard to maneuver herself, she didn't have time to think about how dark it was or about being completely alone with no weapon. As she stopped to catch her breath, she looked at Argent and shook her head. "Why the heck did I say *no* to a gun?"

He tilted his head at her.

"Because my history with guns isn't great?" She tried to make herself laugh, because it was easier than giving in to the feeling of utter dread that settled deeper in her stomach the closer she got to home. "Fair point."

After what she guessed was at least an hour, finally, Laura pulled onto her street. It was quiet. When she'd left with Jerry and Barb all those days ago, it had been daylight and there had been people milling about. Now, everything looked different. Some houses had been boarded up; others had broken windows. Before the accident she'd been partial to late night runs, and she knew Alex still indulged himself in them if he couldn't sleep or if he needed to release some tension from the kids or work or their arguments.

Looking up, she blinked slowly at an unlit streetlamp. She could picture its orange glow, always flickering a little, in and out, in and out. She shivered and reached down to weave her fingers into Argent's fur. After days stuck in the gymnasium with very little in the way of exercise, except for Laura throwing a ball for him on the grass outside, he was clearly very pleased to be out on a walk. Even if it was late, and dark, and cold.

Outside the house, Laura kept tight hold of Argent's leash. He stopped and looked at her, confused as to why they weren't charging up to the front door calling for Erik, and Scarlett, and Alex.

"You remember what happened in there, boy?" Laura patted her lap and Argent instantly sat up on his hind legs, put his big paws on her knees, and leaned into her. Wrapping her arms around his neck, she nuzzled into him and sighed. "I have to tell them. I have to tell Alex and the kids. But I have no idea how."

When she released him from her embrace, Argent stayed where he was and simply stared at her.

Laura realized she was crying. "Why? Why do I have to tell them?" She wiped her cheek with the back of her hand. "Because they are my world. All we have now is each other, so I have to be honest." She sucked in her breath and held it as she counted to five. "I have to be honest so that we can have a fresh start."

"Good morning." Alex's deep gravelly voice greeted her before she'd even opened her eyes. His beard tickled her neck as he kissed her behind the ear.

"What time is it?"

"No idea." Alex pushed himself up onto the pillows behind them and scraped his fingers through his hair. "We have no clocks, no jobs. The kids have no school. Which means we don't have to get out of bed." His eyes were twinkling and Laura started to blush.

"Alex, shouldn't we be, I don't know, doing something useful?"

"The twins and I took care of everything. We've cataloged our supplies. Erik has put together a handy little toolbox of anything he thinks might come in useful if we encounter another broken generator.

We'll need to head out for more in a few days, but we're good for now."

Laura rested her head on her husband's shoulder. Right now, you wouldn't know that anything was any different from how it had been a few weeks ago. Sun was filtering in through the window. Their bedroom looked the same. Same photos on the walls, same dresser, same closet.

As her eyes came to rest on the closet, Laura swallowed hard and quickly looked away. Alex hadn't commented on what state the house had been in when he and the twins had returned, but he'd been so pleased to see her last night that he hadn't commented on much at all except to say she was foolish to travel all that way alone.

"I'm fine," she'd replied, pulling Scarlett onto her lap for a hug and smiling at Erik. "I'm just happy to be home."

"I'll go make coffee." Alex was swinging his legs out of bed and fumbling for a T-shirt.

"Coffee? Did Erik fix the coffee machine?" Laura could hear the delight in her voice.

Alex chuckled at her and leaned in to kiss her forehead. "No, love. But he did find the camping stove in the garage."

"Oh. Right." She rubbed her neck. Every muscle in her body was hurting. Alex saw the gesture and perched on the bed next to her.

"Stay here. Rest. I'll bring breakfast and then we'll do the grand unveiling."

Laura frowned.

"Your new chair." Alex was grinning. He was acting the way he did at Christmas and on birthdays—as if they were the happiest, most in-love couple in the world.

"Right." She folded her arms in front of her stomach. "After that, though, Alex, I need to talk to you. You and the kids."

Alex stood up and nodded, clearly not picking up on her serious tone of voice. "Course. Sustenance first, though. Right?"

A few minutes later, Alex returned with the first hot cup of coffee Laura had seen in days. She was almost salivating by the time he handed it to her. "Oh my!" She breathed in the smell and wrapped her hands around the cup. "I can't believe we have coffee."

"Our own little palace," Alex said.

"What's for breakfast?" Laura could smell something but couldn't quite work out what it was.

"Toast and eggs." Alex grimaced a little. "Scarlett's cooking."

Laura slurped her coffee and tried not to laugh. She was remembering the time they went camping when the twins were younger. They couldn't have been more than eight and they decided to surprise Mom and Dad with breakfast in bed. The result was raw sausages, burned bacon, and inedible eggs.

"You're right. I'll go check on her." Alex nodded toward the door. "Join us in a minute? When you're ready?"

Laura told him she would, then leaned back against the headboard and concentrated on enjoying every mouthful of coffee. When she'd drained the entire cup, she finally made herself get out of bed.

She'd washed almost as soon as she got home last night—desperate to get the smell of the high school gymnasium out of her skin—but now it was daylight she couldn't avoid looking at herself in the bathroom mirror.

"You have to do this," she whispered. "You have to tell them. Today."

When she emerged, as if he knew she needed company, Argent was waiting for her. He walked in front of her until they reached the living room, then stopped and looked up.

"It's okay, boy, you go relax." Laura gestured to the couch and smiled as Argent snuggled into it.

In the kitchen, the twins were standing in front of the family's camping stove, nudging one another. "That toast is going to burn," Scarlett snapped at Erik.

"At least it'll be cooked. Your eggs look raw," he snapped back.

From where he was leaning against the counter, Alex looked up and smiled at Laura. "There you are. Everything okay?"

"You don't have to keep checking on me, Alex, I'm fine." Laura noticed the tension in her voice and mentally kicked herself for it. Trying to smile, she added, "I can take care of myself."

As Alex's eyes scanned her face, something tugged at Laura's stomach. He was looking at her strangely. As if he was thinking, *I know exactly how well you can take care of yourself.*

She glanced toward the back door. Like the living room windows, it was boarded up, but that didn't stop her picturing what was out there.

"Food's ready!" Scarlett yelled triumphantly as she waved at the pan on the stove.

"Great," Laura smiled. "I'm starving."

At the table, eating breakfast as a family for the first time in years, Laura watched the twins as they chattered loudly about everything they'd done since they arrived back at the house.

"It sounds like you two have really grown up recently," she said, smiling.

"You don't know the half of it. Wait until we tell you about the prison." Scarlett's eyes sparkled as she spoke.

"I'm not sure your mother needs to hear that now," Alex said gently.

"Actually—" Laura spoke before she even realized she was going to. "I do want to hear it. Of course, I do. But I have something to tell you all first."

"Shall we do the chair first?" Alex's chair scraped against the floor as he moved to stand up. "I really want to see what you think of it. It's top of the line—"

"Alex…" Laura reached for his hand and squeezed it. "Please?"

As Alex sat back down, the twins glanced at one another. Their smiles had dropped from their faces. Happy families never lasted long in the Banks household. Why should today be any different?

Closing her eyes, Laura bit the inside of her lower lip and breathed in slowly. When she looked up, she spoke to Alex and the twins. "There's something I have to tell you. All of you."

"Laura, you don't have to—" Alex met her eyes and shook his head. He knew. Shoot. Of course he knew. Why else would he have been so keen to avoid talking about anything *real*? To pretend they were on vacation, sleeping in and enjoying coffee in bed.

"Yes, I do," she replied solemnly. "Because I've learned something very important since this all happened. I've learned that the three of you are the most important people in the world to me." She cleared her throat and sat up a little straighter, ignoring the twinge in her back. "Since my accident, things have been tough for all of us. I haven't made things easy for any of you."

"Love, what you went through—" Alex reached for her hand but she didn't let him take it.

"Yes, it was awful. But it was awful for you too. All of you. I'm not sure how we could have handled it differently. I never thought we'd have to navigate something like this, and I'm pretty sure if we're honest with ourselves we'd all say that we did things we weren't proud of."

The twins exchanged a glance and hung their heads.

"But it's time for me to take responsibility for my actions. I was in pain. I took too much medication and I became addicted."

"Laura, you dealt with this in rehab, you don't have to go through it all again." Alex was speaking softly but Laura didn't give in. This time, she wouldn't let him cushion her from herself.

"I went to rehab and I got better but I didn't tell you the whole truth." She looked from Alex to Scarlett to Erik, then put her palms flat on the table as she said, "Ever since I got back, I had pills stashed in the house. I never intended to take them, but I knew they were there and it made me feel… safe."

Scarlett breathed out slowly but Erik looked confused. Shrugging, he said, "But you didn't take them, though, did you?"

"No." Laura shook her head emphatically. "No, I didn't."

"So, then, what's the big deal?" He looked at his sister. "Mom, it's great that you're trying to be honest but—"

"There's more." Laura cut him off and spoke faster this time. "When your dad came to look for you, a man from my support group turned up at the house. He knew I had the pills hidden here. Not because I'd told him, but because addicts know other addicts. I let him in because he said he needed help, but he attacked me."

"What! Mom? What?" Scarlett and Erik almost leaped out of their chairs, but Alex had screwed his eyes closed. He knew. He knew what she did and he was bracing himself to hear it said out loud.

Laura gestured for the twins to calm down. "I'm okay." She tried to smile. "Look at me, I'm fine. But the man—Dave—he isn't."

"Laura," Alex muttered softly.

"Dave is dead." Laura said it as loudly as she could. Three little words. "He is dead. I killed him. He tried to kill me and I shot him. Then I wrapped him up in the rug from your dad's study and I dragged him outside and hid him under the table in the yard."

She was speaking to the twins because she couldn't bear to look at Alex's face.

Scarlett's eyes looked like they were going to pop right out of her head. Erik, on the other hand, was eerily silent. Then, all of a sudden, he exploded in a clap of laughter. "Seriously? You shot a guy? And buried him in the yard?"

Laura nodded slowly.

Erik was grinning. Scarlett looked at him and started to laugh too.

"No, kids, this isn't funny. I took a man's life." She looked at Alex, expecting to see hurt or fury or disappointment in his face. Instead, he began to smile. "You're not mad?" she asked, almost at a loss for words.

"Mad at you?" He pulled his chair closer to hers and grabbed her hands between his. "For protecting yourself?" Alex stroked the side of her face and met her eyes. "You don't think I'd have done the same thing if I was here? You think any one of us wouldn't have shot this guy to protect you?"

Laura raised a hand to her face. Her cheeks were wet. She was crying. "But, the pills? I lied to you about them."

Alex shook his head. "And now you've told us the truth. So that's the end of it. Okay? No more beating yourself up. No more carrying this awful weight around with you. It's over. It's in the past." He looked up at the twins and without him even needing to ask they got up from their seats.

Scarlett wrapped her arms tightly around Laura's neck and Erik slipped his hand into hers.

"From now on, this family has a fresh start. Right?" Alex looked at each of them in turn. "We stick together and we look out for each other. Agreed?"

The twins nodded.

"Agreed," Laura whispered, allowing herself to lean into her daughter's embrace.

For a moment, no one moved. Then Erik said, "Seriously though, Mom?" When she looked at him, he was grinning. "You're a total badass."

Laura shook her head but couldn't help smiling. "Yeah," she said. "I guess I am."

24

MOLLY

TWO WEEKS LATER

For a moment, when Molly opened her eyes, she forgot she was sleeping in the old French classroom. Staring at the ceiling, and a large poster of the Eiffel Tower, she could almost hear the hum of people gathering beneath it, staring up at its belly, marveling at its beauty.

Nearby, someone began to open the blinds. Sunlight streamed in. Not hot, but bright.

"Rise and shine." Carmel, who was wearing tight jeans and a tighter shirt, waved at them and told them it was time for breakfast.

Pushing herself upright, Molly reached for her hoodie and pulled it over the gray vest she'd been permitted to take from the clothing pile. While it was a little small, it was easy to wash and dried quickly.

“We’re coming.” Molly pulled her hair into a ponytail and used a headscarf to push it back from her eyes, standing up as Carmel opened the door and started hurrying them along.

The other women in the dorm looked just as tired and browbeaten as Molly. Most had spent the last fourteen days picking the bones of the train for extra supplies. Diego had three guys working on the generator, but so far they’d had little luck. A couple of times it had clunked and spluttered, and everyone had held their breath as they waited for it to spring to life. But it never had.

Apparently its circuits were fried and it needed some replacement parts. Diego had issued all scavengers a list, but Molly wouldn’t have been surprised if the whole thing was a wild goose chase; if the engineers were simply too scared to tell Diego the machine was broken beyond repair.

While the scavengers went all over town looking for supplies, engine parts, and any morsel of fuel not yet siphoned off from people’s abandoned cars, Molly had been restricted to duties inside the school. Diego hadn’t said as much, but he suspected her of being the one who told the cops about his gun supplies, and he wasn’t foolish enough to allow her the privilege of fresh air.

As they trudged down the hallway toward the cafeteria, Molly tried not to look at the artwork on the walls; it reminded her too much of what should be happening here. At first, when she’d told Lucky they would stay, she’d tried to start an evening club for the kids. Partly as a way to have some contact with Jenna, partly because the thought that none of them would ever read a book again made her want to scream. After two days, Diego had put a stop to it.

“If you have time to read books, you have time to do extra work,” he’d snapped, clearly still confused about why she hadn’t left and suspicious of her every move.

After that, the books had disappeared. Every single one of them.

In the cafeteria, Molly spotted Lucky. He was picking at a bowl of dry breakfast cereal. No sugar—that was reserved for Diego's favorites.

From the table at the far end of the room, Molly selected a protein shake. Plain, not flavored. She'd seen some coffee-flavored ones being brought in a few days ago, but clearly they were too fancy to be shared.

"How'd you sleep?" Molly sat down next to Lucky and sipped her shake, willing herself to believe it tasted of something better than old classroom chalk.

"Okay." Lucky moved his spoon around his dish and sighed. He was desperate to leave, but at the same time, seemed to have accepted the fact that if there had been no news of his parents by this point, they were unlikely to find anything if they went searching.

"I might try and go past my house today," he muttered. "We're starting to go over the gardens on that side of town. Diego wants to add fresh fruit and vegetables to the grocery supplies. He's hoping some folks have veg patches or whatever."

Molly pressed her lips together and tapped her fingernails on the side of her shake carton. "Lucky, it's too risky. You know what's happened to others who haven't stuck to their tasks."

Even as Molly spoke, she couldn't quite believe what she was saying. Had she really allowed them to become so entrenched in Diego's way of doing things that they were too scared to veer off course a little to look for a family member?

Instead of protesting, Lucky nodded.

"Did you hear what happened?" Molly turned to see Becky Simmons sliding onto the bench next to her.

Molly shook her head.

"Diego caught someone trying to sneak food to the zeros. He *shot* them." Becky's eyes were wide and she was wringing her hands together, but she seemed more enthralled by the drama of it than worried about the loss of life.

"Damn it!" Molly bit her lower lip and pushed her shake away. It wasn't right that they were eating when others were starving. "The only reason they're not working is because they're sick," she muttered.

"And they're sick because he kept making them go into that train," Lucky added.

Molly and Becky both dipped their heads; Lucky was right. Laura had told Molly before she left that Chase suspected something toxic was released into the air when the train went up. He'd tried to persuade those who were sick to go with him, but the ones who were only coughing a little thought they'd be okay. A few days later, they became so sick that Diego had to allocate an entire classroom as a medical ward.

"They say he's getting rid of them," Becky whispered, leaning in closely. "The sick people? They go into the medical ward but they don't come back out."

"He wouldn't do that." Molly shook her head, but she didn't believe it. Diego had made it very clear where he stood—if you wanted to stay, and be given food, you worked. If you didn't work, you were disposable.

"O'Neil." A guard marched up to her and rapped his knuckles on the table. "You've been reassigned. You too, kid. You're both on the hauling team today."

"The hauling team?" Molly swallowed hard. She didn't want to be anywhere near that train. "Cruz told me I was to stay inside the school."

"Cruz changed his mind," the guard snapped back. "So finish your food and get going."

Molly glanced at Lucky. Slowly, they got to their feet. "He must be running low on numbers if he's trusting me to go outside," Molly muttered.

"Hauling?" Lucky asked as they made their way into the hall.

"Pulling wreckage that Diego can use to build his wall," Molly said, already feeling the burn in her muscles as she thought about having to spend the next twelve hours shifting heavy pieces of scrap metal from the derailed train.

"Why do we need a wall anyway?" Lucky said, sounding nervous.

"Well, Diego's either completely paranoid and thinks we're going to be attacked at any moment—" Molly shook her head.

"Or he's right and we *are* going to be attacked at any moment." Lucky widened his eyes.

"Let's hope it's the former," she said.

Reaching the front of the gym, which was now being used as the main entrance to the school where people were checked in and out, Molly paused and breathed in deeply. She'd barely breathed even a molecule of fresh air for two whole weeks.

"Name?" A guard holding a clipboard, with a shotgun slung over his back, stood in front of her and tapped his pen loudly.

"Molly O'Neil."

The guard ran his finger down the list. "Haulage," he said. "Over there."

With Lucky, Molly headed to the group of people who were waiting to be taken to the train. On the other side of the parking lot, a second group were getting ready to go patrol the woods; a daily activity that Diego now insisted on as part of their "ongoing security protocol" even though Molly knew the real reason. She'd overheard him and his men talking about the dead prisoners in the woods, and if Diego was patrolling up there it meant he was worried about it. Worried that whoever it was might be a threat.

Looking down, Molly breathed in sharply as she noticed a faded bloodstain on the sidewalk. She had no idea what had happened to the bodies of the police officers who were shot. Rumor was Diego had burned them.

"You're sure you haven't seen any signs of Colton or the police?" Molly had asked Lucky this question several times, but as they headed out of the school gates, she couldn't help asking it again.

It had been two weeks, and she'd heard nothing. Surely if he was alive and okay, he'd have found a way to contact her? He wouldn't have just left them there in the school. Which meant he probably wasn't okay, and that whatever had happened to him was her fault.

As if he could read her mind, Lucky whispered, "You were right to tell him about the guns, Miss O'Neil. It's not your fault, what happened."

Molly nodded but looked purposefully at the guard up ahead, indicating that Lucky should keep his voice down. So far, no one had figured out that she was the leak. She needed to keep it that way.

"All right, folks!" The guard had stopped in front of a rolled-over train car. It was half on, half off the tracks and looked like it had already been given the once-over by Diego and his crew.

"There's hardly anything left," someone said loudly.

"Which is why your job is to get these doors off and over to the building yard."

"The doors?" Molly asked. "How the heck are we supposed to—"

Without even stopping for breath, the guard marched over to her and grabbed her wrist. He was squeezing it so hard she thought it might snap. "I don't give a damn *how* you do it. You just do it. Got it?"

Molly nodded, and as the guard let her go, she stepped back, rubbing her wrist.

As someone up ahead tried to take charge and said they'd attempt to loosen the hinges, Molly and Lucky positioned themselves at the opposite side of the door. With two others, they prepared to try and lift the door if the hinges were freed.

"Okay, nearly there!" the guy on the hinges shouted. "Brace yourselves!"

There was a moment's stillness, then the door lurched downward, its full weight coming free. Molly and the man next to her struggled to keep hold of it. Her arms were burning. She'd just about secured her grasp, even though her lower back was throbbing with the effort, when she heard Lucky gasp. The door shifted.

"Who let go?" someone yelled. The door creaked.

Molly looked at Lucky. He'd let go of the door and was holding his hand to his chest.

"Drop it!" Molly shouted. "Move away and drop it! Someone's hurt!"

The second the door was down, she stepped away. Lucky's hand was bleeding profusely. Although he was holding it up, blood was pouring from it, dripping onto the rocky ground beneath their feet. His face had lost all its color and even his lips looked gray.

"Crap," someone nearby called out. "The kid needs medical attention."

Waving at them to shut them up, Molly pulled her headscarf free and wrapped it around Lucky's palm. Nausea tugged at her stomach as she noticed the flap of skin that had been sliced loose. "Sit down," she said, tugging him away from the train. "Here." She guided him onto a discarded piece of wood and bobbed down in front of him.

"Hey!" The guard stormed over and glowered at them. "Back to work."

"He needs medical attention. He's a *child*," Molly spat, standing up and gesticulating wildly at Lucky. "He's badly hurt, which should never have happened since he had no business being here."

The guard paused, glanced in Lucky's direction at his increasingly pale face and the blood that was seeping through Molly's scarf, then nodded. "Fine. Go back to base, but you'll both miss a meal for this."

"Fine!" Molly helped Lucky to his feet and started to walk away. "Don't worry," she said quietly. "You'll be okay. A few stitches and you'll be fine. Nothing to stop you at least going on veg picking duty."

As Lucky tried to smile, Molly swallowed hard. This wasn't good. Not good at all. What was she thinking, making him stay here? Why didn't she make them leave when she had the chance?

At the high school, Molly refused point-blank to allow Lucky into the medical wing without her. Reaching instinctively for the back of her jeans, she had to remind herself that her gun was no longer there—

that she'd given it to Chase. Despite occasionally wishing she still had it, she was glad she'd made the decision. The morning after the shooting, Diego had searched every single person before allocating them a number and a work duty. If he'd found a weapon on her person, he'd have kicked her out—or worse—and she doubted he'd have allowed Lucky to stay with her.

"Are you a doctor?" she asked as a woman walked over and began to examine Lucky's hand.

She had long brown hair, tied in a ponytail, and was wearing a pair of glasses with a scratch across the left lens. "A vet," she said, "but don't worry, I can do stitches." Gently, she turned Lucky's hand over then looked up at Molly. "We can't use anesthetic for cases like this. You'll have to hold him still while I stitch him up."

Lucky looked green around the edges and reached for Molly's hand. Squeezing it tightly, he said, "Do I really need stitches?"

"I'm afraid so," the vet said. Then, gesturing to a nearby nurse, she asked them to clean the wound while she prepared her supplies.

Motioning for Molly to move away from Lucky, as the nurse dabbed antiseptic wipes on Lucky's palm, the vet lowered her voice. "Under normal circumstances, he'd be fine but—"

Molly inhaled sharply. "But?"

"We're not permitted to use antibiotics for something like this. There simply aren't enough."

Molly's hand bunched into a fist. Not enough? Diego had raided every pharmacy in town. "Without antibiotics, it could get infected?"

The vet nodded, glancing at Lucky. "I'm so sorry. It's not up to me. We've been given instructions. I don't even have access to the antibiotics."

Molly closed her eyes and turned away so she could take some deep breaths. She'd only just turned around when the door opened.

"O'Neil, I was told you left your work duty?" It was Diego. Next to him, Jenna was staring wide-eyed at Lucky and the pile of blood-stained wipes beside him.

"Lucky injured his hand. He'll be fine, but he needs to rest, and he needs antibiotics."

Diego pushed the door open farther and stepped inside. Peering at the cut on Lucky's hand, he shook his head. "It's a minor wound, he'll be fine. He's young, healthy. Doctors hand out antibiotics like candy these days. There's no need for it."

Molly opened her mouth to reply but, next to Diego, Jenna offered a quick shake of the head. Molly looked away and ignored her. "If we give him antibiotics now, we'll prevent the worst-case scenario. Surely it should be a decision for a medical professional, not—"

"Not…?" Diego stared at her, willing her to finish her sentence. When she didn't, he said, "If we treated every patient based on a possible worst-case scenario, Miss O'Neil, there would soon be no medicine left for those who really need it."

"Like the ones with the terrible coughs?" Molly stepped forward and waved her hand around the room. "Where are they, by the way? All the sick people who keep coming in here? Where are they now?"

Next to Diego, Jenna's eyes were wide and watery. There were dark shadows beneath them and a red mark on her temple that looked like it might be turning into a bruise. She was thin, too, much thinner than she had been a few weeks ago.

Diego didn't flinch. Turning away, dragging Jenna with him, he called, "You may take the rest of the afternoon, but your dinner portions will be halved." As he reached the door, he said, "And that's me being generous because the boy is Jenna's friend."

Molly waited until the door had closed before hurrying over and peering through the glass window in the top of it. Diego had his arm around Jenna and was heading back toward the gym.

When she turned around, the vet motioned that she was ready to start stitching. Lucky looked terrified. Like Jenna, he too looked thin. He'd always been a scrawny teen, but after two weeks at the CAL he was almost emaciated.

Molly reached up and let her fingers graze her collarbone. She wasn't in great shape either. Every morning, getting out of bed became a little more difficult. Was it any wonder the people on haulage duty didn't last very long?

"Okay, ready?" the vet asked Lucky.

He nodded and looked away as Molly positioned herself behind him and put her hands on his shoulders. Next to her, the nurse held Lucky's arm. For a moment, he was still, but as soon as the vet's needle met his skin he cried out. The vet worked quickly, but every stitch made Molly flinch.

Finally, it was done.

Lucky had managed to stay still, but he was shaking. Molly helped him to his feet and put her arm around his waist as they trudged back toward his dorm room. His hand was thickly bandaged, and he was holding it against his chest, walking slowly, barely a shuffle.

Even when they were stuck in the prison, nothing like this had happened. The teens had been scared but they hadn't been physically hurt. Now, Lucky was in desperate need of *real* medical care, and Jenna… well, Jenna was clearly suffering at the hands of Diego, whether she'd admit it or not.

Molly helped Lucky back to his dorm, then set him down on his bed and put her hands on her hips. He looked up at her through glassy eyes, exhausted by the trauma of what had happened.

"Lucky," she said. "Enough is enough. We can't stay here any longer. Since we can't simply walk out the door, it's time we started planning our escape."

25

COLTON

"Okay everyone, thank you for coming." Hicks was standing in the middle of the room holding a warm beer. In a semi-circle around him, the seven remaining officers on the Fairfield police force stood solemnly watching.

For two weeks, Colton and Hicks had been holed up at the police station with the few officers who'd remained after their failed attempt to take control of the high school. In the aftermath, most had decided to hunker down with their families rather than keep fighting. Some had left town. Two had joined Cruz. The CAL, they called it. Every time Colton heard that acronym, it made his blood boil, and it made him sick to think that men who called themselves cops had switched sides.

For two weeks, Colton had expected Dukes to step in and arrange something—anything—in memory of those who'd lost their lives fighting. Of course, he'd done nothing.

Their bodies—the bodies of Chief Bailey and the men and women who'd died that day—had been disposed of by Cruz. They hadn't even been buried properly, and Dukes didn't have the courtesy to agree to a service.

"Too much to do," he'd said. "Pointless," he'd said.

Colton's fingers tightened around the bottle he was holding. He wished it was a candle, but beer was a less precious resource than light.

"I think Colton wanted to say a few words," Hicks said, stepping back and gesturing for Colton to take center stage.

Colton blinked at him. They hadn't discussed who would say what. He certainly hadn't expected to be put up front, even though the whole thing had been his idea. "Well, ah," he said, clearing his throat. "I didn't know the Chief as well as all of you. I didn't know many of your colleagues either. But I know they gave their lives fighting for the people of this town. So, why don't we go around the room and share a few memories?" He nodded at Hicks to start.

"Okay, okay, sure," Hicks glanced behind him at the door. They were in the basement among the old cardboard box files and ancient evidence bags. Dukes was off shift. Sleeping, they hoped, in the Chief's old office. They didn't have much time. "Well, the first time I met the Chief, I was a rookie…."

As Hicks began to tell his story, Colton breathed slowly and purposefully. He was trying to remain present. He was trying to do the Chief the honor of keeping his own anger and frustration at bay, but it was hard. Real hard.

"What the hell is this?" Dukes' voice, just as loud and disdainful as Colton had predicted it would be, filtered in from the doorway.

He'd hoped they would have a little longer before being discovered, but at least they'd made the effort. "To the Chief, and to all those who lost their lives for the folks of this town." Colton raised his beer bottle. The seven cops opposite him hesitated for a moment. then did the same, muttering a mixture of "cheers" and "to the Chief".

When Colton turned around, Dukes was practically beet red. Fury was written all over his face. "I thought I told you—no, in fact, I *know* I told you—there was to be no wasting of police time."

"You did." Colton put his arms behind his back and gestured for the others to leave the room. As they skulked out, only Hicks stayed by his side.

"And you disobeyed me?" Dukes looked from Colton to Hicks and back again.

"I did." Colton tilted his head to one side and refused to look away.

Dukes paused for a moment, then narrowed his eyes and leaned forward. Snatching the beer from behind Colton's back, he tossed it into the corner of the room where it shattered. *That'll stink by the morning,* Colton thought. "Both of you, you're out on haulage duty for the rest of the day. Go. Now."

"Not sure what I expected him to do to us, but this ain't so bad," Hicks said. He was lifting a heavy backpack onto the back of a wagon. It was stuffed with supplies they'd secured from a grocery warehouse on the edge of town. Next to him, Colton heaved up two large water bottles.

"It's been two weeks, and the best Dukes can think of to do is to haul the supplies left on our side of town back to the station, so Cruz doesn't get his hands on them. *This* is what was so important we couldn't spare fifteen minutes for a memorial service." Colton was struggling to let it go.

"We tried," Hicks said, shrugging. "The Chief would have appreciated the effort."

"You find any ibuprofen in there?" Colton asked, trying not to feel irritated by Hicks' lack of outrage.

"Sorry, man." Hicks took his pill bottle from his pocket and shook it. There were four pills left, but Colton had refused to take them. He needed some, but there was no way he was taking Hicks' last pills. "Sit up front, I'll get the rest."

Colton rubbed his knee and glanced at the wagon. Sure, he could rest. He could sit down and let Hicks do the rest, but what would that make him? Besides, too much time sitting meant too much time thinking, and he couldn't let himself think about what Molly and the kids were going through back at the school.

"You kidding? Let you have all the fun?" Colton smiled and limped back toward the warehouse.

An hour later, they arrived back at the police station. "What did he say to do with this stuff?" Hicks asked.

Colton shrugged. "Take it inside, I think. Let's go check first." He climbed down slowly from the wagon and walked up to the front entrance. Prepared to flash the badge he'd been given so he could prove he was on their side, Colton approached the officer guarding the doors.

"We need to unload the wagon. Do we go round back?" Colton asked, slipping his badge back into his pocket.

"Might as well leave it where it is," the officer said. "We're rolling out."

"Rolling out?" Colton exchanged a glance with Hicks. "Out where?"

"Go talk to Dukes," the officer replied. "He's on the second floor."

Inside, Colton stopped and looked at the empty booking desk and the vacant cells. The whole place was a wreck, had been since they'd taken up residence here, but now it was a chaotic wreck. Officers were coming and going, carrying, fetching, moving things around.

Upstairs, Dukes was looking at a large, spread-out map, indicating a path that led past the prison and away from town. When he saw Colton, he looked up. "Good, you're back. We need your help to load everything onto the remaining wagons. Andrews should have brought them round to the front of the building. We need to move fast."

"Sir? We're leaving?" Hicks moved closer to the table and looked at the map.

"We've done all we can here," Dukes replied. "We're heading for Bangor. They have a larger police force, and there's a military base nearby. They may need our help to get the grid back online."

"Sir, with all due respect, how can we help get the grid functioning?" Colton spoke before he was able to stop himself. Despite the frustration burning like acid in his throat, he was doing his best to remain civil. "We'd be better off staying here and protecting the townspeople. If you want to make contact with the military, send a scouting party. I'd be happy to volunteer."

Dukes sucked in his cheeks and stared at Colton for a moment, then moved forward, puffing out his chest like a gorilla who wanted a fight. "You've had your orders. Pack up the station. Load the wagons. We leave in one hour."

Colton opened his mouth to reply but changed his mind. Fine, if Dukes wasn't going to do the right thing, Colton would do it himself. He'd go with them to Bangor, find whoever was in charge, and bring the army back to secure the high school. Dukes might be willing to leave the people to suffer, but Colton wasn't. Especially when one of those people was Molly.

"Yes, sir," he said through gritted teeth. "One hour, sir."

True to his word, an hour later, Dukes was standing at the front of the station, ready to leave. Six wagons were lined up. Four already had drivers. Dukes had staked a claim on the fifth, and Hicks looked at the sixth.

"Looks like we're carpooling," he said to Colton, but before he could climb up into the front, Dukes walked over and held out his hand.

"Colton, the badge you were borrowing. I'd like it back, please."

Colton paused and glanced at Hicks, but did as he was instructed and handed back the badge.

"It's the end of the road for you, Marine."

Colton bit the inside of his cheek and pushed back his shoulders. "End of the road?"

"You're not a cop." Dukes cast a withering look at Colton's leg. "And you'll slow us down. We're done with you."

"Slow us down? Sir, we're traveling with wagons." Hicks tried to laugh, to lighten his tone. "Come on, Dukes. I know you two haven't always seen eye-to-eye, but Colton's been an asset. Heck, how many more officers would we have lost in the shootout if it wasn't for him?"

Dukes breathed in deeply. His fingers were on his holster. "You know what, Hicks? For that, you're out too." Dukes held out his hand. "Give me your gun, officer."

"Dukes, you can't do this." Hicks shook his head in disbelief. "This is my own personal weapon, not police issue."

"You think I give a damn who issued it?" Without even blinking, Dukes pulled his gun and pointed it at Hicks.

Hicks pulled his too, and the two men stood staring at one another, weapons raised, neither moving, until Colton put his hand on the barrel of Hicks' gun and shook his head. "It's fine, Hicks," he said, reaching into his own holster. "Give him what he wants."

Colton handed Dukes his gun and nodded for Hicks to do the same. For a moment, Hicks didn't move, but then he cursed and handed over his weapon. Turning around, Hicks kicked an empty can so hard it flew into the air. Colton followed him.

As they watched the wagons pull away, Hicks muttered, "What do we do now?"

"I have no idea." Colton looked toward the end of the street. Just around the corner, Cruz had started making his wall. Molly was on one side of it. He was on the other, except now he had no weapons and only one ally. His chance of helping her and the kids escape the CAL had just taken a pretty steep nosedive.

26

COLTON

"There's nothing here that's any use," Hicks said as he punched a nearby wall. "They took everything." He looked up at the incident board that Dukes had been using to plot out what had become known as the vigilante murders in the woods. "Everything except this." Hicks shoved his hands into his pockets, as if that might stop him from punching anything else, and added, "You know what? I reckon Dukes got scared. Between Cruz and whoever's been bumping off escaped prisoners, he knew he couldn't handle it."

Colton ground his teeth. Hicks was right, of course, but they'd spent too much time worrying about Dukes. He was gone now. It was time to focus on their next move.

"We'll wait until it's dark, then head out," Colton said—a statement not a debate. "Cruz might have men watching the streets. Heck, whoever's up in the woods might too. Once it's dark, we can at least *discreetly* look for shelter elsewhere." Colton sat down in the high-backed chair behind the booking desk and rubbed his knee. It was at least three hours until sunset. The rest would do him good, even if the hunger pangs in his gut wouldn't. "Here," he said, "we're sitting ducks once they realize there's only two of us."

"You think they will?" Hicks asked.

"Cruz has men all over town. They'll notice a bunch of wagons loaded with cops," Colton replied. Leaning forward, he put his head in his hands. He was exhausted. It had hit him like a two-ton truck the second Dukes and the others had left; he'd been pushing himself. To fit in, he'd been pushing through the pain in his leg. Yet it had all been for nothing. They'd ditched him anyway.

"I need some shut-eye," he said, barely looking up.

There was a pause, in which Colton assumed Hicks was contemplating telling him not to beat himself up, or that Dukes was an idiot, but he didn't. "I'll keep an eye out front."

When the door closed, Colton allowed his eyes to close too. At least he could rest.

As soon as the sun was down, the two of them left the police station carrying nothing but the two bottles of water they'd found in the bottom drawer of a vending machine. Looping around the outskirts of Midtown, to avoid the CAL barrier, they headed for one of the streets that had been undamaged by the fire.

Occasionally someone ducked out of a doorway, looked at them as if they were terrified of being shot or mugged, then ran off down the street.

"Looks like we're not the only ones using the cover of darkness to avoid Cruz. He's got the whole town scared witless," Hicks said as a teenage boy bolted across the road in front of them and disappeared down an alleyway.

Colton didn't say anything in response. Guilt was tugging at his insides. Guilt and shame because, for a few days, he'd felt like he was worth something again. He'd remembered what it felt like to take charge, to help people, to be someone that folks listened to. Not just the school bus driver with the bad leg.

Now, he was back where he'd started. No good to anyone and, this time, desperate for pain relief to ease the ache in his leg.

"How about this one?" Hicks was looking up at a building with a balcony that wrapped all the way around the second floor. "Good lookout spot?"

Colton nodded. He couldn't bring himself to feel anything other than resignation. "Sure. We'll check it out."

Inside, Hicks made straight for the kitchen and discovered it was completely empty. The cupboards were bare, the fridge contained nothing but mold, even the knives were missing.

"I'll go look at the balcony," Hicks said, gesturing to the stairs.

"Okay." Colton sat down at the large empty table. He wished he had a drink. Whiskey. On the rocks.

A few minutes later, Hicks returned. "It's good," he said. "Great vantage point for the school and the train tracks."

Colton nodded at him. "That's good. Good work."

Hicks was opening a nearby drawer, mumbling something about the fact that right now even a can of boiled carrots would be better than eating fresh air for supper, when they heard a noise in the hallway. The front door was rattling.

"Down," Colton whispered, sliding from his chair to take cover behind the table.

Hicks followed suit and reached instinctively for his holster. Remembering it was empty, he sprang to his feet and began to frantically search the kitchen for anything he could use as a weapon.

"There's nothing there, get *down*," Colton snapped.

"What about these?" Hicks spun around, holding up a meat mallet and a marble rolling pin.

"Not quite up to date on my bludgeoning training," Colton muttered, taking the rolling pin and turning back to watch the door.

As they watched and waited, straining their eyes in the darkness, nothing happened.

Then someone began to pound on the window behind them.

"Crap!" Colton spun around, raising his rolling pin. A face was peering at them through the glass.

"Let us in!" the face shouted before pressing its mouth up against the glass and blowing hard, puffing out its cheeks.

"What is he doing? Is he high?" Hicks looked at Colton.

Colton rolled his eyes and put down his makeshift weapon, almost tempted to laugh. "It's okay. I know him." Swearing and getting to his feet, Colton watched as Hicks opened the door and Tommy and Zack Hargrove tumbled in.

"What are you two doing here?" Colton asked, half smiling at the sight of familiar faces.

"We were going to leave town but…." Zack glanced at Tommy and something passed between them. An argument? One of them wanted to go and one wanted to stay?

"But Zack chickened out," Tommy laughed. "Better the devil you know, and all that."

"We've been watching the police," Zack added, ignoring his brother's chicken comment. "We saw them abandon the station. We were going to check it out when we saw you two."

"So, you followed us here?" Colton raised his eyebrows.

"Yeah," Zack said, swinging a backpack from his shoulder. "And it seems like it's a good thing we did. You look like crap."

Colton was about to reprimand the student for his language, but before he had a chance, Zack opened up his bag and tossed Colton a beer and a bag of chips.

He did the same to Hicks, and Hicks grinned.

"When did you leave the school?" Colton asked after taking a long swig of warm beer.

"After the shooting," Zack muttered. "Cruz is crazy."

"Was Miss O'Neil still there?"

"Still there," Tommy answered. "Don't think she felt right leaving everyone."

"But you boys were planning to skip town?" Hicks asked from across the table.

Tommy shuffled a little uncomfortably. "We were, yeah, but we decided to stick around and gather some supplies. Then we saw what Diego's lot were doing and… I dunno, I guess it felt wrong to leave when you were all still here."

"Which is what I said from the beginning," Zack cut in.

Watching the two of them, Colton took another drink. As Tommy produced a candle and some matches, he nodded to himself. Four men. Cruz had half a town under his control and they only had four men, but four was better than two.

"How do you feel about Cruz?" he asked, looking from Tommy to Zack.

"Like he's a class-A psychopath," Tommy replied quickly.

"Then how do you feel about taking down a psychopath?" Colton watched the brothers carefully. They exchanged a glance, then nodded.

"Good." Colton raised his beer. Hicks did the same. "That's what I hoped you'd say."

27

MOLLY
TWO DAYS LATER

Although Molly had hoped Lucky would be transferred back to veg picking duty, she had woken the day after the accident to discover that both of them had been put back on haulage. Yesterday, he'd struggled through the day, trying to avoid using his injured hand, his energy utterly depleted from his reduced food supplies the day before. Every now and then, she had stepped up and helped him before being yelled at by one of the guards.

By the end of the day, she'd been desperate to take Lucky and leave, but she had two problems; she couldn't leave without Jenna, and she couldn't leave while Lucky was so gravely ill. In this state, he wouldn't make it down the street let alone to a hospital.

Molly had spent the night tossing and turning, despite being exhausted. When morning came, she hurried to the cafeteria and waited for Lucky to appear. It was almost time for the breakfast things to be cleared away and for them to be herded up to go out to the train tracks when she realized Lucky wasn't going to show up. Quickly, she headed to the boys' dorm and knocked on the door. It was empty except for Lucky, who was sitting on the edge of his bed. He was feverish and pale. He was holding his hand, and he looked like he'd been crying.

"Lucky?"

The boy looked up at her and shook his head. "I don't think I can do it, Miss O'Neil. I don't think I can do it today. It'll kill me." He said the world *kill* as if he genuinely believed it might.

Molly sat down next to him and put her hands on his shoulders, angling him toward her. "Yes, you can," she said sternly, despite the fact that as she took in his gaunt, shaky frame, she wasn't sure how he was going to do it either.

Lucky met her eyes and nodded, but when he tried to stand, he almost fell back down. Molly touched the back of her hand to his forehead.

"You're burning up," she muttered. "Okay, come with me."

Heaving Lucky to his feet, Molly helped him stagger down the hallway and toward the medical wing. At the door, the vet who'd seen them before agreed to check Lucky's wound and, almost as soon as she peeled back the bandage, her face turned gray.

Molly flinched at the smell.

"It looks like it's infected," the vet said softly.

"So, he gets antibiotics now, right?" Molly asked, folding her arms in front of her stomach.

"I'm so sorry, I can't." The vet looked toward the door, where a guard with a gun was watching them. "The best I can do is clean the wound, but it's going to hurt."

Lucky shook his head and shrank back. "No, I'm fine. Please don't touch it."

"Will it help?" Molly asked, trying not to look at it.

"It might." The vet smiled thinly.

"Do it." Molly positioned herself behind Lucky and put her hands on his shoulders. "You can do this, Lucky. I'll hold on to you."

As he reached up and took hold of her fingers, Lucky winced. The vet had barely touched him and his eyes were already watering.

Molly breathed in deeply and counted to ten.

"Okay, here we go…." The vet was holding a pair of tweezers. At first, when she started debriding the wound, Lucky bit his lower lip, tensed up, and closed his eyes.

A few seconds in, he'd begun to scream and was shaking from the pain. This was worse than the stitches, much worse.

"For God's sake, give him something!" Molly yelled.

"I can't." The vet shook her head. She looked tearful, too. "I'm sorry. The best you can do is keep him still so I can work."

Wrapping her arms around Lucky's upper body and pinning him to her, Molly forced herself to look away. A tear escaped and rolled down her cheek; this was all her fault. If she'd taken Lucky and Jenna and left weeks ago, this would never have happened.

After what felt like forever, the vet had finally finished. Loosening her grip on Lucky, Molly met the vet's eyes. "Where do they keep the drugs?"

The vet looked back down, focusing on Lucky's hand. "I can't…."

"Please. I'm not asking you to do anything. Just tell me where they are. Surely, you can see this isn't right? He needs help."

The vet glanced up. Lucky was on the verge of passing out from the pain and seemed almost delirious. She looked at the guard, then back at Lucky's hand. "The chemistry storage closet." As she whispered, she turned to the tray beside her and took an alcohol wipe.

"All right." Molly slid away from Lucky and stood up. "Can you keep him here until I return for him?"

The vet nodded. "Yes. I'll keep him here."

"Okay." Molly ducked to meet Lucky's eyes. "You'll be all right, Lucky. I'll be back soon."

On her way out, Molly did her best to hold her head high, but when she reached an empty section of hallway, she leaned against the wall and took a deep, shaky breath. Was she really going to do this? Was she really going to try and steal from Diego?

Patting her hair, her fingers touched against the headscarf she'd been wearing since she got here. She'd washed it, but it was stained with Lucky's blood. The thought made her grit her teeth and stand up straighter. Yes, she was doing it.

Molly knew the high school like the back of her hand. If she had an advantage, that was it. She knew that the chemistry storage closet could be accessed from the physics classroom. Years ago, they'd stopped using that way and boxes had been piled up against the physics door. If she was lucky, no one knew the door was there.

Ducking into a nearby dorm, Molly grabbed a sleeping mat and bundled it up with some blankets; it was commonplace for people to move rooms, especially when entire dorms were frequently becoming full of people with respiratory issues. So she tried to look as if she was doing something she was supposed to be.

Passing a guard in front of the cafeteria, she shot them a steely glare. “I’m on night duty and I can’t get a wink of sleep with all the idiots who are coughing back there. Sort it out, would you?”

“Shut it,” the guard replied. “Find a corner, get your head down, and quit moaning.”

Molly tipped her chin up and stalked past. When she rounded the corner, she threw the mat into an open doorway and began to run. Reaching the entrance to the science block, she paused. A woman with a shotgun was standing in front of the chemistry classroom door. Molly looked around. She was standing next to the girls’ toilets. Her mind reeled back through a selection of memories; she’d taught a substitute lesson in a nearby classroom once and had been interrupted halfway through by what sounded like a poltergeist. As it turned out, one of the girls had figured out that rattling the pipes in the toilet caused a knocking noise that could be heard in the biology room.

Ducking inside, Molly looked around, grabbed a toilet brush, and ran over to the pipes at the far end of the toilets. With all her might, she pulled her arm back and began to whack it. Again and again and again. When she stopped, she threw the brush down and hurried back to the door.

Peering around the corner, she nodded—it had worked. The guard had disappeared.

As quickly as she could, she darted down the hall. She paused outside the chemistry room but didn’t let herself enter; they’d have another guard outside the storage room. They were bound to.

Instead, she entered the classroom next door and paused for a moment. The physics room was empty. The storage closet was at the far end, blocked by a bookcase. Molly made a beeline for it and pushed the unit to one side. As she turned the handle to the closet, she held her breath, but it worked.

The door opened and Molly was met by a stack of cardboard boxes containing Bunsen burners and glass vials. As quietly as she could, she moved two. Just enough for her to climb into the center of the closet, then she began to scan the shelves.

Through the glass window of the door at the other end, she could see the silhouette of a guard and prayed they didn't turn around.

At last, she spotted a bottle of aspirin and a second bottle of a medicine she recognized as being an antibiotic. She paused, her fingers outstretched. She wanted to take all of it. Every single bottle, for Lucky and for those who needed them, but the only way this would work was if no one realized what she'd done until it was too late.

Stuffing the bottles into her bra, Molly turned around and climbed back over the boxes. When she'd repositioned them, she closed the door, dragged the bookcase back into place, and took a deep breath. She allowed a smile to twitch at the corner of her mouth, but then braced herself to head back out.

Pulling the door open just a little, she looked right. The guard hadn't returned. Quickly she sprinted for the hallway, the pills rattling as she ran.

She was looking over her shoulder when she hurtled smack into someone's chest. "I'm late for work duty," she said, stepping back. "I'm just…."

Her mouth dried up and the words she was trying to say disappeared.

In front of her stood Diego Cruz and three of his men. Behind him, Jenna was staring at her with wide eyes.

Diego rubbed his clenched fist and looked her up and down. "Well, well, well. The schoolteacher."

28

MOLLY

"Where are they?" Diego held out his hand. "The drugs you stole from me. Where are they?"

Molly's brain was moving too slowly. She couldn't weigh up her options quick enough. With a clenched jaw, she reached into her shirt and removed the bottle of aspirin. "Here."

Diego frowned at it. "And the rest?"

Molly shook her head. "Diego, please. Lucky *needs* antibiotics. If he takes them, he'll be back to normal. He's a good kid. A good worker."

"I don't care." Diego's bluntness surprised her. "He's not worth a week or more of our supply. We've got to save that for the ones who matter. That kid? He's nothing to me." Diego twitched his fingers at her. "Hand over the rest or I'll have you searched."

“Jenna….” Molly looked from Diego to his daughter, trying to catch Jenna’s eyes. “You and Lucky are friends.” However, Jenna didn’t look up. She was turned toward the wall, her hair obscuring part of her face. When Molly looked at her hands, she could see she was shaking. Taking a step back, Molly shook her head. “Sitting on a pile of meds when people are sick and dying makes you a monster, not a leader. This isn’t right!”

Diego narrowed his eyes. To the men standing either side of him, he spat, “Search her.”

As two of Diego’s men took hold of her arms, and another took great delight in reaching into her shirt for the second bottle, Molly strained against them. She wanted to kick them where it would hurt. She wanted to spit in their faces. She wanted to run, but that wouldn’t help Lucky.

“What do you think we should do?” Diego was speaking to Jenna.

Molly looked from Jenna to her father. Slowly, Jenna lifted her head. Across the side of her face was a large unmistakable bruise. Molly bit back a gasp. Instinctively she lurched forward, but the men holding her arms pulled her back.

Jenna bit her lower lip. Her thick dark hair was greasy, her face pale, and her clothes dirty. She sucked in her cheeks and shoved her hands into her pockets. “She stole from us, and Lucky is no use to anyone. They should leave. Kick them out. Let them fend for themselves and then see how they like the way you run things, Dad.” Jenna glanced at Diego, and he nodded slowly.

Rubbing his chin, he said, “You don’t think that’s a little… lenient?”

Molly was studying Jenna’s face. Was that a flash of panic? Moving from one foot to the other, she shook her head and cleared her throat. “No. They helped me once,” she said. “Miss O’Neil got me out of the prison. People know that. This is a fitting punishment.”

Diego put his hand firmly on Jenna's shoulder. "Good. You're learning." Then to the men holding Molly, he said, "See to it. The kid too."

With a gun to her head, Molly was marched past the medical bay, where the guards retrieved Lucky, and then the two of them were taken right through the belly of the school.

"They're doing this so everyone can see us," Lucky muttered, cradling his hand.

"Don't talk." Molly nodded at him. "Save your energy."

In the gym, people parted to let them through. Molly caught a glimpse of Becky, dismantling the Lost and Found board because Diego had said it was a waste of resources. She didn't move, just weakly held up her hand and lowered it. Molly mouthed to her that everything would be okay, but she didn't know if Becky had understood.

Outside, they were loaded onto a horse-drawn wagon. One guard in the back with them, one driving.

As they drove, the sun dipped lower in the sky. They were heading for the edge of CAL territory. Over the train tracks, past the wall Diego was building, past the police station and toward the woods.

When they reached the police station, Molly sat up, craning her neck to see whether anyone was there. Deep down, though, she knew they weren't—there was no way Diego's men would risk riding straight past the station if the cops were still in town.

Molly closed her eyes and sank back down.

Finally, after what felt like forever, the wagon stopped. They were on a dark road with thick woods on either side of it. Possibly near the prison. Possibly the other side of town—she couldn't tell anymore.

"Get out," said the guard in the back.

Doing as she was told, Molly climbed down, then helped Lucky do the same.

"Walk." The second guard had joined the first. Both were pointing their shotguns at them.

"How do we know they won't just kill us?" Lucky muttered.

Molly wanted to tell him it would be okay. She wanted to say that of course they wouldn't. Instead, she said nothing. As they walked, eventually they heard the wagon start moving. When they turned back around, it was gone.

Molly put her hand on her chest and took a deep shaky breath. Tears had started to run down her cheeks, but she didn't wipe them away. "I failed you," she whispered. "I failed both of you."

Next to her, Lucky sat down on the ground and tucked his knees up under his chin.

Molly sat down too. The road was quiet, empty, abandoned. They had nowhere to go; they couldn't go back to town, and if they headed away from town, she had no idea what they'd find. Her shoulders started to shake. Before she could stop herself, she was sobbing. "I'm sorry, I'm sorry, Lucky." She tried to catch her breath.

After a while, when she'd stopped crying and was pulling herself back together, Lucky looked at her and said, "It's not your fault… Jenna? She wanted to stay with her dad."

"He's hurting her," Molly muttered.

"Yeah, but she loves him. You did all you could."

Molly studied Lucky's face. "When did you get so wise?" she laughed.

"Oh, probably when I went to prison for the day," Lucky said, smiling.

"Well then, oh wise one…." Molly stood up and pulled Lucky to his feet using his good arm. "Where are we headed?"

Lucky looked left and right; then a flash of something Molly recognized crossed his face. "Isn't Jenna's hideout near here?" Lucky pointed to the woods on their left. "That way?"

Molly began to smile. "Yeah, I think it is. All right, let's go."

For a few brief moments, when they began walking, a whisper of optimism vibrated in Molly's chest. Jenna's hideout was far enough away from CAL territory for them not to be discovered. Jenna had shown them all the supplies she kept there, so Molly knew they'd at least have something to eat tonight, and the pills she had hidden were there too. She had no idea what they were, but if worst came to worst, they might at least provide Lucky with some pain relief.

Not long after she had these thoughts, however, doubt started to creep in; she'd already made one terrible decision today. What if she gave Lucky the pills and they turned out to be something terrible? What if they got lost and ended up back in CAL territory? Ran into a raiding party? Got themselves shot? It was only because of Jenna that they'd been allowed to leave. Diego and his men wouldn't be so lenient a second time around.

"Is it this way?" Lucky had stopped. He was leaning against a tree, cradling his bad arm. In the eerie light of the moon, which was only just managing to filter down through the branches above them, Molly could make out some delicate beads of sweat on the boy's forehead. He wasn't well. In fact, she was surprised he was managing to walk at all.

"I'm not sure." Molly looked in the direction Lucky had pointed. "It all looks the same in the dark."

"I'm sure it's this way," Lucky said, accepting her help as he heaved himself into an upright position.

Molly nodded. She had no idea whether Lucky was right or not, but he seemed certain. So she followed him.

As they slowly wove their way through the tangle of trees in front of them, Molly tried to pull her thoughts away from what would happen next and focus on what was happening right now. Right now, they were safe. They'd escaped the CAL and they'd survived. That had to be a good thing. Didn't it?

"Miss O'Neil." Lucky had stopped and was squeezing her arm.

Molly looked at him. "What is it, Lucky?"

"There. Right there." As Lucky reached out a shaky finger and pointed at something in front of them, his legs wavered and he stumbled into Molly's side.

Slotting her arm under his, Molly heaved him up. She was practically holding him upright; if she let go, she was pretty certain he'd fall to the ground.

"We found it," Lucky whispered.

Molly looked up. Her breath caught in her chest; Jenna's hideout was illuminated by the stars above the clearing. The logs, the tarpaulin, the remains of a fire. Pulling Lucky with her, Molly hurried toward it. When she lowered him onto one of the logs, he groaned, sank to the ground, and leaned his back against it.

"Wait there." Molly ran straight to the tarp, ducked underneath it and pulled aside the piece of plywood under which Jenna kept her things.

Taking out the plastic bag, she thrust her hands inside and felt her way through the objects. Matches. Water. Protein bars. First-aid kit.

"Here we go." Molly crouched down in front of Lucky and smiled at him, even though his eyes were barely able to focus on her face. "Drink this. I'll get a fire started, then I'll see what Jenna's got squirreled away in her first-aid kit."

Lucky accepted the water she'd offered but didn't speak.

Turning to the spot in the middle of the circle, which had previously housed a campfire, Molly bit her lower lip and exhaled slowly. Her thoughts were trying to run away from her. They were trying to convince her that Lucky was in dire need of help, that their situation was bleak, that it was going to get worse instead of better because they were all alone and had no one to go to for help. But she couldn't let that happen.

Using her hands to guide her through the darkness of the trees surrounding the clearing, Molly searched for firewood. As she moved, she tried to focus on the feel of the wood beneath her fingers, on whether it would make good kindling, and on straining her ears for any signs of movement.

Once or twice, she felt a familiar twinge of panic in her chest and had to stop to catch her breath. Alone in the dark like this, there was a time—not so long ago—when that twinge would have spiraled into a blind, paralyzing panic. There was a time when she'd have been so terrified by the blackness around her that she'd have been unable to even think straight.

Now, however, as panic fluttered beneath the surface of her skin, she almost laughed at it; darkness was a preposterous thing to be afraid of. Death, hunger, pain, losing the ones you cared about… those were the things you should fear. Not *darkness.*

When she returned to Lucky, his eyes were closed. His breathing was deep and a little shaky. Molly pressed her lips together and tried to remember what she knew about lighting fires. As she arranged the kindling, she said, as lightheartedly as she could, "You know, a few years ago, I took one of those wilderness survival courses." She glanced back at Lucky, but his eyes remained closed and she had no idea if he was asleep or listening to her.

"You heard me telling Colton about my cabin? Well, I inherited it from my grandfather. He loved it. We both did." She took out the matches and struck one until it lit. "I remember going there when I was a kid and thinking that, one day, I'd run away from everything and go live in the woods with my grandpa." Molly smiled at the memory, then laughed ironically. "Obviously, I didn't anticipate an EMP being the reason I'd want to run away."

Leaning in and blowing gently on the fire, Molly watched the flame desperately try to ignite.

"I was actually quite good at this in the course. Got full fire-lighting marks…."

"Well, I'd hope so. You are a teacher." Lucky's voice was thin and gravelly, but Molly breathed a sigh of relief as he spoke. When she looked at him, he'd pushed himself a little further upright and was watching her. "It smells funny." He wrinkled his nose.

"Pine," Molly replied. "Pinecones make *great* kindling. The sap ignites real easy and they keep burning long enough for the other wood to catch fire." She smiled at him. "Plus, they smell *great*. Not funny."

Lucky's lips twitched into a smile, but when he leaned forward to take hold of Jenna's plastic bag, he winced.

Leaving the fire, which was finally starting to take hold, Molly sat down next to him. "I'll do it," she said, opening up the bag. "Okay, we've got food." She handed him a protein bar and was surprised when he didn't rip straight into it. "And the first-aid kit."

"Please God let there be drugs in there," Lucky said, leaning closer as Molly unzipped the kit.

Please God... her thoughts echoed Lucky's. She didn't want to have to fetch the mysterious pills she'd stolen from the prison. She didn't want to risk giving them to him. She couldn't take it if it went wrong.

"There." Lucky pointed at a small bottle tucked into one of the kit's inside pouches. "What's that?"

Molly narrowed her eyes. "Vicodin… where the heck did Jenna get Vicodin from?"

Lucky pointed at the label. "I don't recognize the name. Maybe she bought it from that kid—Frank—the one who sold stuff at school."

Molly looked up and folded her arms, her teacher voice instinctively taking over from her normal voice. "There's a kid who *sells stuff* at school?"

Shrugging, Lucky said, "Frank Thomas? He's—"

Molly waved her hand at him. "You know what? It doesn't matter." For a moment, she closed her eyes. Her gut twitched with nostalgia—for a time when she'd have taken this nugget of insider student knowledge, stormed into school, and demanded a plan of action be drawn up to tackle the selling of prescription drugs on school property. When she opened them again, she shook her head and said, "Vicodin isn't ideal. We still need antibiotics, but it'll help with your pain. Maybe reduce your fever."

Lucky held out his hand. "Right now, I'll take anything." After swigging two back with a mouthful of water, he sighed and looked at the protein bar.

"You should eat it," Molly said. "Even if you don't feel like you can. We need to get your strength up."

"So we can get out of town?" Lucky asked as he opened the bar.

Taking a bite of her own, Molly looked at him and sighed. "Ridgeview Hospital might be overrun, but at least we'd stand a chance of getting you some proper meds." She paused and shook her head. "I just don't know what there is for us here now, Lucky."

For a long moment, neither of them spoke. Then Lucky put down his food and closed his eyes. He still looked feverish, shivering and sweating at the same time. "My parents are gone, aren't they?"

Molly glanced at him. He was leaning his head back against the log, his good arm wrapped across his stomach for warmth. A few weeks ago, her instinct had been to lie. They were past that now. Lucky deserved her honesty. "I think so, yes. I think they'd have showed up by now if they weren't."

As Molly watched the slight teenager beside her, she saw him suck in his cheeks and blink quickly up at the stars. Briefly, he glanced at her. "You can tell me now, Miss O'Neil. If you saw them die. If they were inside the house when it burned down but you didn't want to tell me. I'd understand."

Molly sat up and put her hand lightly on top of Lucky's. "No, Lucky. I didn't see them. I didn't make it upstairs. So there's no way to know for sure if they were there or not." She paused and took a deep breath. "I'm sorry, Lucky. I wish I could give you an answer."

Lucky sniffed loudly and wiped tears from his face with the back of his hand. "I wish you'd lied," he said quietly. When Molly frowned at him, he added, "I wish you'd told me they were dead. At least then, I wouldn't be wondering whether they left me on purpose. Whether they saved themselves and forgot about me." As Lucky spoke, his voice cracked and his tears came thicker and faster.

Watching him, Molly felt as if her heart might break clean in two. Before she could speak, however, Lucky took a deep shaky breath. “I’m going to choose to believe they’re dead, Miss O’Neil.” He met her eyes and nodded. “I’m going to choose to believe that I don’t have a family because they died. They loved me, and they died waiting for me to come home.”

Molly paused. In her old life, she’d never have reached out and hugged a student. She’d have said what she was supposed to say, offered as much comfort as she could, then urged them to talk to the school’s guidance counselor or their parents. But this wasn’t her old life.

Putting down her water bottle, Molly wrapped an arm around Lucky’s shoulders and hugged him. As they both stared at the flames dancing in the fire, she took a deep breath and said firmly, “You still have a family, Lucky. You have me. We might not be related, but after everything we’ve been through, I’m afraid you’re not getting rid of me.” She smiled as Lucky looked at her. “We’re sticking together. You got that?”

A smile ghosted over Lucky’s lips. “Yeah, I got that.” But as he closed his eyes and drifted away into a fitful sleep, Molly’s mind wouldn’t let her rest.

She might have been able to help Lucky, but she’d been in charge of five kids on the day the EMP hit and at least one more of them still needed her help.

29

COLTON

For two days, Colton, Hicks, Zack and Tommy had spent almost every waking minute observing the CAL and their activities in the town. While Hicks and Tommy seemed keen to move quickly, Colton had persuaded them that haste would not help them. They were outnumbered, which meant they had to be smart and they had to know what the CAL were doing, when they were doing it, and how.

From the upstairs of the house they'd chosen to hide out in, they had a good view of both the school and the train tracks. Taking it in turns to watch, while the others headed out scavenging for any useful supplies Diego's men might have missed, it soon became obvious that the CAL were both ruthless and methodical. Every day, a different team of workers would arrive at the train to pick it over, taking almost anything that could be useful for the wall Diego was constructing.

Entry and exit from the school was strictly controlled, and more than once Colton saw the guards taking great pleasure in bullying people of a lesser rank than them.

"I could try and make contact with one of the kids from the school?" It was early evening. Hicks was cradling a bottle of beer. Their last one. Looking up at the ceiling, toward the balcony where Zack was taking his shift on observation, he added, "Take Zack with me. Get him to point out a kid who'd be least likely to tell tales, try and get some insider knowledge?"

Next to Colton, Tommy shook his head. "I love my brother, but he wasn't exactly one of the popular kids. I don't think his presence would help."

"We can't trust anyone from inside the CAL," Colton said gruffly, rubbing the flat of his palm over his ever-lengthening hair; a few weeks ago, it had been short and smart. He'd need to remedy that soon or it would become a distraction.

"Surely there's someone?"

"There is." Colton cleared his throat and cast a glance at Tommy. "Molly O'Neil. She's the only one we can trust, but we haven't seen her for days."

"You think they figured out it was her who told us to raid the school?"

Colton had been trying not to think about that; when his mind started to wander, when he started to think about what Molly might be going through if Diego had figured out she was the one who betrayed him, a cold sweat broke out at the base of his neck.

He was about to tell Hicks that Molly was the kind of woman who could take care of herself when the sound of hurried footsteps on the stairs interrupted his train of thought.

"Colton?" Zack lingered on the bottom step, bracing himself on the wall as he hung his upper body into the room. "You need to see this. Quick."

Pushing his chair loudly back from the table, Colton headed after Zack. With a couple of days' rest under his belt, his knee was doing better, but he'd reached the end of Hicks' painkillers and had just two pills left. In his hurry, he forgot to use his good leg first and as his bad leg jarred on the first step, he winced.

Behind him, Hicks asked if he was okay.

"Fine." Colton put his hand on the banister and used it to help him ascend.

Out on the balcony, Zack was crouched down, the setting sun at his back just as Colton had taught him, pointing through the railings toward the school.

Without speaking, Colton and the others crouched down next to him. Zack handed Colton a pair of binoculars they'd found back at the police station. Their only pair. "Is that—?" Colton swallowed hard as his voice faded.

"Miss O'Neil." Zack nodded.

"And Lucky?" Colton wrapped his fingers around one of the metal rails in front of him and looked harder, as if he might suddenly discover he was mistaken.

"What's going on?" Next to him, Tommy was peering toward the school. "They're taking them somewhere?"

"Two armed CAL guards," Colton said, trying to take in every last detail. "Looks like the kid's injured."

"They're being kicked out?" Hicks asked.

“Or taken away to be....” Zack allowed his question to disappear, unspoken but understood.

“They wouldn’t go to the effort of driving them elsewhere,” Colton replied, even though he wasn’t sure he believed it. From their vantage point, even with the binoculars, he couldn’t make out the expression on Molly’s face and wasn’t sure if he was glad of it or not. Pressing the binoculars harder against his face, Colton watched until the wagon disappeared out of sight, then motioned for the others to follow him back inside.

“Zack, you’re the fastest.”

Zack nodded and glanced at his brother.

“Follow them. Stay out of sight. Figure out which direction they’re headed in, and we’ll rendezvous on the corner of Main Street near the old coffee shop.” When the others looked at him for an explanation, Colton added, “If we’re going to take on Diego, we need all the help we can get.”

“I don’t know.” Tommy had folded his arms in front of his chest and was looking at his younger brother.

“While we stand here debating it, Miss O’Neil could be in real trouble.” Zack had already started toward the stairs. “She never gave up on me. So I’m not giving up on her. I’ll meet you on Main Street.” And with that, he disappeared.

It took Colton, Hicks, and Tommy less than ten minutes to gather the weapons they’d constructed for themselves. No guns, but some knives, some socks filled with rocks, and a slightly cracked baseball bat.

When they reached Main Street, they ducked into the cover of a nearby building and waited. Tommy was beginning to get nervous when they finally spotted Zack, moving in the shadows toward them.

"Did you catch up with them?" Colton asked.

Zack nodded. "They headed for the woods on the outskirts of town. I couldn't go any farther or they would have seen me. I waited. They came back without Miss O'Neil and Lucky, but they weren't gone long so they can't have taken them too far."

Colton reached into his pocket and took out the hand-drawn map of the town that they'd spent the last few evenings constructing. "So they must have dropped them here." He pressed his index finger onto the road that led out of Fairfield and toward Rockridge.

"Isn't this where Jenna's hideout is?" Zack asked, pointing to the woods that stretched out to the west of the road the wagon had taken.

"That's where they're heading." Colton met Zack's eyes and nodded firmly, folding up the map. "It has to be."

"You're sure they wouldn't just keep on going? Head out of town?" Hicks asked. From his expression, Colton could tell he still thought it was a possibility that Molly and Lucky had been driven out of town to be disposed of rather than simply set free.

"Lucky's injured. He didn't look in a fit state to walk anywhere, and we hid some supplies at Jenna's spot," Zack replied.

Colton nodded, shoving the map into his pocket. "I agree. Let's go."

As they walked, and it grew darker, Tommy and Zack strode off ahead while Hicks and Colton made sure they weren't being followed. "You really think we can take on the CAL? Even if we do have two extra bodies?" Hicks asked quietly.

Since they'd met, Hicks had been consistently optimistic, but in the last few days—since he'd been abandoned by his former colleagues—the young man's outlook had noticeably soured. He didn't want to run, he wanted to fight for the town, but he didn't believe they'd succeed, and that was a problem.

"Hicks," Colton said as he put his hand firmly on his friend's shoulder, "as a Marine, I've had fewer men than this on my side and fought bigger battles." His mouth twitched into a smile. "Heck, as a bus driver I escaped a prison in the middle of an EMP with only a teacher and some school kids." He gestured in the direction they were walking. "That teacher." He stopped and met Hicks' eyes. "We can do this. Me and you. Molly. The kids. But we have to work together, and we can't let doubt infect us. Right?"

Hicks bit his lower lip then nodded slowly. "Right." He straightened his shoulders. "Right," he repeated, louder, more confidently.

Colton patted his shoulder. "Good man." Then he gestured ahead to where Zack and Tommy had stopped. "Looks like it's time to head into the woods."

Darkness had settled around them and the woods were illuminated only by the moon and the stars. In any other circumstances, they might have stopped to appreciate their surroundings. Now, however, they kept going through the undergrowth until they saw a flicker of light up ahead.

"I smell pine needles," Tommy said.

"We are surrounded by pine trees," Zack replied sarcastically.

"It's a fire." Colton pointed toward the light. "We move slowly. You three stay in the trees until we know it's Miss O'Neil and Lucky."

As Colton took the lead, Hicks, Zack, and Tommy followed. Two figures were sitting with their backs toward them, facing the fire. Colton inched forward. As he moved, his foot caught a twig that snapped loudly and instantly one of the figures was on their feet, holding a large tree branch, braced to use it.

"Molly, it's me." Colton stepped into the flickering firelight with his palms outstretched. "It's me."

For a moment, Molly didn't move. She looked him up and down, still gripping her weapon, then finally her entire body seemed to crumple. Tossing the weapon to the ground, she rushed forward and threw her arms around him, gently patting his arms. Colton paused for a moment, then allowed himself to hug her back. Squeezing her tight to stop her from shaking, he said, "It's good to see you, Molly."

"It's good to see you too." Molly stayed in his arms for a few more seconds, then pulled back and looked up at him. "How did you find us? Are you all right? Are you alone?" She looked past him, and Colton gestured for the others to come out.

"It's okay, it's them," he called.

As Tommy, Zack, and Hicks walked out of the shadows, the relief on Molly's face was visible. Reaching up to rub at her temples, she smiled. "Tommy? Zack? I thought you boys were skipping town."

Zack shrugged at her nonchalantly, clearly not ready to admit how much he'd been determined to help her.

"Well, thank God you didn't." She looked back at Lucky, then returned her gaze to Colton, her relief fading a little. "Lucky's injured. Diego's restricting medical care, so I tried to steal some antibiotics for him."

"*Restricting* medical care?" Colton followed Molly over to the logs on the opposite side of the fire.

Next to Lucky, Hicks, Tommy and Zack had sat down and were warming their hands over the fire while watching her closely.

"They caught me," Molly said, shaking her head. "Jenna stepped in and convinced Diego to banish us rather than shoot us but—" She stopped and swept a hand across her forehead. Although the firelight was making her skin look soft, it couldn't hide the lines beneath her eyes or the droop of her shoulders. A few weeks ago, Colton would have stopped himself from putting his arm around her. Tonight, he gave in to his instincts.

Molly put her hand on his, as if the gesture was completely natural, and he felt her exhale. "What about you?" she asked, looking from Colton to the others. "What's been going on?"

After introducing Hicks, Colton gave Molly a condensed version of what had happened after their failed attempt at taking back control of the school. When he told her the police had left, and that Dukes had banned him and Hicks from going with them, she put her head in her hands and sighed loudly. As Colton watched her his stomach twisted uncomfortably; this wasn't the Molly he'd expected to find. This Molly was beaten down. Deflated. But the fiery woman he knew was still in there; she had to be.

"Well, I'm not going to stop you from coming with us," Molly said, glancing over at Lucky. "Tomorrow, we're heading for the hospital. I'm going to get Lucky some antibiotics and then we're heading out to my cabin." Waving her hands at the woods, as if the trees themselves were to blame for the situation, she added, "I'm done with this, Colton. You should be too."

Colton frowned and angled himself toward her, untucking his arm from her shoulders. Nearby, Tommy, Zack and Hicks were muttering between themselves. Lucky was still sleeping. "You're done? How can you be done? What about all the people who are still at the school?" He reached for Molly's hands and squeezed them between his. "We can't leave them at the mercy of Diego Cruz, Molly. We can't. Look at what's happened to Lucky."

For a moment, Molly held Colton's gaze, but then she took her hands back and shook her head. "Exactly. Look at what's happened to Lucky. He could die, Colton. He needs medical care and he's not going to get it here." As if she couldn't bear sitting down, Molly stood up and braced her hands on her lower back. "Last time you tried to get into the school, people died. A lot of people. It's not worth the risk. Maybe I'm being selfish, but Lucky's life is my priority now and he needs help."

"And Jenna? What about her?" Zack's voice filtered over from the far side of the fire and Molly looked toward him. Standing up, he walked over to her and brushed his floppy hair from his face. "Erik and Scarlett are okay. The Bankses are good people. They'll take care of the twins no matter what. But…." Zack glanced back at his brother and inhaled deeply. "Jenna's like us. Her dad is no good. I don't know what happened back at the school, but I know that if she sided with Diego it's because he's her *father* and she felt like she had no choice. That doesn't mean we should give up on her. It doesn't mean we should leave her with him."

Molly opened her mouth to reply, but before she could speak, Lucky's shaky voice rose above the crackle of the fire. "Zack's right, Miss O'Neil. Jenna's dad is the reason she has bruises on her arms. She's scared of him, but she's the reason we're still alive instead of lying out the back of the school with bullets in our skulls." Pushing himself up a little straighter, Lucky gestured to the tarpaulin strung between the trees. "She trusted us enough to share this place with us. I don't think we should give up on her. I don't think we should leave her behind."

Lucky's blunt turn of phrase caused Molly to inhale sharply. Pressing her lips together, she looked around the group. Hicks and Tommy were watching, as if they were outsiders because they hadn't been a part of the group from the beginning of this thing.

Turning away, Molly looked up at the stars and blinked slowly. Colton stepped up beside her. "Why can't I, for once, be the one to just run away? Leave. Look responsibility in the face and say *no thanks.*"

Colton shrugged a little. "Because it's not in your nature. You fight for other people. It's what you do."

Molly closed her eyes. When she opened them, she glanced at Colton, then turned back to the group and put her hands on her hips. "Okay," she said firmly. "But let me be clear that I'm going back there for *Jenna*. I want her out of there before anything else goes down. I can't allow her to get hurt."

Colton smiled to himself. There she was; the Molly he remembered. "Agreed."

"Okay, but how do we do that?" Zack asked, looking from Molly to Colton. "How do we get her out?"

Colton saw Molly's lips part into a smile. "I have an idea," she said. "An idea I'm pretty sure will work. But first, we're going to need some help."

30

LAURA

For the third night in a row, Laura was awake and staring at the ceiling.

When she first came back home, for a few days at least, everything had been strangely wonderful. The atmosphere in the house had reminded her of when they had power cuts when the kids were young, before they were old enough to find the lack of internet or tablets irritating and when their eyes had lit up at the idea of board games and candles and family time. It had reminded her of the camping trips they'd taken, cooking questionable meals on the tiny gas stove, washing with cold water, peeing in buckets.

Her confession had led to a new understanding between them and—for the first time in such a long time—they had truly felt like a unit. The way a family was supposed to be. They were lucky. They had each other, and they were going to be *okay*.

But that was before the raids got worse.

She'd been home less than a week when someone from a couple of blocks over had knocked on their door and warned them that the CAL were closing in on them.

"They're going street by street, a different house each night. It won't be long before it's your turn. If I were you, I'd get out," the woman had said, adjusting the backpack on her shoulder and gesturing to the man waiting on the sidewalk. "We're heading out of town, telling as many folks as we can before we leave."

"Where are you going?" Laura had asked.

"Anywhere but here," the woman had replied.

Since then, each morning when Alex had taken Argent for a walk, he'd been told of a different house that had been ransacked by soldiers from the CAL. Men and women with guns who broke in, no matter whether the house was occupied or not, and took what they wanted. Not what they needed. What they *wanted.*

So far, their house had been spared. Alex thought it was to do with the fact they'd seen his shotgun. Laura thought it might have more to do with Argent's teeth. Either way, they knew it wouldn't be long before their house was chosen. They just had no idea what to do about it.

Alex's first plan had been to board up all the remaining windows in the house and turn it into a fortress. The kids had spent an entire afternoon forging almost comical weapons from kitchen equipment while Alex sat polishing the shotgun like an old farmer on a porch.

Wriggling down into the mattress to try and find a comfortable position, because her back always throbbed at night when she couldn't sleep, Laura looked toward the bedroom window. She wanted to see the stars. Without them, the whole house felt too close, too dark, too frightening.

"It doesn't feel like home anymore," Laura whispered.

To her surprise, Alex's voice replied, "I know."

Under normal circumstances, Laura would have flicked on the bedside lamp and suggested making tea if they couldn't sleep. Instead, she settled for a candle and fumbled for the matches to light it with.

As Alex's face became visible, she sighed and pushed her hair from her face. "We have to leave, don't we?" she asked.

"I think we do, yes," he replied.

"Where will we go?"

Echoing the woman from the doorstep, Alex attempted a smile and a sarcastic, "Any place but here?"

Laura smiled back and slipped her hand into her husband's.

"We've got your new chair. Traveling won't be too bad. Maybe we head for the hospital? You said that doctor told you he'd be there if we needed help?"

"He did, yes, but how do we even know if he made it there? He could have moved on already. Or maybe they were so overrun they didn't let him in in the first place." She was trying not to panic, but her chest already felt tight. "Besides, what about all our stuff? How do we transport it?"

Alex shook his head. He didn't have the answers, she didn't expect him to, but he'd be annoyed at himself for not being able to fix it. He always wanted to fix things.

"If we make tea, will it disturb the kids?"

"Maybe, but they've disturbed us enough times over the years." Alex chuckled and climbed out of bed. "You coming?"

Laura nodded, already pulling her shiny new chair closer to the bed so she could ease herself into it.

In the kitchen, Alex lit a couple more candles and turned on the camping stove.

Laura stopped next to Argent's bed and offered him an apologetic look as he put his paw over his face and groaned at her. Looking at Alex, she bit her lower lip and said, "How much gas do we have left? Should we be using it just for tea?"

"Tea is an essential," Alex replied. When he saw that she was serious, he added, "Don't worry. We've got plenty."

As they waited for their little camping kettle to boil, Laura drummed her fingers on her thighs. "Okay, pros and cons," she said. "Let's go…."

"Pros and cons?" Alex folded his arms.

"Reasons to stay versus reasons to go." Laura widened her eyes, indicating that Alex should be the first to speak.

"Right. Well," he said, "reasons to stay—we have a good amount of supplies, comfortable beds, books, games, home comforts."

"Home," Laura repeated. "That's a big one. It's home, and if we leave, I'm pretty sure it means we won't be coming back."

Alex nodded solemnly. "Reasons to go?" he asked.

Laura looked around the room. "We're pretty sure we're going to be robbed any day now, in which case our supplies, comfortable beds, books, and games will probably be stolen."

"Which will negate everything on our previous list." Alex turned to the kettle and took it off the gas. Pouring hot water into two small mugs, he sighed. "We know what we need to do, love. We just need to figure out when and how."

"And persuade the twins to come too."

"Come where?" From behind them, Scarlett's voice filtered into the room.

Laura shifted her chair backward and found Scarlett and Erik, in their pajamas with wild bed hair, staring at them.

"Where are we going?" Erik repeated his sister's question.

"Kids, come sit." Alex gestured to the couch in the living room and the four of them headed over to it.

With the twins next to each other, Alex in the armchair, and Laura in her chair beside him, Alex sighed heavily. "Guys, we're going to have to leave the house."

"What? Why?" Scarlett's reaction was predictable but not as outraged as Laura had expected it to be. Clearly, this wasn't a surprise.

"The CAL are getting more dangerous. The longer we stay the more we risk getting hurt." Laura looked at Argent, who'd padded over to join them.

"We can defend ourselves," Erik said defiantly. "We've got weapons. We'll just show them we're not going to give in."

"I'm not sure it's that simple, love," Laura replied. She was about to add that no amount of *stuff* or supplies was worth risking their lives over when she noticed Argent's ears prick up. Raising her index finger, she shook her head. "*Shhh.*"

The other three froze and stared at her.

From the back of his throat, Argent began to growl.

"Alex?" Laura swallowed hard. "Someone's out there," she whispered.

Argent was standing up, hackles raised, staring toward the front door. Alex put his hand on the dog's shoulder, then moved past him and picked up the shotgun.

"Don't go out there," Laura said, wanting to shout but trying her best not to. "Please, Alex. Don't. Let's go to the bathroom. Like we said. If something happens, we go to the bathroom, lock ourselves in and wait until it's over."

But Alex pointed at Argent. He had stopped growling and was staring at the front door. He tilted his head from one side to the other. Then there was a knock. A loud knock.

"Laura? Alex? It's Molly. Can you let me in?"

Alex looked at Laura, blinked at her, then put the shotgun down and ran to the door. When he pulled it open, Molly practically tumbled inside and Laura clapped her hand to her mouth when she saw who she was dragging along with her.

"Lucky? What happened to him?" Scarlett had rushed over and was helping Molly carry Lucky to the couch while Alex secured the door.

Panting, Molly swept her hand across her forehead. She looked thin, pale, dirty and tired. Very tired.

"Get her some water," Laura directed Erik. "Molly, sit down. What happened?"

Molly shook her head. She was so out of breath she couldn't speak. Finally, after taking a few long swigs of water, she managed to say, "Lucky got hurt shifting scrap metal from the train. Diego wouldn't give him antibiotics. I tried to steal them. They threw us out."

Scarlett and Erik exchanged an alarmed look while Laura gestured for Molly to drink some more water.

"Whoa," Alex breathed. "And you came straight here?"

Molly shook her head. "No, I went to the woods. To Jenna's hideout. Colton, Zack, and Tommy caught up with us there. They're going to attack the high school, try to run the CAL out of there, but first I need to get Jenna out. She's still there. Her father won't let her leave." She exhaled slowly, her breath beginning to return to normal.

"They're going to attack the high school?" Erik asked. "Who? The cops?"

Molly shook her head. "The cops are all gone. It's just Colton and one other guy called Hicks." She took another sip of water.

"Two of them are going to take on Diego? That's madness," Scarlett said.

"I know." Molly met Scarlett's eyes, but then turned back to Laura and Alex. "Listen, I'm so sorry to do this to you, but I don't have much time. I brought Lucky here because I need you to take him to the hospital. He *has* to have proper treatment or he's going to die."

On the couch, Lucky was barely conscious enough to react to what Molly was saying. He was sweating and his skin looked almost gray. A bloodied bandage on his hand indicated an injury that was beginning to smell.

Laura looked at Alex but didn't need to say anything.

"Of course," he said. "Of course we'll take him. We were thinking it was about time for us to leave town anyway."

"Does he need painkillers?" Erik asked, his face growing paler as he looked at his classmate. "We have some in the first-aid kit."

"Painkillers would be great," Molly replied. "Scarlett, could you help your brother so I can talk to your parents?"

Hesitantly, Scarlett stood up, but did as she was told and followed Erik from the room. When they were out of earshot, Molly leaned forward onto her knees and said, "Are you sure about this? You're sure you want to take your family away from here?"

"We're sure," Laura replied, reaching for Alex's hand. "We owe you a great deal, Molly, but apart from that we can't stay here much longer. We know that."

"Okay." Molly stood up and Laura noticed her wobble a little.

"Molly, you should take a minute. Sit down. Rest."

"I can't." Molly put her hands on her hips and inhaled deeply. "I have to get Jenna out of the school before Colton and Hicks make their attempt. I just needed to make sure Lucky was going to be okay."

"And when you've got Jenna? What then?" Laura was following Molly back toward the door.

"Then I'll come find you."

"Good luck." Laura stopped in the hallway.

Molly nodded at her and opened the door. "Thank you. Be safe, all of you. I promise I'll see you soon."

31

JENNA

Despite being only mid-morning, it was blisteringly hot. Summer in Fairfield was rarely this warm, and Jenna couldn't help feeling like the weather was mocking them. No aircon? See how you like *this*.

Up ahead, her father was walking with large, exaggerated strides—a habit he'd always had and which she'd always felt was to make up for the fact he was shorter than most men. Pacing up and down, he'd occasionally shout at the workers on the wall to keep going, work faster, or to remember that if he wasn't satisfied with their performance, they wouldn't be eating supper later.

Jenna's job, it seemed, was to sit and watch. To marvel at his authority and to learn how to maintain control over other people. Every now and then, her father would glance over at her, and she'd raise her eyebrows to indicate she was impressed. He seemed to like that.

Despite it being hot, Jenna was still wearing a long-sleeved top. She'd absentmindedly rolled her sleeves up and now pulled them back down. The bruise on her forearm was turning a yellowish shade of green and she hated to look at it. With it out of sight, at least she wasn't forced to remember how she'd received it.

Shuffling uncomfortably on the cinderblock she was sitting on, Jenna winced as a middle-aged woman—who she knew as Becky—stumbled and fell with a crash into a pile of materials near to the wall.

Instantly, Jenna's entire body stiffened. She looked at her father, hoping he hadn't spotted it, but of course he had. Barely missing a beat, he strode over and pulled Becky to her feet. Inches from her face, he spat, "One more incident like that, Miss Simmons, and you will be on laundry duty the rest of the week. And you know what that means!"

"Y-y-yes, sir," Becky stuttered and pushed wisps of hair from her face. Her clothes were dirty and she looked exhausted.

"It means *basic* rations and sleeping outside."

As Becky nodded and hurried back to her post, Jenna hopped down from her spot and walked over. Hesitantly, she touched her father's elbow. "Dad?"

"What?" He whipped around and tugged his arm away.

"It's just an idea but… perhaps we should look at using only the strongest workers for the wall? I know you want everyone to do their bit but…." Jenna tried to adjust her tone, to make it more scathing, more cynical, more like her dad's. "Using people like *her?* Like Miss Simmons? It's slowing things down."

As her father examined her face, Jenna held her breath. Finally, a smile spread across his lips. "You're right. Starting tomorrow, we'll siphon off the weakest recruits and consign them to permanent laundry duty."

Jenna opened her mouth to tell him that wasn't what she'd meant, but he put his hand firmly on her shoulder and squeezed. The gesture made her flinch.

"Seems like you're finally getting a brain in that head of yours. Must be all the time you've been spending with your father."

Trying to smile, Jenna waited for him to remove his hand and turn away before breathing out. It had always been this way with him; a compliment wrapped in an insult. She didn't remember a time when he'd *ever* praised her properly. The way other parents did. For most of her life, she'd told herself that it was how he showed her he loved her; that he was tough on her because he wanted her to be tough, to be able to look after herself. But that excuse was wearing thin.

Closing her eyes, she pictured her hideout. The others had teased her for keeping a copy of *Swiss Family Robinson*. What they didn't know was *why* she loved that book; she loved it because it was about a family who pulled together. A family who wound up in an almost impossible situation and who made the best of it. When the EMP hit, she'd imagined that finally this might be what happened to her and her father; she'd imagined them bonding over the difficulties they were about to face. She'd imagined taking him to her hideout, showing him it was the perfect spot to shelter from the rest of the town. She'd imagined him telling her she'd done a great job finding it, and saying it was just the two of them now. Them against the world. But, of course, that hadn't happened.

The closest she'd come to feeling like part of a family was when she was in the prison with Miss O'Neil and the others. Back there, she'd felt respected, cared about, looked after. Here… Jenna looked up at her father and tucked her short hair behind her ears. Here, she was just another body. Just another person to be ordered around and yelled at.

She was trying to stop her mind wandering toward Lucky and Miss O'Neil, and how far away from the town they'd be by now, when one of the patrolmen nearby shouted for her father's attention.

"Sir! There's someone on the perimeter!"

Jenna's breath caught in her chest. It had been days since anyone who wasn't a part of the CAL had dared to approach. Immediately, her heart began to beat a little faster.

"Jenna!" Her father gestured for her to follow and broke into a run. Jenna jogged after him and they stopped just inside the perimeter of sandbags and junk that had been set up to indicate the beginning of CAL territory.

"Who was it?" Her father grabbed the patrolman's arm and scowled at him. "You let them go?"

"I'm sorry sir, I didn't see."

"Jenna, get over there and check it out."

As her father pointed to the other side of the barrier, Jenna swallowed hard; he had no idea who was out there and he was willing to send her over to look? Rubbing at her arm, she nodded. "Yes, sir."

At first, when she climbed over, she saw nothing. Just an empty street with empty houses. As she moved, her foot caught against something. She stooped to pick it up.

"What's that?" Her father was peering over the barrier. "Give it here." He held out his hand and Jenna climbed back over. "A book?" he scoffed and turned it over in his hands.

"*Swiss Family Robinson*," Jenna muttered, unsure whether she wanted to smile or cry.

"Sir, there seems to be a note?" The patrolman was pointing at the book. Jenna's stomach clenched. Every muscle in her body was twitching with the desire to grab the book back and run away with it.

Slowly, her father took out a piece of paper. At first he frowned, but then he scoffed. "Looks like it's from your little friends," he said. "Utter gibberish, of course."

"What does it say?" Jenna asked quietly.

For a moment, she thought her father might tear the piece of paper into shreds and throw them into the air. But then he thrust it at her and said, "Like Jenny Montrose in the treehouse, you're finally where you belong."

Jenna's eyes scanned the words.

"Looks like they've realized you belong with your family." Her father rolled his eyes, dropped the book to the ground and turned away. Already, he'd moved on and was gearing up to tell the patrolman that if he let someone that close to the perimeter again, he'd be the next person sent out to the woods.

Jenna stooped down, picked up the book and slipped it into the back of her jeans. Re-reading the note, she chewed her lower lip. "Jenny wasn't ever in the treehouse," she muttered. "She was only ever in the cave at the end of the book."

As her father stalked away, Jenna returned to her lookout point and tucked the paper into her pocket. Miss O'Neil didn't make mistakes. She was trying to tell Jenna something; she was telling her that her *real* family were waiting. All she needed to do was go find them.

32

MOLLY

"It's been almost an entire day," Tommy said. "We can't wait indefinitely."

"What if she's not coming?" Zack asked, glancing at his brother.

"She's coming," Molly said, crossing her arms in front of her chest. "I saw her pick up the book. I watched from the shadows. She found it, and she's coming."

"Maybe she doesn't want to come." Tommy had been on edge all day. He was stoking the fire and boiling some water to make coffee, but was barely able to concentrate on the task. When he'd revealed he'd found a can of out-of-date instant stuff at the back of someone's cupboard, Molly had almost died with gratitude. Now, despite her nerves for Jenna, her mouth was watering in anticipation of it.

"She'll be waiting for darkness to fall," Molly said firmly.

"And if she doesn't turn up?" Zack asked, handing his brother two of the takeout cups they'd scavenged from a nearby Starbucks so he could pour hot water into them.

"Then Colton will get her out when he and Hicks go for the CAL." Molly accepted a takeout cup and didn't even wait for the liquid to cool before taking a long, slow sip. Usually she laced her coffee with two large spoonfuls of sugar. Today she didn't care. It was the first caffeine to hit her veins in nearly three weeks, and it felt *heavenly.*

All afternoon, she'd been trying to sound as if she believed what she was saying, but deep down, she knew that if Jenna was still inside when Colton and Hicks started their raid on the CAL, things could go very wrong. Colton had made it clear to her that he couldn't guarantee Jenna's safety and, reluctantly, Molly had agreed this was Jenna's choice. They'd given her a sign that they were waiting for her. If she chose not to come, then the consequences had to be on her.

Despite telling herself that over and over, however, Molly still felt sick to her stomach when she thought of what Colton had planned for when darkness fell. Concentrating on the coffee, she looked up at the patch of sky that was visible above the clearing.

"As soon as it's dark, we're going to help them," Tommy said firmly.

When Molly had returned from taking Lucky to the Banks home, she'd found Colton and the other three poring over a map of the town, formulating a plan. Colton had insisted that Tommy and Zack stay behind with Molly to wait while he and Hicks headed to the school, and Molly could tell Tommy was finding it a difficult task to swallow. Inaction didn't suit him. It didn't suit her either.

Slowly, still sipping her coffee, and praying the Bankses were already making their escape from town, she nodded. "We wait until darkness falls," she said. "If she's not here an hour after sunset, then you can go."

As the sky darkened, Tommy and Zack readied themselves to head to the school. Molly was pacing up and down. CAL workers were sent to bed an hour before sunset. If Jenna was coming, she should be here soon.

Although she'd told Tommy and Zack to wait an hour after sunset, in reality none of them had any way of judging the time. Eventually, Tommy stood up and said, "Okay. I'm sorry, Molly, but it's time we left."

Molly put her hands into her pockets and tried to loosen her shoulders. Nodding, she said, "All right."

"Are you coming?"

Molly held her breath in her chest for longer than normal, then slowly released it. She was trying not to think about what might be happening at the school. She was trying not to picture Jenna betraying them, telling Diego that Molly was still in town and trying to snatch her away. Or, worse, Jenna being caught betraying her father as she tried to escape.

"No," she said. "I'll wait here for Jenna. If she's not here by sunrise, I'll head after the Bankses and we'll all meet at Ridgeview Hospital. That's where they're heading."

Tommy nodded. Next to him, Zack seemed a little more reluctant than his brother to leave. He was extending his hand to shake Molly's when something moved in the bushes. He stopped in a freeze frame. All three of them stared at the trees.

"Jenna?" Molly's heart skipped a beat as Jenna stepped into the clearing. On her shoulder was a backpack bulging with supplies. Staring at them, she smiled weakly.

"I knew you'd understand my message." Molly rushed over and pulled Jenna into a tight embrace. "I knew you'd come."

"I did." Jenna pulled back, adjusting her backpack on her shoulder and looking at Tommy and Zack. "But where are the others?" Her eyes widened slightly. "Is Lucky—?"

"He's okay. He's with the Bankses. They're taking him to Ridgeview Hospital to get treatment for his injury."

Visibly relaxing, Jenna dropped her bag to the ground and smiled. Tucking her hair behind her ears, she glanced at Zack. "You okay?" she asked casually.

"Yeah. I'm okay." He scuffed his foot against the ground. "Glad you got out. Was it okay?"

As Jenna started to tell Zack how she'd managed her escape, Molly approached Tommy. "I think we should send Zack and Jenna on ahead. If they go now, they could catch up with Laura and Alex. At least that way, we know the kids are safe."

Tommy looked over at his younger brother. After finally being reunited, he was clearly reluctant to leave him, but eventually he nodded. "Agreed." He was about to put a hand on Zack's shoulder and tell him their decision when another crack in the bushes made him stop.

Looking at Molly, he said, "Colton? He's not back yet, surely?"

Molly frowned. Gingerly, she moved forward, noticing Tommy reach down for the knife he'd been keeping in his shoe.

She was staring into the darkness of the bushes when, slowly, a face appeared. “Well, well, well. Look who’s here.”

Molly stepped back, her fists clenched at her sides.

“Dad?” As her father stepped into the clearing, Jenna’s voice was barely a whisper. Behind Molly, Tommy raised his knife.

“I wouldn’t if I were you.” Diego shook his head. When he raised his hand, he was holding a handgun.

33

COLTON

"You're sure we can do this with only two of us?" Hicks asked, peering out from their hiding place in the trees opposite the school.

"Two is better than twenty," Colton whispered back. "We can take them by surprise."

Hicks cast him a skeptical glance but nodded all the same.

"When the guards change, we slip around the back. From what we've observed the past few days, there's only ever one guard on duty on the side door. A big guy. Big muscles, but it's all for show. He spends most of his time with his girlfriend when no one's looking." Colton narrowed his eyes at the front of the gym, watching for the smallest sign of movement. "That'll be our in."

"And then we separate?" Hicks said, repeating what they'd already discussed as if he needed to commit it to memory.

"You create a distraction in the main hall. Molly's certain all the guards will flock to see what's happening."

"And you'll go wake everyone in the dorms?" Hicks said.

Colton nodded. "The armory is on the way to the dorms. If I can, I'll take out the guard, get in and get some weapons. Then I'll wake everyone and get them out. As many as I can as quickly as I can." Colton raised the knife he was holding. "The less noise I make, the longer they'll stay focused on you."

"What if…." Hicks swallowed hard. He was young. He'd been a cop for all of five minutes and now he was being thrust straight into the line of fire. "Last time, they knew we were coming."

"This time, they don't," Colton replied. "Last time, they were ready for us. This time, we will take them by surprise. They know Dukes and the other cops left. You need to *make* them think we've stormed the place looking for Molly. Talk to them. Use your words. They won't shoot you if all you're doing is talking."

Hicks nodded, but he was still worried. He was marching into the CAL camp without a gun; of course he was worried.

Colton met his eyes, praying he didn't live to regret persuading Hicks to do this. "We've got to try. We're the only ones left who care about the people stuck in that building."

"And if Jenna betrayed you? If she told her father about the note?"

Colton studied Hicks' face and thought of Jenna. Maybe he was naïve. Maybe he was foolish, but in his gut he *knew* she'd do the right thing. If an old fool like him had figured out that a bunch of misfit students, a teacher, and an ex-con were the best family he'd ever had, then

Jenna would have figured that out too. “She won’t betray us,” Colton said, narrowing his eyes. “She—”

Colton was cut short by the expression on Hicks’ face. His eyes had widened and he was pointing at the school. “Is that her?”

Colton spun around and lifted his binoculars. “That’s her!” He had to fight the urge to shout. Repeating himself in a whisper, he said, “That’s her. That’s Jenna.” He watched as Jenna stood with her hands on her hips, talking to the two guards at the front exit. Eventually, they parted and let her go. As she walked, she checked behind her to make sure she wasn’t being followed, and then ducked into the shadows of the parking lot and disappeared.

Colton breathed out slowly but, almost as soon as it arrived, the wave of relief that had washed over him was erased. Another figure had exited the gymnasium. A figure that caused the two guards at the front to step aside.

“Crap. It’s Diego.” Hicks had spotted him too and was looking at Colton. Diego talked with the guards for a moment, then pushed one —hard—in the shoulder so that he slammed backward against the wall. “Is Jenna leading him to Molly?” Hicks asked.

“No, he seems mad. Mad at them for letting her go.” Colton was trying to make out what Diego was saying, but his lip-reading had never been much good.

After a little more yelling, Diego stormed back into the building, dragged out a guard to replace the one he’d shoved, then strode off in the same direction Jenna had taken.

Colton swallowed hard. “Shoot. He’s following her.” He moved to charge forward but Hicks grabbed his elbow and pulled him back into the trees.

"I know you want to help her, but Diego's gone… with him out of the way this is probably the best shot we're ever going to have at getting people out of there. At reasoning with people." Hicks let go of Colton and stood back a little as if he was trying to give him space to come to his senses.

Colton pinched the bridge of his nose and let out a low growl. Hicks was right—he knew that—but it didn't stop him from wanting to sprint back to the woods and warn the others.

"Colton?" Hicks looked toward the school. "We've got to do this. Now."

Eventually, Colton straightened his shoulders and nodded. "All right," he said. "Let's go."

As Colton had predicted, they found the side door to the gym open a crack and, inside, the guard who was supposed to be on duty leaning up against the wall mumbling into the neck of a thin leggy woman with big blonde hair. Hiding behind the door, Colton gestured for Hicks to step in first. As soon as the guard saw him, he uttered a loud, "Hey!" but before he could push the blonde away and reach for his gun, Colton had jumped from his hiding place and knocked the guy out cold while Hicks took care of the woman. With his hand over her mouth, Hicks told her they weren't there to hurt her, then took out a strip of cloth from his pocket and tied it in a gag to stop her from speaking.

While Colton used a cable tie to secure the woman to a drainpipe outside, Hicks dragged the muscular guard out and used his handcuffs to do the same. "Take his gun," Colton said. "But only use it if you have to. If they see you're armed, they're more likely to shoot."

Hicks nodded, relieved to finally be armed, then looked down the hallway.

"Good luck, buddy. See you on the other side." Colton patted Hicks' shoulder, then pulled him into a quick hug.

"See you, Colton." Hicks stood back, took a deep breath, then ran for the door that led into the gym.

While Hicks began to shout, a commotion started inside the gym. Someone was ringing a bell. Others were yelling for backup. Sticking to the shadows, Colton waited. And waited. He waited while guard after guard stormed past and barged into the gym. When their footsteps finally stopped, he snuck out and followed the route Molly had given him.

At the armory, he paused. He could see the silhouette of a guard inside the door. Briskly, he knocked and entered.

Clearly not expecting anyone, the guard spun around and fumbled for her weapon. Colton lifted his hands. "I'm a friend," he said. "I'm unarmed."

Although she looked tough, this woman clearly wasn't a cop or a soldier. She was trembling too much to be trained.

Colton watched her. He was about to try and reason with her when she opened her mouth. She was going to scream. He couldn't let that happen. Lunging forward, Colton slammed his hand over the woman's mouth and took her to the ground. In one seamless movement he'd rendered her unconscious, but he didn't have time to stop and feel bad about it.

Grabbing a weapon of his own and one spare, Colton headed in the direction of the dorms. There were four. Old classrooms that had been turned into rows and rows of cramped sleeping bags. At the first,

Colton looked back and forth to check that, as he suspected, the guards were gone, then strode in.

From their sleeping bags, the people Diego had nearly worked to death watched him with wide frightened eyes. Guilt twisted in his gut. How had things gotten so bad so quickly?

"I'm a friend," Colton said quietly, shoving his emotions away from the surface. "I'm with the police and I'm here to help you take back the school from Diego and his men. We don't have a lot of time. Diego isn't here right now, so this is your best shot at freedom." When no one moved, Colton raised his voice. "If you stay here, you'll get sicker and sicker and you'll die. That's the reality. Cruz doesn't give a damn about you. All he cares about is his wall. He's turned this school into a prison camp, and you can stop it, but only if you act now."

"How?" someone shouted. "The guards are armed. We have nothing. Some of us haven't eaten in days. How can we—"

Around the room, people were starting to murmur. They wanted this, they just needed to believe it could happen.

"Right now, there is no one guarding the armory and my friend is creating a distraction out front. If we work together, we can win this."

Colton started to move to the door. "Those who want to fight, come with me. Those who are too weak, work your way through the other dorms. Spread the message. Fighters come to the armory. The sick and the frail find somewhere to hide until it's over." He was at the door and turned back to look at them. "Or you can stay here and do nothing. It's your choice."

After the smallest pause, two young men jumped up and ran over to him. Another followed. A woman. Three more. *Finally*, Colton thought, *we're doing this*.

34

JENNA

Jenna couldn't understand what was happening; she knew her dad hadn't followed her. She *knew* it! She'd been so careful; she'd waited in the parking lot—she wasn't sure for how long, but she'd waited, watching to make sure he didn't emerge through the gates. She'd even taken the long way around to get to the clearing.

"Did you really think Jenna would betray me?" Her father was grinning, but it wasn't the congenial, joyful grin she saw other kids' fathers use. This was a contorted grin. It curled up at the edges and showed off the gold cap on his front tooth.

Jenna's breath caught in her chest. She hadn't betrayed Miss O'Neil—she'd *never* do something like that. Miss O'Neil was the only one who'd ever truly looked out for her.

"She got your message and she told me about it." Her father reached into his pocket. Behind her, Jenna felt the others move backward as if he might be drawing another weapon. What he brandished, however, was not a weapon. It was her copy of *Swiss Family Robinson.*

"I didn't!" Jenna cried out, looking at her teacher and praying that Miss O'Neil didn't believe she had led him here.

"Don't worry, Jenna," Zack shouted. "We believe you."

As Jenna smiled thinly at her friend, her father started to laugh. The sound sent a violent shiver from the base of her spine down into her ankles and she felt her legs wobble. Her forehead was throbbing with the memory of the last time he'd laughed like that; when he'd smacked her right in the face as punishment for dropping a box full of food supplies, then told her to toughen up when she'd started crying.

Still laughing, truly pleased he'd caught her out, her father weighed his gun up and down in his hand. Jenna swallowed hard and, even though they'd barely said two kind words to each other their entire lives, she moved closer to Zack. He was standing next to Miss O'Neil, quietly simmering with the same kind of rage she'd witnessed back in the prison. Except, this time, it seemed like they were on the same side.

"It's about time, young lady, that you learned to truly respect your elders." Her dad's fist clenched and unclenched. He looked at the bruise on her head.

Jenna moved back. She was shaking from head to foot. She should have stayed put. Staying would have been easier; at least then no one else would have been at risk of being hurt. Miss O'Neil stepped in front of her. "Leave her alone," she said defiantly, putting her hands on her hips.

"How did you know I was here?" Jenna spoke before she could stop herself, partly because she was desperate to know but partly because she needed to make sure the others believed she had nothing to do with this; more than anything, she couldn't bear the thought that they might buy her father's lie.

Still holding his gun, moving it slowly from pointing at one to another of them, her father tilted his head and chuckled. “Your problem, Jenna, is that you constantly underestimate me.”

Jenna tugged on her sleeve and blinked at him.

“It never occurred to you that I’d understand the message from your teacher, did it?”

“I—”

“Tell me.” He moved closer but Miss O’Neil moved too, determined not to allow Jenna to be reached. “Where did that book come from? *Swiss Family Robinson*!” He spoke the title as if it was a curse word.

“It was Mom’s. It…” she trailed off. Her skin had gone cold.

“Wrong!” Her father laughed again and shook his head. “It was *mine*. I know that book inside out.” He waved his hands around the clearing. “And this place? You thought this was your secret spot?”

Jenna closed her eyes. She almost couldn’t stand looking at him.

“Well, it was mine first. Before me, it was my big brother’s. Before him, our cousin.”

When Jenna opened her eyes, her father had lowered the gun a little. “*I* gave you that book. *I* brought you here when you were little. You might remember if you hadn’t spent your entire life being an ungrateful brat.”

Jenna scraped her hands through her hair. She hadn’t known any of that. If she had, she’d have been able to prevent this, but she’d put her friends in danger. They’d stood up for her. They’d risked their own safety for her and now she’d brought her father right to them.

In front of her, Miss O’Neil held up her palms and said calmly, “Mister Cruz, Jenna doesn’t want to go with you. She chose to come with us. We'll keep her safe. Surely, as her father, you want what's best for her?"

For a moment, Jenna's heart trembled with the notion that her dad might agree. That he might shrug and tell her to go if that was what she wanted.

Of course, he didn't.

Practically spitting in Miss O'Neil's face, he raised his gun at her and shouted. "You think I'm going to let you take my daughter?! She's *mine*. Mine! She does what I tell her to do."

As Zack and his brother moved slowly toward Miss O'Neil, preparing to protect her if necessary, Jenna took a deep breath.

"No." She spoke quietly at first and then louder. "No! I'm done. I'm not going with you." And then she hurtled into the darkness.

Running as fast as she could, dodging fallen branches, straining her eyes in the darkness, she headed away from her hideout and back toward town. Behind her, she could hear feet. Her father's feet. But she could also hear Miss O'Neil shouting for her. She needed to get her father away from Miss O'Neil and the others, and she knew exactly where to take him.

On the outskirts of town, Jenna headed east. In the direction of the one place her father hadn't deigned to show her on their many tours of CAL territory—the bunker he'd had fitted out for his own use. The bunker she'd followed him to one night, and which clearly had not been designed to have room for her.

Reaching it ahead of him, she shoved her hand into her pocket and took out the one thing she'd been hoping she wouldn't have to use—the set of keys she'd stolen from her father while he was sleeping. Selecting the largest one, she held her breath and prayed it would work. When it clunked loudly in the lock of the one-story concrete building, she pulled open the door and hurried in. From outside, the floodlights powered by the CAL's emergency generator let in a thin sliver of light that highlighted row after row of supplies. The supplies her father had been siphoning off from the high school. For him and him alone.

Leaving the door open, Jenna dashed behind it and froze, stock-still, her breath coming fast. In her shaking hand, her father's keys shook.

"Jenna!" His shadow appeared in the doorway. "Jenna…" he repeated, quieter this time. "I know you're in here. Actually, I'm impressed you knew about it… and that you had the *guts* to steal my keys." As he moved farther inside, he began to look behind the piles of supplies. "I guess you were planning to steal from me as well as run away? Give my hard-earned goods to your little friends?"

Jenna's entire body was shaking. She was desperate to move but frozen to the spot at the same time. *Okay, Jenna. Do it. Do it now!* Releasing a guttural scream to power herself forward, she sprang from behind the door, but just as she was about to reach it a hand clenched around her wrist.

She turned. Her father had hold of her and was glaring at her, his eyes full of fury. At first, she began to wilt. She shrank back and swallowed hard, ready to apologize and beg him not to hurt her. Then she stopped. She looked at his hand, saw the whiteness of his knuckles as he tightened his grip, and instead of shrinking she made herself bigger. He wasn't much taller than her and he definitely wasn't as stocky. She'd been on the high school wrestling team. She was strong.

"Let go of me." She stared at him and refused to look away. "Let. Me. Go."

"You really think I'm going to—"

Before he could finish speaking, Jenna used every ounce of power inside her, pushed past the exhaustion and the lack of food and the fear, and shoved her body weight into her father's chest. As she lunged at him, she yelled and propelled him away from her.

He stumbled backward, wide-eyed. He released his grip.

Without missing a beat, Jenna turned, ran outside, and slammed the door shut behind her.

As her father started to shout and push against it, she used the last molecule of strength in her body to hold it closed, shoved the key into the lock and turned it.

As it locked, she stood back, panting for breath.

"Jenna Maria Cruz! Let me out! Unlock this door. Now!"

Jenna stared at the door and listened to her father's words, waiting for the familiar feelings of guilt and desperation to settle in her stomach. When they didn't come, she pushed up her sleeves and braced her hands on her hips.

Walking up to the door, she pressed her palm against it and said loudly, "You wanted this place for yourself. You didn't plan to include me. Well, you've got your wish. Bye, Dad."

Then she put the keys down on the doorstep, turned away from him, and walked away.

35

MOLLY

Hurtling through the woods, Molly fell to her knees twice and hauled herself back up. Branches scratched her arms, and she was pretty sure her leg was bleeding, but she didn't care. All she cared about was reaching Jenna.

Tumbling out of the woods, Molly blinked at the floodlights, which had been set up around the boundary of the CAL territory. It hadn't been like this a few days ago; they must have finally got the generator working, and she prayed that the Bankses had made it out unnoticed.

Still blinking, Molly froze. Up ahead, someone had stepped out of the shadow of a building. She narrowed her eyes, poised to run, then let out a short sigh of relief. "Jenna?"

Molly ran forward. Jenna stood still, waiting for her. As Molly pulled her into an embrace and looked around frantically for Diego, Jenna's shoulders started to shake.

"Are you all right? Jenna? Where's your father?"

Through heavy tears, Jenna spluttered, "He's gone. He's locked up. He can't hurt us."

"Oh, Jenna." Molly squeezed the girl as tight as she could and kissed her forehead. "I'm so sorry. I'm so, so sorry."

Pulling back, Jenna swiped her eyes with the back of her hand. "Why are you sorry? You saved me. I'm the one who put you all in danger. I should have stood up to him sooner. I should have…."

"No." Molly shook her head and put her hands firmly on Jenna's shoulders. "Absolutely not. This is not your fault. Your father is responsible for his actions. I'm just sorry I couldn't support you more. I'm sorry you had to handle him by yourself."

Nodding, Jenna started to cry once more, then folded herself back into Molly's arms. For a long time, they stood together, not moving, and then Molly heard Tommy's voice.

"Molly? People are escaping from the school. They're starting to head out of CAL territory and no guards are following them. I think Colton did it."

Molly looked at Jenna and, with her arm around her shoulders, smiled. "Okay, then let's head to the road and wait for him."

At the edge of town, Molly and the others huddled together and watched as people filtered past them, some running, some staggering, all heading away from the high school and from Fairfield as fast as they could. How long should they wait for Colton before heading for the hospital? She hated to even think it, but the more people who got there first, the less chance there was of finding the medication Lucky needed.

It was almost sunrise when, finally, they saw Colton's frame lumbering toward them. Molly's heart fluttered in her chest and she fought the urge to run toward him. Next to him, Hicks was limping too. Under other circumstances, Molly might have laughed at the pair of them, but instead she waited until they'd reached her and then hugged them both.

"You're okay?" she asked looking at Colton while pulling water from Jenna's backpack—which they'd retrieved from the hideout—and passing it to them.

Colton took a long swig and wiped his mouth with the back of his hand. "Fine. We're fine."

"The school? The CAL?" Molly looked from Colton to Hicks and back again.

"It's over," Colton said gruffly. "It's all over."

"A lot of the guards switched sides quickly," Hicks said. "The others have been handcuffed and locked up. I'll put a team together and transfer them to the police station later so I can figure out what to do with them. There are some cops who didn't leave town who I'm hoping will come out of hiding when they realize what's happened, and some good guys from back there who helped get everyone out."

Molly looked at Tommy and Zack, who were both grinning.

Patting Hicks on the back, Colton nodded at him. "You were great back there, kid. Really great."

"Finally, we can instill some order. *True* order," Hicks said. "Fair order."

Colton looked at Molly, who had stepped back and was watching him. She knew his instinct would be to stay, so she smiled and tilted her head. "It's okay," she said. "You can stay, Colton. I'll catch up with the Bankses and Lucky and follow through with the plan—get the kids to my cabin. When things are fixed here, you can catch up."

Brushing his hand over his longer-than-usual hair, Colton blinked at Molly, then turned to Hicks. "Hicks, you and I work well together. I couldn't have survived the past few weeks without you, and I sure wouldn't have done what we did today if I was alone."

Hicks nodded and slapped Colton's upper arm.

"But…" Colton glanced at Molly, then at Jenna, Zack and Tommy. "I've found the people I want to serve with. I'm with them. Until the end."

Hicks breathed in deeply. He was disappointed, perhaps even a little nervous at being left in charge, but he understood. After he and Colton embraced, patting each other on the back, he turned back toward town.

He'd moved only a few steps when Jenna pulled free and ran after him. "Sir?"

Hicks stopped and looked at her.

"My father is locked in a bunker on the edge of the CAL perimeter. The key is on the doorstep. He's armed but inside there are a lot of supplies. All the stuff he stole from the school. I know he's not a good guy but—"

Hicks nodded at her and pursed his lips. "Thank you, Jenna. I'll see to it he's arrested, and I'll try to make sure he's not harmed. If it's okay with you, and since he has supplies, I might let him stew awhile to give me time to weed out anyone who might be contemplating another insurrection."

Molly watched as Jenna's shoulders relaxed and she gave Hicks the briefest of nods; she'd done her bit. Finally, she could leave her father behind.

For a long moment, the six of them watched Hicks walk away. When he was out of sight, Molly slipped her arm through Jenna's and looked down at Colton's leg. "You okay to get going?" she asked.

"Yeah," he said. "I'm okay."

As they began to walk, he was still limping, but Molly supposed that was going to be a permanent feature until he was able to rest it for more than a few hours at a time. "You want me to make you another splint?" she asked, nudging his side.

"I might wait until we get to the hospital," he replied, smiling at her. "Thanks all the same."

Molly opened her mouth to speak, then paused.

"What is it?"

"It's just…" She lowered her voice and looked away from him, her throat constricting a little as she realized she might be about to cry. "I'm glad you're safe, and I'm glad you're sticking with us."

When she looked up, Colton's jaw was twitching as he bit back a smile. "I'm glad too, Miss O'Neil. Can't think of anyone I'd rather survive the apocalypse with."

"Ditto."

At the river on the western side of Fairfield, a few miles from the hospital, they stopped to allow Colton's knee a break, and to finally eat something.

Sitting beside Colton, Molly noticed the Hargrave brothers muttering to one another. "You okay, boys?" she asked, in what she realized was a very teacherly voice. Trying to soften it, she smiled.

Glancing at his brother, Zack stood up and put his hands into his pockets. He was looking down at his shoes. When he looked up, he cleared his throat. "Well, the thing is…."

"Speech!" Jenna shouted, giving him a big grin.

Zack rolled his eyes but couldn't resist his own smile. "The thing is, me and Tommy were planning to go someplace. Some place different. So, we were thinking we'd stick with you as far as the hospital and then…" he trailed off sheepishly, and rubbed the back of his neck with his palm.

Molly frowned and looked at Colton, who shrugged at her as if to say this was the first he'd heard of any plan to head off on their own.

"Tommy has some friends who have this cabin."

"I see." Molly pressed her lips together. She knew it had been too good to be true. Zack and Tommy were leaving. Once again, their numbers were dwindling.

"Miss O'Neil has a cabin," Jenna cut in. "In the woods somewhere, right?"

Molly nodded. "Right. After we make sure Lucky is okay, I was going to suggest that we all…." She looked at Zack. "But if you and Tommy have other plans, that's fine. You should do what's right for you."

Zack looked down at his brother.

"Bull crap." Jenna's voice made Molly jump.

"Jenna?" She widened her eyes at her.

"No. It's not fine. We should stick together. We've been through all this and you're just going to leave?"

"I didn't know you cared," Zack muttered, although he looked like he might start to blush.

"A few weeks ago, I wouldn't have. But now?" Jenna looked to Colton, who nodded in agreement.

"Miss O'Neil looked out for us from the start. If she's willing to take us with her to her cabin, I say we'd be idiots not to go." She looked from Zack to Tommy. "No matter how nice your friends are."

Standing up and putting his hand on Zack's shoulder, Tommy took a small piece of paper from his pocket and handed it to him. "It's your choice, buddy. It's you and me now, so you tell me what you want to do and I'll do it."

Zack moved his index finger over the piece of paper. As he looked up, he began to grin. "Then I say, sure. Why not? It'll be like a school trip."

"Not like the last school trip, I hope," Colton chuckled.

Zack grinned again, then turned toward the river, gave Tommy one final glance and—when his brother nodded at him—tore the paper in half and threw it into the water.

Molly stood up and watched the two waterlogged pieces drift under the bridge, then turned around and, with her hands on her hips, said, "Actually, I don't think it will be like a school trip. We're a family now, which means it is *definitely* time you all stopped calling me 'Miss O'Neil'."

"So, we call you *Molly*?" Jenna wrinkled her nose as she asked the question.

"Yes, Jenna," Molly chuckled. She was about to tell Jenna and Zack to try it out when a loud bark interrupted her.

She looked around. At first she couldn't see anyone, but then she spotted a familiar group. A woman in a wheelchair. A dog, a man, and three tall, skinny teenagers. Her heart almost skipped a beat. Up ahead, the Bankses were waving at her. As Laura and Alex hung back with Lucky who was moving slowly, Erik and Scarlett hurtled toward them and—to Molly's surprise and delight—practically threw themselves at Jenna and Zack.

Molly glanced at Colton and he nodded at her. The kids' faces had lit up. They were chattering at one another, clamoring to be the one to tell their tale first.

"All it takes is a snack and some soda, and they're good as new," Colton said.

"They're amazing." Molly smiled at them. Next to her, Tommy nodded in agreement. "How can they adapt so easily?"

"Kids are resilient," Colton said, taking another swig from his water bottle and gesturing to Alex and Laura.

As Molly followed him toward them, she smiled to herself. The kids were safe. Sure, there would be memories they'd have to overcome. Scars from what they'd seen. But scars meant they had survived. Scars meant their wounds were healing.

Looking at the sun rising over the water, Molly breathed in the morning air and held it in her lungs. It was a long walk to the hospital and then to the cabin, but they had each other. Soon, they'd be safe. Finally, safe.

EPILOGUE

DIEGO

THREE DAYS LATER

Diego had no idea how long he'd been in the bunker. With the door closed, not even a flicker of light was able to make it inside, so there was no way to tell whether it was night or day outside. He'd slept four times, so maybe he'd been there four days? Surely, though, Jenna wouldn't have left him there for four days? She wouldn't have had the guts.

Remembering the look on his daughter's face as she shoved him away from her, Diego tried to ignore the twisting sensation in his gut. She'd never looked at him like that before, and he couldn't put into words what it had been. Disgust? Contempt? Disappointment? Maybe all three.

The schoolteacher was to blame. Of that he was certain. Before Jenna had gotten caught up with Molly O'Neil and her gang of misfits, she'd toed the line. Before O'Neil, she'd never have dared to defy him like that. She did as she was told.

Diego was so angry with the teacher that for the first however many hours or days he had denied himself the pleasure of reading to pass the time, simply because it reminded him of her too much. O'Neil was an English teacher, wasn't she? He could picture her standing at the front of the class, taking pity on kids like Jenna. Kids from the *rough* neighborhoods. Congratulating herself at the end of the day for taking them under her wing, and telling herself she was some kind of savior because she gave them the time of day.

Well, Molly O'Neil knew nothing. *Nothing.* About him or his family. She proved that when she left her cryptic little note for Jenna. No way would it have occurred to her that Diego would have figured it out, because he was stupid. Right? He was nothing. Just a volunteer firefighter without two brain cells to rub together.

But he showed her, didn't he? He caught them out, and he'd catch them out again as soon as he was free.

Pushing himself up from the pile of blankets he'd been sitting on, Diego shook his arms to release the tension in his muscles. He thought about doing some exercise. Jogging on the spot. Jumping jacks. Push-ups. But he was tired. He had food and water, but the lack of light was messing with his head. Making him sleepy. Lethargic.

Looking at the shelves he'd spent so long stocking, he sucked in his cheeks and rubbed the knuckles of his left hand into the palm of his right. Why the hell hadn't he brought something to write with? Something to write *on*? He could have put his thoughts onto paper, untangled them, figured out how he was going to find that schoolteacher and punish her.

First, of course, he'd take his daughter back. That would be the teacher's first punishment. But what then? What could he do to show her how much he truly *hated* her?

Turning away from the shelves, he reached for the kerosene lamp he'd set up on top of some boxes of canned foods and turned it down. He had plenty of fuel and matches, but a sneaking, heavy sensation in his gut reminded him that he had no idea how long he'd be here. If Jenna really was gone, who would come for him?

Would anyone from the CAL notice he was missing? Would anyone *care*?

Shoving thoughts of friendship and rescue from his head, he looked around the bunker and surveyed what was left of his empire; enough food and water to last him a few months at least. But a man needed more than food and water to survive.

He was about to drop and force himself into a set of push-ups, because even pain or discomfort would be a distraction from the thoughts that were starting to drive him mad, when he heard a noise outside. A clanging noise just beyond the door.

At first he was certain he was imagining it, but then a pounding started. Pounding against metal.

Ha! She'd come back. Of course she'd come back. No way would his only daughter abandon him.

Diego stood up and reached for his gun. He wasn't going to use it, but he wasn't going to just smile and welcome her with open arms; she'd have to earn his forgiveness.

Slowly the door slid open and daylight poured in. He blinked quickly, a searing pain shooting across his forehead. Temporarily blinded by the brightness he was unaccustomed to, he held out his hands to try and shield himself from it.

"Jenna Maria Cruz, I'm angry but I appreciate that you are doing the right thing." He continued to blink. The silhouette in the door was larger than he'd expected it to be.

As his vision cleared, he narrowed his eyes at the figure in front of him.

A figure that was definitely not his daughter.

"Who are you?" He raised his gun and flicked the safety off. "Who the hell are you and what do you want?"

A man. A cop, maybe, in uniform of some kind, was holding the key to the bunker and staring at him. Dropping it to the ground, utterly unfazed by Diego's gun, he stuck out his hand. "Diego Cruz? I'm Victor Fox. I've been looking for you."

Diego hesitated but when Fox kept his hand outstretched, he lowered his gun. The guy wasn't armed, or at least he didn't seem to be. "Looking for me?" Diego inched slowly forward. "Why? Who are you?"

"I'm the guy who's about to give you what you want…."

END OF ENDURING ANARCHY

DARK NATION BOOK TWO

Escaping Anarchy, February 9th 2022

Enduring Anarchy, March 9th 2022

Surviving Anarchy, April 13th 2022

PS. Do you enjoy post-apocalyptic books? Then keep reading for exclusive extracts from ***Surviving Anarchy, Fractured World (EMP Aftermath Book One)*** and ***Survive the Fall (EMP: Return of the Wild West Book One).***

THANK YOU

Thank you for purchasing Enduring Anarchy
(Dark Nation Book Two)

Get prepared and sign-up to Grace's mailing list
to be notified of my next release at www.GraceHamiltonBooks.com.

Loved this book? Share it with a friend, www.GraceHamil-
tonBooks.com/books

MAKE AN AUTHOR'S DAY

There's nothing better than reading great reviews from readers like yourself, but there's more to it than simply putting a smile on my face. As an independent author, I don't have the financial might of a big NYC publishing house or the clout to get in Oprah's book club. What I do have, as my not-so-secret weapon is you, my awesome readers!

If you enjoyed this book, I'd be incredibly grateful if you could leave a quick review. Simply TAP HERE or just leave a review when prompted by Amazon at the end of this book. Alternatively, head over to the product page for this book on Amazon and leave a review there —look for the WRITE A CUSTOMER REVIEW link.

No matter the length (short is fine!), your review will help this series get the exposure it needs to grow and make it into the hands of other awesome readers. Plus, reading your kind reviews is often the highlight of my day, so please be sure to let me know what you loved most about this book.

ABOUT GRACE HAMILTON

Grace Hamilton is the prepper pen-name for a bad-ass, survivalist momma-bear of four kids, and wife to a wonderful husband. After being stuck in a mountain cabin for six days following a flash flood, she decided she never wanted to feel so powerless or have to send her kids to bed hungry again. Now she lives the prepper lifestyle and knows that if SHTF or TEOTWAWKI happens, she'll be ready to help protect and provide for her family.

Combine this survivalist mentality with a vivid imagination (as well as a slightly unhealthy day dreaming habit) and you get a prepper fiction author. Grace spends her days thinking about the worst possible survival situations that a person could be thrown into, then throwing her characters into these nightmares while trying to figure out "What SHOULD you do in this situation?"

You will find Grace on:

BLURB

The world is broken. And it can't be fixed…

Before an EMP blast shattered her world, Molly was a high school English teacher. Now, she's responsible for keeping five teens, four adults, and a dog safe in a world where the bad guys are out to get them. It's time to retreat and they head out to her family's cabin deep in the Maine woods where they can be safe. But when they arrive, it's clear that someone has been there.

Fixing the cabin may be more than the group was prepared for. Winter is coming and there's food to gather, wood to chop, they need to find a reliable source of water, and the cabin needs to be winterized. Still, it's their best chance for survival…

But Molly and her charges can't hide forever. Diego Cruz wants his daughter back no matter what, and there's stories that the woods around town are haunted by the bogeyman who is none other than Victor Fox, a former prison guard. Diego wants Jenna back and Victor wants that fugitive Molly is harboring, and they're both willing to do whatever it takes to achieve their goals.

Molly knows that if they're going to survive, they need to choose their battles carefully. The old world is gone, and there's no going back. But if they work together, a new world can rise from the chaos…

EXCERPT

CHAPTER ONE

JOE

When Joe stopped running, all he could hear was his breath faltering in his chest. As he dragged mouthfuls of air down into his lungs, he leaned forward onto his knees. His sweatpants were too tight. Not his. Borrowed from the trunk of an abandoned car which, miraculously, hadn't been looted yet.

They were almost cutting him in half. He stood up, hands on hips. He was too loud and too clumsy for all this. His breathing was loud and his big old clown feet—as his mother had called them when he was a teenager—were loud too; snapping twigs, tripping over the uneven ground, drowning out the sounds of the others so that he'd barely heard Rick when he shouted, "Stop, we've lost him!"

Joe pressed his lips together and exhaled slowly. He'd never been an athlete. He was slim, but not in a muscular way, and too tall to be graceful. He'd tried it all—hockey, football, soccer, basketball—and he'd been unceremoniously booted from every team he'd attempted to join. He was *not* the kind of guy who should be running through the woods in the middle of the night with four other now ex-cons. In fact, he shouldn't even *be* an ex-con. A 'con' of any kind. He wasn't that kind of guy. He'd done everything right, his whole life. Until he hadn't.

Right before the power went out, he'd been days away from his appeal and a chance at freedom.

"You're free now, aren't you? What are you complaining about?" Rick had said to him when he'd drunk one too many cups of prison punch and gotten so morose he'd threatened to start something with one of the bigger inmates just so that he'd be put out of his misery.

"Free?" Joe had laughed so loudly that a spray of saliva had peppered Rick's chunky face. "You think *this* is freedom?"

"Ain't no guards in charge of us no more," Rick had replied, wiping his face with the back of his hand. "We could walk right out the door if we wanted to."

Joe leaned against the tree beside him and shuddered as a gnarly branch fingered the back of his neck. That was how it had started. Joe had gotten up from his chair and said, "Well, come on then. What are we waiting for? Others have done it. Why not us?"

At first, Rick had shaken his head and said, "Nah, man. We're safer in here. Ain't you heard about the bogeyman in the woods? The one *killing* inmates?"

Totally out of character, buoyed by desperation and booze, Joe had laughed in Rick's face and called him a coward. Rick had clenched his fist. From nearby, Franko, Jim and Luiz had hurried over to see what was going on. A few hours later, the decision had been made; they were finally going to leave Fairfield. Bogeyman or no bogeyman, now that Dougie was gone and people were doing whatever the hell they liked, outside was better than in.

That had been two weeks ago. Two weeks that felt like two years.

Joe strained his ears, trying to hear sounds outside of his own body so he could figure out where everyone was. In the belly of the woods, it was too dark to see them. Rick had a lighter but he'd probably left it back at the hideout.

"Rick?" Joe whispered into the still night air. "Franko?"

No one replied.

Joe flattened his palm against his chest and tried to push down the panic that was tightening in his rib cage. What if they'd left him? They had vowed to stay together, but perhaps they'd decided they'd stand a better chance without him. Perhaps, when he was sleeping, they'd decided between them to sacrifice Joe to the bogeyman who was chasing them so they could get away.

If they'd left him, where would he go? How would he survive if he was *alone*?

He wasn't as smart as Franko or Rick. They were the ones who'd thought of changing out of their prison-issue clothes so that no one realized who they were. He wasn't streetwise like Luiz either, who'd swapped a bottle of pills for information and been told that they'd arrived just after a massive showdown at the high school. A bunch of civilians who called themselves the CAL had been running things, but they'd been overthrown and were now regrouping on the other side of town. They were, according to Luiz's source, not people you wanted to get caught up with.

"Rick?" Joe tried again, louder. This time, Rick answered.

"Joe, over here." He was tapping something, maybe his knuckles, against a tree trunk. Joe followed the sound. Finally, up ahead, something flickered. Thank God--he'd brought the lighter.

As the others gathered around, Rick gestured for them to huddle together. The warmth of the other men's bodies made Joe realize that his arms were cold. It was late summer, which meant the nights were growing cooler. The prison had been unbearably hot, but out here, at this time of night, whispers of fall were in the air.

"You sure we lost him?" Luiz's deep voice rumbled. The flame from Rick's lighter illuminated his chin, making his entire face look much more menacing than usual.

Franko and Jim nodded.

"How the hell did he find out who we were?" Joe asked, folding his arms in front of his chest. "We were careful. So careful."

"Probably Luiz's *contact*," Franko spat. "The pill guy? I knew it was a bad idea to trust him."

"I didn't tell him anything about us." Luiz stood up and squared his shoulders.

Waving his lighter a little, Rick told them to settle down. "It doesn't matter how he found out about us. He did. Which means our plan to sit pretty in that nice little house on Longfellow is out the window." He paused and looked at each of them in turn. "We've got to leave town."

"And go where?" Joe asked. "Where do we go if we leave town?"

"My old man used to take me fishing up near Fullers Woods. It's about forty miles north of Fairfield. Plenty of cabins up there. Far enough away that I doubt anyone will try and look for us," Jim offered. As the only one of them who was local to Fairfield, his suggestion prompted a series of nods from the others.

Joe exhaled slowly. Okay. A plan. They had a plan.

"What was that?" Rick snapped his lighter closed and put a heavy hand on Joe's shoulder.

"What?" Joe whispered.

"I heard—"

"STAY WHERE YOU ARE AND PUT YOUR HANDS IN THE AIR!" a voice boomed out from the trees. At the same time, bright white light flooded the spot where they were standing.

Joe tried to shield his eyes. It was too bright. He couldn't see a thing.

"Put your hands up and surrender!" the same voice yelled.

Rick's hand disappeared from Joe's shoulder and he felt him move away. At that exact moment, a shot was fired. Into the air, but close. Joe's ears began to ring.

As his eyes adjusted to the light, he realized the others were lining up beside him with their hands raised. He copied them. Behind the light, four men with shotguns and flashlights stepped into view. *Flash-lights? They have working flashlights?* Joe's heart fluttered as he wondered, for just a fraction of a second, whether the power had come back on.

"Well, well, well…." Someone was pushing their way to the front of the men with the guns. He was large, older than the rest, and had a saggy chin that implied he'd once been much rounder in the face. He was holding something, and Joe couldn't tell whether he was happy to have found them or furious.

"Shit," whispered Jim. "That's him. Victor."

"Quiet!" The large man pointed at Jim, then looked slowly at the rest of them, each in turn. "In case you don't know, my name is Victor Fox."

Joe felt Jim inhale sharply.

"Until a couple of months ago, I was a guard at Fairfield Prison." He narrowed his eyes and shook his head. "But I don't think I had the *pleasure* of becoming acquainted with any of you gentlemen."

"We'd sure as hell remember a gut as big as that!" Luiz's loud brash voice caused Joe to flinch. All four of the shotguns twitched toward him, but Victor gestured for them to remain still.

Ignoring Luiz's attempt to start an exchange of insults, Victor Fox lifted the object he was holding. It was a big black binder, and he was pressing his palm to its cover as if it was the Holy Bible. "So," he said, flipping it open and glancing over his shoulder at the men with the guns. "Let's see who we've got here."

Victor began flicking slowly through the pages. Each one contained a mug shot and a list. Some of the pages had big red crosses through them. Others had sticky notes and doodles that looked like maps. Joe's mouth was sandpaper dry. He cleared his throat.

"Nervous, are you, son?" Victor looked up at him and smiled with the corner of his mouth. "Well, you should be." He took a step closer. "You must have thought all your Christmases and birthdays had come at once when the power went out. Freedom! Just like that. All your crimes, absolved. After all, there are no records anymore. No one to care if you serve your time. No one to make sure you *pay* for what you did."

Joe looked at Rick, who shook his head at him.

"Well, that's where you're wrong." Victor licked his lower lip. "Because I have records, and I will make sure you pay."

"Oh yeah, how?" Luiz tipped his chin up at Victor in a way that made Joe's skin crawl; he was going to get himself killed.

"I'm going to lock you back up, of course."

"Lock us up?" Luiz laughed loudly. "You seen the inside of the prison lately? Good luck getting us back in there without getting your own head blown off."

Victor opened his mouth to reply but then closed it again, smirking a little as he returned to his binder. "Ah, here we are." His eyes widened and he tapped the page. "Life sentence for murder and sexual assault." He shook his head and tutted loudly. "Should have just gotten the chair. Would have saved everyone so much time and money." Sighing, Victor reached for his gun.

Joe turned to Luiz, looking frantically from him to Rick.

"That's not right," Luiz said loudly. "That ain't—"

Victor stepped forward, but he wasn't looking at Luiz. He was looking at Jim. "James O'Malley, I hereby sentence you to death."

BANG!

Joe slapped his hands over his mouth and stumbled back as Jim's body wavered. Thick red blood oozed from his temple, and then he fell. His head landed on Joe's foot. "Oh my God," Joe whispered as a clot of nausea formed in his throat. He reached down and started pulling at his sneaker, desperate to get it off his foot. To get the blood away from him. "Oh my God, oh my God."

"You bastard!" Luiz lunged forward, screaming. Rick was screaming too. Franko bolted in the other direction, but four shots followed him.

One. Two. Three. Four. Into his back. He fell face first onto the ground.

"Run! Run!" Rick yelled at Joe and dove into the trees. Luiz was on the ground, two men holding his arms.

Joe was frozen to the spot. He couldn't move. *No one's watching you, Joe. They're focused on the others. It's now or never!* A voice, perhaps his own, perhaps God's or his mother's or Roxy's, echoed in his ears.

He turned and ran, but he'd barely made it three feet when something hit him in the thigh. A sharp, searing pain, like nothing he'd ever felt before, ricocheted up and down his leg. He stumbled, trying to drag himself forward, but fell to the ground.

Fractured World (EMP Aftermath Book One)

BLURB

No power. No law & order. No safety net. The world as everyone knows it is over.

Laurel is stabilizing a patient in the ER when the power goes out. As she struggles to keep her patients alive, she faces an ugly truth—the world as everyone knew it is over. The smart thing to do is run and try to survive, but Laurel refuses to leave her patients behind—least of all her sick mother. There's only one choice to make. She'll have to stay and fight.

Bear is done fighting. War and PTSD have cost him everything—his job, his self-respect, and his wife - Laurel. But when he can no longer deny the old world is gone, he gains a new purpose. Laurel is hundreds of miles away from his mountain cabin, but he knows she needs him.

After so long being a lost solider, he finally has something worth fighting for. The highways are clogged with dead cars. Frantic survivors want his truck, his tools, his supplies. He'll face treachery, desperation, and endless miles of unforgiving wilderness, but he's going to find his wife. Together, they can survive anything.

He just has to reach her.

Grab your copy of Fractured World (EMP Aftermath Book One)
Available July 13th 2022
(Available for Pre-Order Now!)
www.LeslieNorthBooks.com

BLURB

Survival of the fittest becomes harsh reality in the blink of an eye.

Greg Healy isn't fooled. The hunting trip is merely a ploy contrived by his wife and mother to force Greg and his father to end their estrangement. Not even Greg's teenage daughter or his father's hunting buddies along for the ride will be enough of a buffer to heal the rift of long-standing resentments. But the helicopter has barely dropped them in the remote Canadian wilderness when they discover their new equipment is dead with no explanation. Now they'll have to rely on each other and resort to Old West ingenuity to find their way home—before the hunter becomes the hunted.

For seventeen-year-old Darryl Healy, things aren't much easier on his grandparents' cattle ranch. Not when his highly intelligent and successful mother keeps hounding him about college applications. But college quickly loses its allure when the lights go out after a cyberattack. Frightening responsibilities fall squarely on Darryl's unproven shoulders as a power-hungry politician is determined to confiscate the ranch's resources—by any means necessary.

Danger and death await the Healy family as each group attempts to navigate this terrifying new post-apocalyptic world while the vast wilderness separates them. When deceit arises from within their ranks, they'll face threats as lethal as the grizzly bears and mountain lions lurking in the shadows.

And in order to survive the nightmare, a deal with the devil might be their only saving grace.

EXCERPT

Chapter One

The rotor blades kicked up such a fierce cloud of dust and debris that Greg had to shield his face with his hands. The limbs of the trees whipped wildly, and the backwash of the rotors made the cold air sharp, stinging his exposed flesh. And then the helicopter was moving away, its deafening roar shifting tones as it flew out across the valley. Greg brushed stray leaves and dirt off his shoulder and watched the bright-blue Bell 407 disappearing in the pale eastern sky. As it went, he felt civilization going with it.

Well, we're in the wilderness now, he thought. *No backing out of this.*

Still, he remained frozen in place until the sound of the helicopter had completely faded. Only then did he turn, willing himself to move. The others were scattered across the clearing already against a backdrop of massive lodgepole pines, black spruce, and larch trees that dominated the mountainous area. It was raw British Columbia wilderness, just about as far from civilization as you could get without parachuting into the tundra.

All of their gear that had been unloaded from the helicopter formed an impressive pile. Greg's father, Tuck, was already working hard to arrange the bags and boxes of tarps, ropes, blankets, and more. The leathery old man was all skin and muscle these days. Somehow Greg's father had retained his farmer's strength, though his flannel shirt and jeans hung loose, and he'd shriveled a bit in recent years. As Greg watched, his father grabbed a massive tent pack and heaved it off the pile like it was nothing.

Well, this is it, Greg thought. *Quality time with the old man. It's now or never. Marion wants me to make this work, so I'd better make it work.*

He sighed and crossed the clearing. The pressure was on. Tuck heard him coming and turned. Greg's father looked so much like him, it was as if someone had taken Greg's broad face, shrink-wrapped it over his skull, and charred the skin slightly in an oven. That was an uncharitable assessment, of course, and Greg knew it.

"Hey there, Dad," Greg said. "Can I help you out?"

Tuck was heaving the packs off the pile, carrying them over to the tents and setting them down one by one in a neat row.

"Suit yourself," Tuck replied, in that rough voice of his. The man had a remarkable ability to make the least little comment sound like a complete and utter dismissal.

He doesn't mean it. That's what Marion would say. That's also what his mother would have said. Greg's wife and mother were thick as thieves when it came to this forced reconciliation.

Greg grabbed a big bundle of sleeping bags that had been lashed together and worked it off the stack. As he did, Tuck picked up another one of the tent packs and hoisted it up like a hay bale, carrying it over to the others.

Greg heard what sounded like distant thunder, and he glanced up at the sky. The only clouds to be seen were gathered just above the tree-tops to the west, but they didn't seem threatening.

"Well, looks like we might get rain during our first night camping. A nice, chilly autumn rain. I suppose I don't mind."

"If it drops a few more degrees, we might get snow," Tuck replied. "You can handle a little precipitation, I hope. The big city hasn't coddled you that much."

"I can handle whatever," Greg said, struggling to lug the sleeping bags over to the tents. "I just hope it clears up by morning. I plan to hit the river tomorrow. I'd like to get some fishing in first thing in the morning."

"I was thinking we ought to hike the area first," Tuck replied. "It's always best to get a lay of the land."

Already a disagreement. Greg was caught between wanting to keep the peace and wanting to go his own way out of sheer, hateful habit.

But their friendly little father-son chat was interrupted when Dad's buddy walked over and proceeded to have one of his coughing fits.

Eustace Simpson was a former smoker whose lungs and throat had yet to fully recover. He was a huge burly chap with an impressive red beard and a massive Cro-Magnon cranium. He wore a thick, red flannel jacket that strained at the buttons, and his hands were calloused and rough. Eustace was an acquaintance of Tuck and Tabitha Healy, and he also claimed to be an avid fisherman and hunter. However, Greg had his own reasons for accepting the man's invitation, reasons he hadn't shared with anyone, though he wondered if the man sensed his purpose.

Eustace knows I'm an environmental lawyer, Greg thought. *Surely it has crossed his mind that I have my eye on him.*

"Sun's going down," Eustace said in his deep voice. "We'd better get these tents set up before it's too dark."

"I got you covered, buddy," said Tommy Riedel, a small guy with a scruffy beard—one of Tuck's other friends. "Let's do this."

"Dad."

The last member of their camping trip was Emma, Greg's fourteen-year-old daughter. She was a bit heavy on the eye shadow these days, and Greg thought it made her eyes look bruised, but he still saw the round-cheeked little girl she'd once been. She had her mother's brown eyes, and wisps of blonde hair poked out of the edge of her toque.

"Dad, I want to set up my own tent," she said, coming up beside him. "By myself. I know how to do it."

"Are you sure?" he asked. "It's not a simple setup like a dome tent. You've never set one of these up before."

"I can do it. Watch me." She brushed past him.

Emma's long-range plan was to become a park ranger, and she wanted to prove herself this year. She'd made that very clear. Greg was tempted to give her a bit of advice anyway, but he bit his lip and walked over to Eustace instead, helping him unfold the support poles for his much larger tunnel tent.

"What do you think?" Eustace said, taking in the surrounding wilderness with a broad sweep of one arm. "I keep a nice campsite, eh?"

"It's a lovely area," Greg replied. And, indeed, he was excited to see what it had to offer. He'd never camped this far from civilization, and the looming mountains and towering forests were breathtaking.

"Everyone thinks we mess with the land," Eustace said, "just because we're a natural gas company. But you can see for yourself. This is virgin land. We haven't done a damned thing to hurt it."

I'll be the judge of that. We already know more than you think, pal, Greg thought, as outwardly he merely said, "Looks that way."

Tuck's little friend Tommy was flitting about the camp, apparently too excited to focus on any one task. As Greg watched, he tried to help Emma set up her tent, but she shook her head and waved him off.

"I did it, Dad," Emma said. She'd set up her tent in record time, and although it didn't look perfect—sit seemed slightly out of alignment—it was serviceable. Greg gave his daughter a round of applause.

"Excellent," he said. "I couldn't have done better myself."

She gave him a withering look that suggested she didn't believe he meant it. "Well, now I'm going to start the campfire. I can do that, too!"

She moved to the center of the camp and began clearing a firepit among the rocks. Greg was genuinely impressed with his daughter—not just her ability but her self-reliance. He'd tried to encourage it in her over the years, and it seemed to have taken root.

That'll serve you well, kiddo, he thought.

As she began stacking up kindling, Greg went to his gear and picked out a small plastic suitcase. He undid the combination lock and popped it open to reveal a rather expensive satellite phone tucked into foam padding.

Time to make a call, he thought. *Marion will want to know we're settling in.*

The phone looked somewhat like an old Nokia cell phone from the early 2000s, though it was larger and had a much longer, thicker antenna. It was packed with a charger, a backup battery, and a bunch of other attachments and accessories that he rarely used. He worked the phone out of its padding, tucked it into his shirt pocket, then walked across the campsite, trying to appear like he was taking a casual stroll. Best to be far from Eustace, just in case he had to mention the case.

Greg pulled the sat phone out of his pocket and pressed the *on* button. It usually took a few seconds to turn on, so when it didn't respond right away, he didn't think much of it. He double-checked to make sure he was pressing the button firmly. When it still didn't respond, he pressed the button a few times repeatedly, shook the phone, and pressed the button one more time.

Battery must be dead, he thought. He went back to the briefcase, grabbed the charging cable, and plugged the phone into the backup charger. He gave it a few seconds, then tried to turn it on again. Still nothing.

"You've got to be kidding me," he muttered. "This damn thing is practically new. I tested it yesterday. *Yesterday*."

With a pocketknife, he worked open the battery case, then swapped out the battery with the extra in the briefcase. This time, he pressed the power button as hard as he could and held it there for almost a full minute. The phone still didn't turn on.

"Son of a—" He bit off the curse. Emma was close by, her fire already crackling. Marion didn't like it when he cussed in front of her.

"Dad, look. It's already going pretty good."

He looked over his shoulder and saw his daughter adding sticks to a small, steady fire. She was doing a great job, but the sudden anxiety spoiled the moment for him. He needed this stupid phone to work.

"Very nice," he managed to say, then turned and smacked the satellite phone against his palm.

He tried the power button one last time and got no response. Disgusted, he tossed the phone back into the briefcase, dumped the battery charger on top of it, and slammed the briefcase shut.

"Problem?"

He looked up into the bony face of his father. Why did the man always look like he'd sucked on a lemon?

"The stupid sat phone is dead," Greg replied. "It was working this morning. Somehow, between the time we left the hotel and the time we landed at the campsite, it died."

"Well, we *are* supposed to be roughing it, after all," Tuck replied. "Maybe nature did you a favor."

"I need…we *need* that phone," Greg said. "What if there's an emergency?"

"We have first aid kits," Tuck said.

"I promised Marion I'd get in touch with her so she'd know we all arrived safe and sound."

Eustace walked over then, brushing his big, ruddy hands on the thighs of his jeans. "Take the battery out. Let it sit overnight inside your tent. Maybe the cold messed with it. Try it again in the morning."

"That's…" A stupid idea. But it wouldn't help his cause to say it, so he pressed his lips together instead. "Yeah, I'll try that, Eustace. Thanks."

He picked up the briefcase, carried it over to where he intended to set up his tent, and dumped it on the ground in disgust.

The batteries were brand-new. The phone was working just a few hours ago. It doesn't make any sense.

Made in the USA
Monee, IL
22 April 2022

95239653R00184